The Case of the Not-So-Fair Trader

by

Jim Stevens

The final approval for this literary material is granted by the author.

Third printing

ISBN: 978-0-98492472-1

For Doris

1

Hit me with your best shot

Nine out of ten people will tell you that the trigger finger makes the difference.

That's incorrect.

It's your feet. You line up your shot with your feet, not your finger, eyes, hands or body, but your feet. Plant them firmly on the ground, hip's distance apart, and that's where, and only where, you'll find perfect balance.

Face the target. Head up, shoulders square. If a level were laid across your shoulder blades, the bubble would rest clearly between the lines.

Then move.

Bend at the waist, twenty, thirty degrees at most. Pull your weapon up slowly, hold it in your hands gently as if it were a firstborn. Feel the smooth surface, the precision that went into its manufacture. Be proud, be respectful and be still, absolutely motionless.

Focus. On the target, the exact spot you want to hit. And don't, whatever you do, close one eye. Talk about a misconception, this is the granddaddy of them all. Do major league baseball players close one eye when the pitch is coming? Did Michael Jordan close one eye shooting three-pointers? Do you close one eye to watch the sun sink slowly in the West? No, no, and no. Keep both eyes open; two are better than one.

Three seconds. This is crucial. Focus for three seconds. If you have to think, your only thought should be that there is nothing between you and the target except opportunity.

Don't squeeze. You want to be loose, free and fluid, muscles relaxed, not tense. Your shooting hand should take control with a slow, deliberate confidence. Let the smooth, rounded contour of your weapon rest in the palm of your hand, index and little fingers steady as your middle fingers carry the weight. All the while your eyes bore into that sweet spot envisioning a clean strike.

Last, but certainly not least, block out all distractions. No matter how much rain pelts on the roof, bad country music plays, or the resounding impact of other shots obliterate their intended targets, block it all out. You are an island. Nothing can invade your space. Allow any blip on your radar screen and you will fail. And failure is not an option.

Ready on the right, ready on the left, and ready on the firing line. Time to put it all to work.

———

Today, it all comes down to one shot. Now or never, ducks on the pond, all the marbles.

I stand straight as a carpenter's plumb line, perfectly balanced, agent of destruction in hand, ready, untouchable and immutable. My fellow warriors are on their feet behind me. I block out their silent hopes and prayers. I can somehow hear. I bend, focus, wait, and take one step forward gliding in a practiced, precision motion. Everything is just right, only triumph waits.

Approaching the line, I take the final step forward and, at the exact millisecond the shot is about to leave my trigger finger, the piercing cry of the devil rings out. A blistering, dissonant, ear-splitting, resounding screech so shrill eyeglasses crack from the falsetto.

"Oh, Mister Sherlock."

My body spasms as if hit with a Taser. I am immobile, frozen in convulsion. All I can do is watch horrified as my shot spirals halfway to the target and takes an unprecedented spin, squirreling out of control until it falls unceremoniously into the trough and rolls hopelessly into the black abyss.

Gutter ball.

I turn to my team, Chico's Bailbondsmen, and each face is the same -- a countenance of disgust, disappointment, failure and heartache. The months, days, hours, bad food, cheap beer, and overpriced shoe rental were all for naught. My fellow keglers stand, their protruding stomachs hanging on oversized belt buckles. Not a word is spoken.

I regain some sense of equilibrium as the sounds of joy ring out to my left. The team from Johnnie's Pastrami leaps into the air, celebrating my failure. Their high-fives crackle against wrist protectors. Beer splashes onto the smooth wood floor. The electronic scoreboard above flashes a goose egg in my last frame, which guarantees with mathematical certainty that the Waveland Bowl Men's Summer League Championship trophy will reside where rye is a religion and Reuben is king.

I stumble to the plastic bench, collapse; my head falls into hands and dips between my knees. Not one Bailbondsman comes to my side; we are all too devastated by the loss to express our discontent. My stomach ties into a Gordian Knot; flesh turns the color of psoriasis red, the mother of all headaches crashes inside my head like two bull goats battling for superiority. I am moved from one torment to another as the voice rings out again.

"I didn't think I was ever going to find you," she said. "Come on, Daddy says we have to get there while the body is still warm."

I rise to my feet, pulled along as a lamb to slaughter.

"And one other thing," she said in her incipient, suburban-raised, staccato voice, "I just love those shoes; they are so retro."

———

My name is Richard Sherlock. I spent nineteen years on the Chicago Police Force, sixteen as a detective. I've shot at seven men, hit four, and killed two.

I am sitting in the passenger seat of a new Lexus 430 as we speed north along Lakeshore Drive. Seems pathetic that this car costs more than my first house and more pathetic that, at this time in my life, I cannot afford either.

"Have you heard of Alvin J. Augustus?" she asks as we go by a line of high-rise condos built along the lakefront, known as the Gaza Strip due to the ethnic make-up of the occupants.

"Yes, Tiffany, but only in passing."

Tiffany, who would name their kid Tiffany? Okay, maybe the guy who owns the store, but who else? You outgrow the name at six; the only contraction is Tiff, and that connotes a fight. The only thing worse than the name Tiffany is sitting next to a Tiffany with diamond studs in her ear lobes that are worth more than my IRA.

"Alvin makes my old man look like a pauper."

"Tough to do."

As we pass Loyola University, she says, "It's a twelve-million-dollar policy. Daddy doesn't want to pay out."

I sit silent, not admitting that I don't blame him.

Traffic is heavy as we proceed through Rogers Park, past Calvary Cemetery and into Evanston. A bit incongruous that the City of Chicago and the City of Evanston are divided by the dead.

"I met his granddaughter, Christina, at the opera once," she says, driving way too fast past a strip of overpriced real estate. "She was weird."

"*You* like opera?" I place a particular emphasis on the you.

"Ah, no. Opera's enough to make anyone hate music."

Our deep, intriguing conversation is interrupted as "Girls Just Want to Have Fun," erupts from the dashboard cell phone speaker. Tiffany ignores the music and the printout of a name across a panel beneath the Lexus stereo system. "Opera, art openings, dinners where they want money for children with flies in their eyes; that's what we have to do to be people like us."

"The injustice of it all."

Horns blare on three sides as Tiffany speeds through an intersection.

"You just ran a red light."

She turns around, looking for patrol cars. "If I get stopped you tell them you're a cop."

"I don't carry a badge anymore."

"Then I'll tell him I'm a nurse. Nurses don't get tickets."

Unfortunately, she's correct. Nurses, politicians, firemen, other cops, and any city employee that wears a tie, are let off with a warning; an unwritten law.

"How did your father find out Alvin died?"

"He has ways."

"He still monitors police bands?"

"Let's just say he has ways."

Tiffany's father, Jamison Wentworth Richmond, CEO of Richmond Insurance, pays disabled guys less than minimum wage to sit in their basements and illegally eavesdrop on police communication systems.

And I complain that my life is pitiful.

"So, how did old Alvin die?"

"He didn't die," Tiffany corrected. "He was murdered. You have to think positive."

———

The Lexus passes two stone pillars and we enter Kenilworth, Illinois. Historians have said these tall columns of precise bricks at one time supported a large gate to keep the Kenilworthians separate from undesirable, common folk such as me. Where the moat and drawbridge once stood is anyone's guess. The town is one of the most exclusive enclaves in America, let alone Chicagoland, with some of the homes filling a footprint larger than a city block. Mostly old money, with ex-senators, CEOs and trust-funders, existing mansion to mansion in the splendor only big, big money can bring. Yes, the rich are different.

Tiffany knows the town like the back of her moisturized and manicured hand. She zips through the twisting streets like an Andretti in a Formula One race. We head east, cut through an alley and end up on an old service road that leads to a private beach.

"Kids used to swim naked out here in the summer," Tiffany says, stopping the car at the edge of the sand.

"You?" I ask, getting out of the car.

"Well, not me; I wouldn't have dreamed of skinny-dipping before I had my breasts done."

I walk towards the lake.

"Mister Sherlock, this way," Tiffany informs me.

To my left is a patch of three-foot grass, bushes, and trees; the spot is littered with teenager trash: cigarette butts, fast-food wrappers, empty quart bottles of beer and malt liquor. Teenagers are the only people who drink beer out of quart bottles. Why, I do not know. There are many tire tracks, old and new, on the service road. Before the beach, mounds of dirt and sand roll gently along, topped with a summer growth of weeds and a few huge rocks here and there.

You couldn't tell if anything was disrupted or not; this fact is disappointing.

"Mister Sherlock, Alvin Augustus awaits us," Tiffany says, standing with her hands resting on her hips.

"Be right there," I say and walk to an indentation between two mounds of sand. I stop, look down and see an empty condom wrapper. If I dug deep, as a good detective should, I would find the condom. I pass. There is a slight, faint odor in the air, sour and unpleasant. I watch carefully where I walk. In the middle of the sand, where obviously the human coupling took place, there is a smooth, white rock about the size of a softball.

"What's that?" Tiffany asks.

"Most people call it a rock."

"I know that."

"Then why did you ask?"

"Mister Sherlock, I want to see the body."

"Don't we all?" I drop the rock.

She follows me up to the sandy path leading to the Augustus property, each step torturous in her six-hundred-dollar Gucci pumps. "Do you have to walk so fast?"

"I get that scent of rotting flesh in my nostrils and I just can't hold myself back."

"Really?"

Tiffany does not have an ear for sarcasm.

We come to a strand of yellow, crime scene tape stretched between the pine trees.

This is dumb.

Who in his right mind would ever consider a thin strip of plastic as a deterrent to anyone? The stuff is flimsy, snaps in two easily, and people walk right into it all the time; but for some reason, whenever a crime is discovered, some genius strings it up as if it were an impenetrable force. Hell, if it works, why don't they put it at the borders to keep out illegal aliens?

I duck under the tape. Tiffany raises it over her head and passes underneath. The difference in our actions speaks volumes.

I raise my hand as if I were the squad leader of the YWCA Indian Guides. "Stop."

Tiffany looks up the rock-lined path, sees a number of people gathered round. "Why?"

"Get behind me."

"A little demeaning," Tiffany says.

"Follow me. Stay close; don't move off the line I set."

Tiffany points to the left, up the path a couple hundred yards from where we stand. "I think the body is over there, Mister Sherlock."

"I doubt if he's going anywhere."

I walk perpendicular to the crime scene tape. Tiffany follows. I move slowly, my eyes never rise from the ground directly beneath me. The rocks are lined up like little soldiers, perfect except for one missing. I consider the one found at the sex scene. I debate whether to go back and get it, put it back in place and return the path to perfection. I don't; too lazy.

"Are we looking for something?" Tiffany asks.

"Yes."

"What?"

"I don't know."

We reach the end of the yellow tape. I take one step to my right and make a close-order drill turn and start back in the direction I came.

"If you don't know what you are looking for," Tiffany says from a foot or two behind me, "How are you going to know when you find it?"

"Trust me; I'll know." I continue to pace across the back lawn of the estate.

After two or three more passes, Tiffany grows even more restless. "This is boring."

"Life is boring," I tell her. "Days, weeks, months, years of one mundane task after another, punctuated intermittently with disappointment, failed expectations, and negative fates; that's what life is all about."

"Not my life."

"Oh, please, do tell your secret."

"Shopping, Mister Sherlock, lots of shopping."

I see a metallic item in the grass, I stop, bend over, reach down to retrieve it, and Tiffany rear-ends me. I catch myself before I hit the ground.

"Sorry about that," she says, "I didn't see your brake lights."

"Don't worry." Hardly the first time I've been kicked in the ass by a woman, and likely won't be the last.

The item is worthless. We continue on my switchback path.

"May I remind you, this is boring," Tiffany says.

"No."

———

No matter how many cities or episodes of *CSI* end up on TV, no crime scene will ever be as pure as the ones they portray. The second after a crime is committed, the scene is always compromised. The wind blows, rain falls, dust settles, bowels move, blood spurts; or some kid happens by on his bike, stops, and turns the victim over for a closer view. I heard of one instance where two tourists found a body in a downtown alley and preceded to pose for pictures with their discovery. They even asked another tourist to use their camera so all three could be in the picture together. There's a vacation slide show the neighbors will never forget.

———

As we traipse through the Augustus back forty, we come upon a garden. Walking alongside, I, and hopefully Tiffany who stays close behind, remain careful not to disturb the rocks lining the walkway. Dirt on the path is as smooth as a baby's bottom and not a bedding plant in the adjacent gardens has been disturbed. If I ever meet the landscaper who did the design on pansies, roses, and phlox, I will certainly give him my compliments.

I stop, think. We are less than twenty-five feet from the actual crime scene.

"What?" Tiffany says impatiently.

I look left, right, up, down, pausing at each as if taking a photo.

"You found something?" Tiffany asks.

"No."

"Then what? Tiffany pleads, "Tell me."

"Can you keep a secret?"

"No, I'm real bad at that."

"Well, then..."

"Tell me anyway."

I pause and look down the way at a tarp covering a huge pile, which undoubtedly includes Alvin. "They might have found him here, but that wasn't where he was killed."

"How do you know that? You haven't even seen the body."

"I don't know," I say, "I just do."

2
Who rocked the stones?

A yellow plastic tarp covers a lump six feet in length, maybe three feet in width, and two high, lying off the path in the middle of a rock garden.

Could there be a greater oxymoron than a rock garden? Rocks don't grow, change with the seasons or bloom; best they can do is gather moss (unless they're rolling) and how attractive can that be? There were hundreds of rocks, some piled in pseudo art sculptures, a miniature Stonehenge, a replica of Mount Rushmore, pieces of red shale stacked in a tribute to Bryce Canyon, a rock waterfall, and a babbling brook. Rocks, rocks, and more rocks; totally absurd. There were rocks piled up in a foursquare like cannonballs in the Civil War, and a rock tunnel for the kiddies to crawl through. Boulders, shiny stones, pebbles, quartz, and quarry stones. The most impressive was the ridge of rocks, landscaped straight upward to a height of ten feet, a triangular wall of stone, two feet thick. Problem was: a section of the wall had collapsed.

I'm about ten feet from the covering when Norbert Keaton gets in my face.

"Sherlock, what the hell are you doing here?"

"Probably a lot more than you."

"Are you looking for bail business?" Norbert, the great detective, has read the inscription on my shirt.

"No, I'm making a fashion statement."

Steve Burrell positions himself beside Norbert, making somewhat of an impenetrable wall. Each so-called detective tips the scales at two-twenty-five-plus, with a body fat index well above the fifty percent range. They were known as Tweedledum and Tweedledee when they partnered at the CPD.

"We don't have to allow you entrance to the crime scene," Steve informs me.

Dumb comment since both Norbert and Steve watched me arrive, pace across the Augustus property, survey every inch, and pick up scraps along my way.

"Insurance investigator, I have a right to be here." This they already know, but can't admit.

"You're supposed to get a waiver."

"Listen," I speak with about as much authority as I can muster. "If it was up to me, this certainly wouldn't be my first choice for a Saturday night out on the town."

The two detectives stand, shifting their weight from side to side.

"Just you keep in mind who is in charge," Steve informs me in no uncertain terms.

"I promise; if anyone asks '*who* is the head ramrod of this wagon train?' I'll tell 'em it's you."

There is a slight pause as I move toward the tarp.

Norbert blocks Tiffany from following me. "Who are you?"

Tiffany's tongue wets her perfect collagen-filled top lip and answers, "Tiffany, nice to meet you."

The four of us gather round the mound beneath the plastic tarp. Steve grips the top edge and asks, "Ready?"

Tiffany steps forward for a closer look, a bad idea, because when Steve whips off the tarp, a raft of foul air hits her nostrils like a blast of baby diarrhea. Her head jerks backward, then luckily forward, as she vomits the remains of a latté colored bran muffin.

I allow her to finish before I lend assistance. "You okay?"

"I haven't done that since going off my purge diet."

I position her behind me and turn to witness Alvin J. Augustus, or at least what's left of him.

The victim is a disgusting, gruesome pile of rotting flesh, mostly underneath some very attractive stones. I move around for different angles and see through the rocks that his bones are broken, limbs twisted, and feet point east and west. There is one large rock resting in the indentation of his skull. Charming. Amazing how one rock could find the exact mark.

I usually dislike what I have to do to make a living, but at scenes like this I downright despise the job.

"Coroner been here, yet?"

"He wasn't too thrilled with it, either," Steve says.

"Can't say I blame him."

"He still around?"

"Said he had dinner reservations and left."

"Who could eat after this?" Tiffany asks.

"I'm certainly planning on it," Norbert says.

The stones cover Alvin like autumn leaves. Blood, which has turned a dark, almost brown crimson, has drained from his wounds and down the brick-designed lane, pooling like a puddle after a thunderstorm. Bits of brain, bone, tissue, and other bodily residue lie in the thick liquid. It reminds me of a Cajun etouffé on a bed of white rice; I'll ask Norbert if that's what he has in mind for his entrée tonight.

"Accidental death, Sherlock," Steve says.

I turn to Tiffany, who has recovered from her gastric mishap. "Hear that?"

"Yes."

"Can I go home, now?"

"No."

"Why not? The police say it's accidental," I plead.

"That's not what Daddy wants to hear, Mister Sherlock."

Steve waxes poetic, "He's out taking a Saturday morning stroll, minding his own business, when something happens, like an earthquake. The rocks come off the ridge and crush him like a cockroach under an exterminator's boot."

"I didn't feel any earth moving," Tiffany says.

"It was a small quake, its epicenter was right here in Alvin's backyard." Steve further explains.

"But I didn't feel anything," she says, "and I'm very sensitive."

"You just haven't found the right man, yet," I conclude.

Norbert offers an additional treatment to corroborate his partner's theory. "Or Alvin's out here, sees a stone out of place, tries to fix it, and the Walls of Jericho come tumbling down."

"This all sounds really good to me," I agree with two of the stupidest theories since the world was considered flat or Iraq had weapons of mass destruction.

Tiffany pulls at my sleeve. "Remember, a twelve-million-dollar policy, Mister Sherlock. Daddy will want no stone left unturned."

"No pun intended."

"Wrap it up, write it up, and seal it shut," Norbert says hopefully.

"No," Tiffany says, "Mister Sherlock doesn't even think this is where he was killed."

The two detectives pause to consider her revelation.

"You were certainly right about not being able to keep a secret," I tell Tiffany.

"So," Norbert asks Tiffany, "how does Mister Sherlock arrive at this conclusion?"

"That's the secret," Tiffany says and smiles to me, looking for a compliment.

"So, come on," Norbert says.

"I don't know how I know. I just know."

"No shit, Sherlock?" Steve says.

Norbert and Steve are not stupid. They both had the brains to coast through twenty years in the Chicago PD, retire with seventy-percent pensions, and take similar jobs with the Kenilworth department, where the worst crimes are committed by drunken teenagers whose parents have very deep pockets for immediate "Let's keep this in the family" verdicts. The two dicks work nine to five, trade on-call weekends, get eleven paid holidays, three personal and three sick days.

I should be so lucky.

They are also smart enough to know this is definitely a murder and that I will do the bulk of their work if they play their cards right.

"He was dragged here," I say.

Norbert and Steve wait for me to explain.

"The path, it's too smooth. The indentations all run in one direction."

"There's lots of other ways he could have got to this spot," Steve says.

"The pattern is too perfect," I answer. "Alvin's body was pulled by his feet, left here, and crushed by a dumptruck load of rock."

"Why would anybody want to do that?" Norbert asks.

"You're the detective," I answer.

I squat down like a baseball catcher, turning toward the body. I know this position is going to come back and haunt me. "Got a time of death?"

"Six to nine hours ago," Steve says.

"Gardener found him around four-ten," Norbert adds.

"What else did the coroner say?"

"Blunt trauma."

"He's really going out on a limb there."

I take a closer look at Alvin's blood-soaked, beige clothing. "The resale value of his suit is virtually nil."

"Linen."

"What?"

"Linen," Tiffany says. "I know because I never wear linen, looks like it always needs ironing."

"Tiffany, I think you cracked the case," I say. "Alvin died of a fashion faux pas."

"Oh, Mister Sherlock."

I wipe at my eyes with both my hands in a last ditch attempt to see if this will all go away. It doesn't.

"You don't really believe that nonsense about this being accidental?" I ask the two burly detectives.

"Let's just say," Norbert says, "we want to."

"People in this town don't like words like murder, homicide, or phrases like 'buried under an avalanche of rock,'" Steve says.

"Can you blame them?"

I move to the head of the body. I am thoroughly disgusted at the rock which scored the direct hit.

"Leave me alone for a few minutes, would you?"

"No problem," Norbert says, leading Steve and Tiffany away.

There is something wrong here, besides the body of a man crushed by a load of stone. His upper body is covered, as are his feet at the other end. A few of the rocks have slipped off the slope and rested on the flat ground. But on his right side, a little past his waistline, there is a clearing and I can see right into his pants and belt. I never studied any laws of physics, but this doesn't seem mathematically correct. More troubling is the one big rock crushing his face and skull. This would be a one-in-a-million shot.

——

Ever since I was a kid I've had this oddball memory. I can take one gander at a scene and literally remember it for eternity. This is not always a big plus when you consider some of the stuff I have

17

witnessed over the years. No matter what the scene may be, the picture enters into my head and prints somehow in my brain forever. Plus, I remember everything I read, every movie I see, person I meet, and food I eat. I have never lost a game of Trivial Pursuit. The only things I can't remember are names; why, I have no clue. I can be introduced to a guy, talk with him and, three minutes later, can't remember if he's Spencer or Spud. But twenty years later, I run into the same guy and recall he lived in Berwyn with his mother and had a cat named Shoes who had to have her tail amputated.

I begin to take a number of mind's eye Polaroids. I move from position to position and lodge into my brain exactly what I see. My pictures have a depth, definition, and feeling that no ordinary camera can capture. The only problem will be how to take the pictures of a blood-oozing, decaying, flesh-peeled-off bones protruding from Alvin and arrange them into an attractive photo scrapbook inside my brain.

Tiffany returns to peer over my shoulder at the rock resting on Alvin's face, as if she were bent over the railing of a pier trying to spot a fish in the water below.

"I think the only thing cracked in the case this far is the victim's head, Mister Sherlock."

"So nice of you to mention."

"But I really think it's great you think he got murdered. We're going to have such a good time finding out who did it." Tiffany adds a giggle of excitement.

The ambulance drives right through the yellow tape and parks ten or twenty feet away. This will do wonders for keeping the crime scene pure.

Norbert and Steve usher over the two paramedics, who take one look at the victim, grab their mouths with their hands and back up quickly.

"Don't feel bad," Tiffany tells the boys. "I let loose when I saw him, too."

I've had enough.

I walk alone up the path to a stone stairway where Xanadu rises before my eyes.

The Augustus home stands as an edifice to the blood of busted stock and commodity traders Alvin was able to financially break and mentally destroy. This multi-thousand-square-foot Greek Revival structure is a testament that a person in business need not invent, manufacture, service, or design in order to reap financial rewards of an incalculable magnitude.

I knew about Alvin J. Augustus; everybody in Chicago knew AJA unless they "lived" under a rock. He was in the financial pages, quoted on the news, threw lavish parties, consulted the mayor. Alvin was to the Board of Trade what Morgan was to banking, Gates to software, and Carnegie to steel.

I notice footprints all over the path and grassy area to my left. Picking the perpetrator's imprint from the many will be impossible. My biggest disappointment is there are no broken branches, ruined pansies, or indented rose bushes -- no sign of an area of final struggle. My hunch that he wasn't killed here is now a certainty.

I'm maybe fifty yards away, but I can see the two detectives and paramedics argue as they clear the smaller rocks off the victim. A wooden stretcher board rests perpendicular. Tiffany is freshening her make-up.

"Hey, Sherlock," Norbert yells out. "Can you give us a hand over here?"

I pretend I can't hear.

Burrell calls out, even louder, "Sherlock, get your ass over here."

I might be stupid, but not that stupid. I walk the other way, deep in detective thought. Out of the corner of my eye, I see Norbert ask Tiffany a question and I can imagine Tiffany's "*you've got to be kidding*" response.

I take a few more steps and turn around to see the detectives and paramedics circle Alvin's upper body, squat down, each grip the rock on Alvin's head, and "on three" lift the weight upwards. Alvin's flesh sticks to the rock like a suction cup and his entire upper body sits up. The four men stop, mid-lift, not sure how to proceed. No doubt the expletives are furiously rolling off tongues. Norbert finally raises his left orthopedic shoe, places it on Alvin's chest and pushes it downward. The pressure holding the skull to the stone releases and Alvin slams back down into a clump of worthless body parts.

Tiffany comes up to me as Alvin is loaded into the ambulance.

"Now what do we do?"

"We?"

"Daddy said I should assist."

"Then why didn't you help lift the rock off Alvin's skull?"

"Oh," Tiffany sighs, "was that totally disgusting to the max or what?"

3
Tell a marketer he's dead

What I did for the back forty, I do for the remainder of the property. Up, down, back, forth, criss and cross, I search for something, but I don't know what. Walk, walk, walk. This is the reason gumshoe detectives still wear ugly shoes with thick gummy soles.

With Tiffany following, complaining of *her* footwear choice, I cover most of the property before darkness falls. There is no moon tonight and I have found not a clue of what went down with poor Alvin J. Augustus.

We move inside to the mansion, where a Hispanic, live-in maid, Theresa, is getting pummeled with questions from Norbert and Steve. The woman speaks only broken English or at least speaks only broken English at this moment.

Tiffany offers her help. "I speak housekeeper Spanish."

An obvious prerequisite for anyone who has never done, nor will ever do, a lick of housework.

For the next fifteen minutes, I meander through the downstairs, trying to get a feel for the life once lived here.

My first thought: uncomfortable.

The furniture is austere, for lack of a better term. It may cost thousands for these high-backed chairs and straight-up sofas, but there is not a place where you could kick off your shoes, lay down and take a nap. The media room has a plasma screen more suited to a drive-in movie theater; but only one Barcalounger sits before it, as if no one could ever agree on which movie to watch. All the floors are made from dark, one-inch, oak planks with the same pattern running across the length of the room. The boards cut from one oak tree, no doubt. The crown moldings are mahogany. All the curtains are made from thick material, maybe chintz. I know little about material except for what I wear. There are six fireplaces, all stone or brick, one so wide a whole cord of wood could fit inside. The house is a newer structure, less than twenty years old, built to appear old and stately, but fools not even me. I guess you could call it faux-old.

What impresses, or actually depresses, me are the windows. Each is huge with inlaid, painted glass artwork usually reserved for churches or cemetery crypts. I can imagine that little natural sunlight filters through during the day. What an awful way to live. One window, or the lack thereof, in the den intrigues me. The eight-inch pane is boarded up; way too high to be a burglar's doing and out of reach for a maid's mop handle during a fit of scrubbing. I make a mental note and continue on.

After her stint as an interpreter, Tiffany informs me, "That woman could never work for me. She uses bleach on all the whites."

She follows me through the upstairs of the house and goes through one conniption after another at the design choices made. "Can you believe this, multi-colored carpeting? My God, we should be looking for a murderer with a sense of style."

I find one room especially curious.

The master bedroom has a bed big enough to sleep the entire von Trapp family and still have room for the dog. The custom sheets alone must have cost a couple of grand, with enough pillows to stock a sultan's harem. The mattress is rock hard on the left and soft on the right. The one blanket is actually two, one side being fat with a duvet cover and the other side thin. There are two plasma-TV screens, one on each side of the room. One nightstand has a phone, an alarm clock radio, and a box holding three prescription bottles. The only label I notice is Ambien. The other nightstand has a reading lamp and little else.

"Like the place, Tiffany?" I ask.

"No, I'm a penthouse kind of a girl." She yawns.

I sense Tiffany has had enough of this peculiar brilliance. "Why does that not surprise me?"

"If we leave now, I can still catch a couple of clubs before closing time," she says.

Norbert is coming our way. I sense he's not far behind Tiffany in his desire to exit.

"Coming back tomorrow?" I ask.

Before he answers, he asks, "Are you?"

"Unfortunately."

"Damn," he says. "What time?"

"After church."

Norbert is surprised. "You go to church?"

"No, but some people do; so I'll wait for them to get home."

"I go to church." Tiffany loves to fill in little tidbits about herself. "The Church of Saint Mattress, I worship upon it every Sunday until noon."

The telephone on the kitchen counter rings. As if on cue, Tiffany picks it up.

"Hello."

She pauses between responses. "Hello. What? No. He's here, but not available. Because he's dead. Yeah, dead. She's not here, either. If she is dead, she's not dead here."

I speak up. "Ask who it is."

"Who is this?"

There is a longer pause; then Tiffany says, "They hung up."

"What did they say when you asked who it was?"

"They said 'they didn't know since they couldn't see me.'"

I lean against a table and cross my arms. "You know, that was probably the murderer on the phone."

"I thought it was a telemarketer."

"Why?"

"Because there was a pause before they started to speak. Somebody's about to try to sell you something when you hear that pause."

"They paused because they didn't recognize your voice."

"Oh."

"Was it a man or a woman?"

"I should have asked that, too?"

"You couldn't tell?"

"It was probably a man; but it could have been a woman with a voice like a man."

"Did the voice have an accent?"

"Well... it sounded kind of weird, now that I think of it. Kinda like someone who'd make dirty phone calls."

"You have a lot to compare that to?"

"I've had my share, although a lot of those were planned."

Steve Burrell comes to where we are standing. "You answer that phone?"

"Yes," Tiffany confesses.

"Who was it?"

"Wrong number," I tell him.

"Telemarketer," Tiffany adds.

Steve tells Tiffany, "You're a lousy liar."

"No, I'm not," Tiffany says. "I'm an excellent liar."

"You always make a habit of answering other people's phone calls?"

"Only if I'm dating them seriously."

I pick up the receiver, dial *69, listen and write on the pad of paper next to the phone what a computer is telling me, hang up, and hand the paper to Steve. "Here's your caller."

Steve dials the number.

"I'll bet it's either untraceable or a pay phone," I say.

"It's ringing." Steve holds the receiver to his ear.

"Mister Sherlock," Tiffany says, "people don't use pay phones anymore."

"Still ringing?" I ask.

Steve hangs up the receiver. "Nobody answered."

"Well, then if it was the murderer, he should be easy to catch," Tiffany says excitedly. "There's not that many pay phones anymore and all cell calls are listed on a giant computer in orbit around the earth."

"Really?"

"I got that from a reliable source," she explains.

"Was the source for sale at the checkout line at the market?" Steve asks.

"Could have been."

"Tiffany," I tell her. "Next time, just ask who is calling."

The day is done. We've all had enough. We separate to make our way to respective exits, us out the back and the detectives out the front. No one says goodbye.

4
My doggone back

I awake on Sunday morning with a pain so sharp it almost levitates me out of my own bed. The agony starts in my lower back, lumbar region, and shoots upward through my body like a lightning bolt through storm clouds. My feet go numb; I can't move my legs. I lay helpless, waiting for the first wave of misery to pass. Partial relief may take one minute or twenty. I scrunch my six-foot frame into the fetal position and begin to rock my upper torso in miniscule increments of movement to loosen my vertebrae. Some days it can take an hour before I can move my legs. Off the bedside table I grab my emergency ibuprofen, pop three in my dry mouth and force them down my throat. Their result won't come for ten minutes, but the result will come. I keep rocking and the pain starts to lessen. I move my toes, which helps my back; but this is misery. Anyone who has ever had back pain can relate; there is no worse feeling than your spine twisted as taut as a wet dish rag.

I've had back problems going on a decade now. Maybe it was too many years sitting in a state-issued, domestic car; maybe it was the strain of the divorce; maybe it was one-too-many criminals wrestled to the ground. Whatever the cause, it hurts.

Today, it is a half-hour between waking and stepping into the shower. I start lukewarm and keep increasing the temperature until it is so hot I could make tea. The jet stream hits my back like one flaming torpedo after another and, with the ibuprofen kicking in, I finally can move like a normal human being.

Yet another aspect of my miserable existence.

Thank God, it is not my kid weekend. The only other plans I had were to attend a victory party at the home office of Chico's Bailbonds, which will certainly not be happening.

I lay on my back, on the floor, feet resting on the couch. I watch, upside down, every local news program that reports on the mysterious, accidental demise of Alvin J. Augustus. From the footage shot early that morning, the yellow crime tape did not do its job once again. There were close-ups of the blood stains, the path, and the rocks. A few of the stories had old footage of Alvin at some art opening or in front of some bank. The weekend anchors and reporters covering the stories were not as well known or as good-looking as the weekday anchors, in the blow-dried, bleached teeth kind of way; but each gave it their best shot in reviewing the lurid details for an audience hungry for a good, gory, death. I wonder if the regular folks watching are snickering at the fact that Alvin won't get a chance to spend all the money he worked so hard to make.

Feeling better, I rise to my feet and make a very easy decision to not clean my small apartment, a common practice I perform on Sunday mornings. Instead, I flip on my computer and make my way onto the internet.

I hate the computer. The fact that my ten-year-old daughter can whip around from one website to the next, while I can't figure out why you have to push START to turn it off, infuriates the hell out of me. How am I going to be able to protect her and her sister from internet predators when I don't know an interface from a Facebook?

I do a search on Alvin J. Augustus. There are a number of internet references. I learn he is/was fifty-seven, had three wives, three kids, a dead mother, and a father missing in action. His name appeared as the defendant on a number of lawsuits. I couldn't tell if any were currently pending. He had no business or social affiliations, wasn't a member of the Rotary, Lions, Elks, Moose, or Knights of Columbus. With all the lawsuits, he probably didn't have time for meetings. The one charity that listed his name as a major benefactor was Alcoholics Anonymous.

Google refers me to a *Sun Times* article from a few years back, from which I learn Alvin J. Augustus was the son of an abusive father and a promiscuous mother. He bolted home at sixteen, talked his way into a job as a runner at the Board of Trade, and put his mind to learning puts and calls. Whether it was corn, wheat, stocks, or pork bellies, young Alvin developed what many said was a sixth sense about the rise and fall of commodity prices. When he became a trader at the tender age of eighteen, he bought when others were selling and sold in the middle of a buying frenzy. He was not right all the time, but he was right more than anyone else. Alvin's business boomed, with no need for employees, patents, factories, warehouses, company cars, bylaws, or boards of directors. He made his money gambling the futures of commodities, currencies, stocks, bonds, and whatever else was on the table. As an aside, the article mentioned that Alvin never played poker, craps, or baccarat, not that he couldn't; he merely considered these games beneath his talents.

I next search "rock murders" and am amazed at the number of singers, guitar players, and drummers gunned down, poisoned, or stabbed in bar fights. I try "murders by rocks" and get some religious nut who lists stoned victims. Pairing the two, I wonder how many of the rock-and-rollers were stoned when they became victims. All in all it is a worthless search. More people waste more time at computers than any other household item, except for the TV.

Noon, my back still hurt, but nowhere near like before, I had no choice but to suck it up and head north.

———

If you are forced to drive an old car, drive a Toyota; all you have to do is keep oil in them and they will last forever. If I can figure this out, why can't Ford and General Motors?

I park my Corolla about a hundred yards from the AJA estate. There are three cars in Alvin's circled driveway, one squad car and two late model Chevys; one has to be either Steve's or Norbert's. I go up the path to Alvin's neighbor, ring the bell and wait.

A woman, mid-to-late thirties, opens and answers. "Yes?"

I show her my license that closely resembles a badge. "My name is Richard Sherlock. I'm investigating the occurrence next door."

"Sherlock?"

"Yes."

She chuckled.

"I didn't get to pick my last name."

"I did."

She opens the door and I step inside the foyer. "I'll get my husband."

"Morris, Barry Morris," says the sixty-something man wearing an awful pair of multi-colored golf pants, approaching me with his hand out to shake.

"I apologize for bothering you, but I'd like to..."

"No bother," he interrupts.

Barry was obviously skilled at interrupting people.

"We didn't see or hear a thing," he says, finishing his sentence.

"Not a thing," his wife, who I doubt was his first, added.

"Did you know the Augustus family?"

"We knew them," he said.

"But it wasn't like we did pot luck," the little missus adds.

"Were you home yesterday afternoon?"

"I was at the mall."

"And I was playing golf."

My first rule of life is to never make assumptions, but I had to assume that Barry owned more than one pair of designer-from-hell golf togs. The thought was unsettling.

"Did you like the Augustus family?"

"No," they answer in tandem.

"Why not?"

They silence in tandem as well.

I decide to wait them out. Give it enough time and he'll say something.

"You know," Barry speaks after about five seconds, "I'm a lawyer and in the legal field we have a name for people like the Augustus'."

"And that would..." I start to ask, but he cuts me to the quick again.

"We call 'em assholes."

A few more pointless questions and I bid adieu to the Morris family.

The family who lived next to the Morris' was not home; neither was the family next to them. My neighborhood canvas was turning up nothing.

Down the block I had better luck, at least in finding people to talk with. The only disappointment was none of the three families heard or saw anything out of the ordinary for a Saturday morning. I was crossing the street to the opposite side of the Augustus home when a familiar Lexus 430 pulled up.

"Mister Sherlock," Tiffany said, hanging towards the passenger window, "I thought you were going to call me."

"I didn't want to bother you," I said, "I was worried that you still might be praying."

"Praying?"

"On the Church of Saint Mattress."

"Oh, yeah."

Tiffany parks the car, facing the wrong way on the street, and gets out with Starbucks in hand, laughing. "You know I forget how funny I am sometimes."

"I don't."

Since it was a hot day, I couldn't blame Tiffany for wearing shorts, but a wife-beater tee-shirt is a little on the casual side, even for investigating a murder. On her feet were three-inch wood clogs with sandal straps from the era of Ancient Rome. Her hair was pulled back into a ponytail and fitted between the canvas and the adjustable plastic strap on the back of her Cubs baseball cap. We made quite a couple pacing up a sidewalk, which seemed longer than a football field.

"Have you discovered any clues yet?" Tiffany asks before I ring the doorbell of a house that reminded me of the stately manor of Bruce Wayne.

"It's still early."

"I know, I'm not even through my first double-loaded, mocha-cappuccino latté yet."

I will not venture a guess at what the man thought, opening his front door to middle-aged me in tennis shoes, jeans, and wrinkled polo shirt, standing next to Tiffany, looking one bad photo out of a Cosmo exposé on "How to look slutty, but cool."

"Can I help you?"

I flash the badge, introduce myself.

"Is it 'take your kid to work day?'" He asks, as his eyes focus between Tiffany's chin and navel.

"We're not related."

He smiles.

Tiffany crosses her arms, ruining his view. "I'm his assistant."

"Do you have a minute?"

The man allows us entrance. "Honey, a detective is here with his assistant."

We are led to a massive kitchen, which opens to a den and sunroom facing Lake Michigan. This is a gorgeous, warm, livable home, the opposite end on the comparison scale to the Augustus' abode.

The wife rises to greet and get a better look at Tiffany. "I'm Mrs. Coulter. You'll have to excuse us; we're in the middle of a crisis."

A teenager sits in the den, curled up on the couch, tears pouring down her face. Tiffany makes a beeline to the girl, who stops crying at the sight of shoes.

"Hugo Boss?"

"Are there any other kind?" Tiffany asks and their bond is secure. "What's the matter?"

"Her dog died," Mr. Coulter said.

"What was his name?" Tiffany asks.

"Lucy." The girl weeps.

"What kind?"

"Labrador." Sniffle, sniffle.

I used to have a Labrador, named Ralph. I loved that dog. Wasn't the sharpest arrow in the quiver, but he was pure white, full of energy, and I could see the dollars rolling in once I had him bred. But I lost the dog in my divorce. Is there no justice for a "man's best friend?" To make matters worse, my ex had him fixed and changed his name to Pumpkin.

"What happened?" I ask the parents.

"She takes Lucy down by the lake everyday and lets her run," Mrs. Coulter says.

"And the dog comes back, goes through this doggie Saint Vitus Dance and drops dead," the daddy says. "I couldn't believe it."

I move closer to the couple. "Where's the dog now?"

"Being prepared for the service," the wife speaks with a "what else can we do?" tone in her voice.

Tiffany and the bereaved one whisper.

I accept the Coulter's offer of coffee and sit at their table to go through a series of questions.

What they tell me, in so many words, is that people who live in these neighborhoods, besides being so far apart in distance from each other, really don't want or need neighbors in the traditional sense. They have their own friends, never need a cup of sugar, and have few complaints since the Village of Kenilworth has such strict rules on what you can and cannot do with your property. These people are hardly the types to hang out on their front porches, sip a cool one, and chat up the people passing by.

"About all I can say is, people do come and go at the oddest times at that house." Mr. Coulter spoke as he sipped his java. "I travel quite a bit and some nights come home at 2 am, and I'll see a caravan of cars pull into the driveway."

"Then for weeks we won't see or hear a peep out of the place," the wife says.

I get the feeling the couple is enjoying this show-and-tell session. This is always my signal to quit. Too much information is sometimes worse than too little.

"Thank you very much." I stand, motion over to my assistant that it is time to go.

Tiffany and the teen, who has ceased the waterworks, hug, air-kiss, and part company.

Outside, Tiffany asks, "Did you find out anything?"

"No, did you?"

"Yes, her parents have her on a budget for clothes and accessories. Talk about torture. How is a girl going to be able to compete at New Trier High School on what's barely lunch money?"

———

Norbert evidently pulled the short straw of the two and is at the house when we arrive. "Should I bother with the neighbors?" he asked.

"No."

"Good."

Except for the media folk trampling the backyard, the place was pretty much as we left it. "Where did they take the body?"

"Downtown."

"When are they doing the slice and dice?"

"Monday," Norbert says sarcastically. "Evidently not everyone has to work on the Lord's day."

"When did you find religion?" I ask the lumpy detective.

"Every Sunday I have to work," he replies and sips coffee from a mug equal in size to a German beer stein.

"Don't you have to use the bathroom constantly using that thing?" Tiffany luckily pointed at his coffee mug as she poses her question.

"The most important tool a detective can have, little lady, is a bladder the size of a football."

Tiffany surveyed his girth, "Obviously, you're well prepared."

"Talk to the gardener yet?" I ask.

"We got an APB out on him."

"You think he killed Alvin for criticizing his pruning?"

"He took a powder. That's as good as a confession in most cases."

"I thought you labeled the case accidental?"

"Oh, yeah." At Norbert's age, memory goes first.

"What's his name?"

"Hector Elondsio."

"Who is scared shitless that someone is going to run a background check, find out he's illegal and ship him back to Juarez."

"Okay, okay, so maybe he's not the best suspect."

"He's probably on his way back to Mexico as we speak."

"Poor Hector," Tiffany bemoans, "he's going to be the only Mexican to have to sneak over the border both ways."

———

In the house, I retrace my steps of yesterday in reverse. I am trying to see things from a different angle; too bad it doesn't work.

Tiffany tags along, she looks in each closet. "I love labels."

"Where is the wife?" I ask Norbert.

"Flying in from Palm Springs, evidently her husband's death has put a serious dent in her vacation plans."

"No one goes to the Springs now," Tiffany says.

"She did."

"And it's like a 190 during the day."

"But it's a dry heat." I put in my ill attempt at humor.

"Sounds like tummy-tuck time to me," Tiffany offers her answer to the mystery.

———

Theresa has nothing better to do than make us all lunch. Norbert has a ham-and-pepper cheese on white with mustard and mayo, topped with sliced kosher dill pickles.

"Hey," he says, "try it; you'll like it."

Theresa whips up a tuna salad for me and Tiffany nibbles on carrots and cucumbers with a bran muffin for her entree.

"Sundays are the best day of the week to flush your system." She offers way too much information for my tastes.

Before Norbert inhales the second half of the sandwich, he pushes a yellow legal pad in front of me. "Steve gets a bit territorial; but if you just happen to see this, it won't bother me much."

On the pad is a step-by-step listing, a cop's to-do list with corresponding dates, times, and locations.

I make mental notes. "Want me to lead or follow?"

"For now, follow."

After the feast, I go outside and retrace the steps I made yesterday. Nothing new.

All in all, a totally worthless day. Detectives have lots of worthless days, not like on TV when all crimes are solved in less than an hour.

I go home. I call my kids. Kelly and Care both get on the phone and go on and on about how great it was riding their new horse.

I couldn't afford to own a horse when I was married, so how my ex is able to afford one now is beyond my comprehension. The entry of my girls into the horsey set unnerves me because about all I know of horses is not to stand behind one.

I tell the girls I love them and can't wait to see them on Tuesday.

I watch the news. Alvin's story has dropped to the last fifteen minutes, packaged between the weather and the sports. By tomorrow it will be off the air.

———

First thing Monday morning I get an anonymous phone message informing me that partial lab results are in and if I happen to be in Kenilworth, at a certain restaurant, around lunchtime, a copy might be available for viewing.

I arrive at 12 noon on the dot. Norbert is manning the rear booth, slurping the soup of the day. "Great lentil soup in this place," he says. "You wouldn't think so, this town being so Waspy."

It's lunchtime, but I order breakfast, the most important meal of the day.

Norbert pushes four pages of stapled report across the table.

I read quickly.

"Blunt trauma." Norbert pushes the empty bowl away to make room for his next course.

"I drove all the way up here to hear that?" I put the report down. "Did you order a full tox screen?"

"I can't do that for an accidental death."

"Why not?"

"Not in the budget."

"Norbert, we're in Kenilworth."

The food arrives and Norbert digs in. I continue reading.

The text is mostly lab mumbo jumbo. I wait for something to jump out, but it is pretty much boilerplate: blood loss, position of the body, vital statistics, and a medical ya-ya of how an avalanche of rocks, falling from a height of approximately ten feet onto a human being, will cause irreparable harm and/or death. The report is hardly appetizing.

"No fingerprints. Maybe it was accidental."

"They're called gloves, Norbert."

"No footprints, loose hairs, dandruff, thread, snot, or sweat on Alvin or on the rock."

"So, look for someone in a Hazmat suit who likes to toss boulders around for fun."

"I'm telling you, Sherlock; we could be onto the perfect crime."

"There is no such thing."

"Oh, come on," Norbert stops chewing. "I could commit the perfect crime if I wanted to."

"Go ahead, Norbert, steal a quarter."

I fold the pages in half. "Can I keep this?"

"I won't read it again," Norbert says, lifting his Monte Cristo sandwich. "You might also want to know that the feds called to voice their displeasure that Alvin would no longer be available for their investigation of insider trading at the Board of Trade." Norbert takes a bite, but continues to speak. "But you didn't hear that from me."

This information is worth the price of admission.

I pick up my fork and eat. My eggs are perfect. Why can't I learn how to poach an egg?

"You think somebody killed him to shut him up?" I ask.

"Steve thought it might be a contract or a mob hit, a wake-up call for any other squealers," Norbert says between bites, "but I think even the mob has more class than that."

I agree. "But who would want to rock him out, when a baseball bat is so much better suited to bashing in a person's head?"

"I heard the mob has switched to using those aluminum bats, much easier to clean and they sink when you toss them into the lake."

"Technology," I say, "it's everywhere."

I eat; Norbert devours. A piece of pie magically appears the second the last French fry enters his mouth.

"What do ya think, Sherlock?"

I should be asking, not answering. "Everything's not kosher."

"Alvin wasn't Jewish."

"Nobody kills a guy dressed in a linen suit on a Saturday morning, drags him home and buries him under an avalanche of his own rocks."

"Yeah, does seem kind of odd."

The waitress lays the check between us. "Insurance company give you an expense account?" Norbert asks.

"No,"

He pushes the tab my way. "Well, they should."

5

Parts is parts

On my drive back into the city I have time to contemplate the case, but I don't. As I pass through Lincoln Park, I look to my right and see what was once the Lincoln Hotel, which was the landing spot of Northside guys who had been kicked out of the house. I could smell the cheap disinfectant, stale smoke, bad booze, and the cloud of depression that came along with each room's monthly rental. After the little lady gave me the boot, the LH was my home.

What a memorable time. Estranged from the wife, kicked off the force for what most cops would consider a normal reaction, missing my kids terribly, fat, out of shape, back killing me daily. I was broke, living off credit cards, depressed, a real pleasure to be around.

Job-wise, I had been blackballed out of any department in the suburbs, the sheriff's department wouldn't touch me and the feds wouldn't admit I existed. Leaving town was out of the question because of my kids. I should have started a new career at the takeout window at a McDonald's, but instead I accepted a job as an insurance investigator with the promise that the hours would be my own. My second mistake was borrowing money from my new employer to pay off the credit cards. Dumb move. Once you owe your soul to the company store, it's tough to get back. Now, when Richmond Insurance calls, Richard Sherlock has no choice but to answer. I feel like an on-call OB/GYN in a Mormon polygamist compound.

————

I arrive at the morgue, not Cook County's, but the *Sun Times*.

One of the great things about living in Chicago is that they have two great, but different, newspapers: the *Tribune*, which is a high-brow broadsheet, made to read while sipping morning coffee at home -- and the *Sun Times*, a tabloid written for the working class stiff who pages through while riding the bus or "L" to work. The only time I ever read the *Trib* consistently was when Mike Royko took the big bucks to write for them; since his death over a decade ago, I'm back to the *Times*. There was no greater newspaper columnist than Mike Royko.

With the internet, few venture into the microfiche daily annals of yesterday and yesteryear. I am welcomed with open arms and files by a clerk named Theobald, a man who looks like he has worked below ground his whole life; he's whiter than Tide.

He helps me look up every article written about or that mentions Alvin J. Augustus. This is boring, tedious work. My eyes tire as the pages zip across a large black screen. I search for a hook, an angle, something that jumps out that doesn't make sense. I adjust and re-adjust the focus to read what I already know. After three hours, I'm toast; my eyes as blurry as the two bottom lines on a Snellen eye chart.

As I reach the street, my cell phone comes alive with an American Idol wanting to "Breakaway." Care, my youngest installed a ring tone on my phone, and I have no idea how to remove it.

There are three messages: Tiffany, Norbert, and Theresa, the Augustus' maid.

Norbert thanks me for lunch and drops in that the Mrs. is back in town. Theresa asks, in much better English, if I could call or stop by, and Tiffany screams "Mister Sherlock!"

I return Tiffany's call.

"You didn't call me," she says instead of Hello. "Daddy said I was to be kept in the loop."

"You were in the Loop."

"No way."

"You told me Monday you're in the Loop for your facial."

"Not that loop."

"My bad." If there is one expression I hate, it is, "my bad."

"I can reschedule my zits getting popped, any day. We're on a case." She pauses for effect. "Dammit, you should have called me, Mister Sherlock."

"Sorry."

She calms down. "What are we doing tomorrow?"

"Tomorrow's Tuesday."

"Ah, duh."

"Tuesdays, I see my kids."

"So?"

"That means I don't work. I pick them up at two, we hang out, cook dinner; I get to be a dad."

"Ah... there is a twelve-million-dollar policy at stake here."

"Not my money."

"But it could be mine someday," she says in no uncertain terms. "I'll pick you up tomorrow at ten."

———

Tiffany arrives at my apartment at ten-thirty; being fashionably late applies to all Tiffany destinations. She wears a yellow sundress, flip-flops, and her hair is pulled back in a ponytail.

"I don't know why we are wasting our time going back to see that woman," Tiffany says driving back through the Northshore. "I mean bleach not only destroys good fabric, but you can smell the fumes while you wear it."

"How many lattés have you had this morning?"

"Three, I'm going to have to make a pit stop if we hit traffic."

Tiffany is ready to burst by the time she parks behind the black-and-white in Alvin's driveway.

"You wait for me before you question her," Tiffany orders before running into the house the moment Theresa opens the front door.

"Mister Sherlock." Theresa steps onto the porch.

I put up one finger to stop her before she speaks. We wait until Tiffany returns and says, "Thanks, I needed that."

The three of us walk around the house, down the driveway, and into the back acreage.

"Mister Sherlock, I worry about Hector," Theresa tells us.

"Why?"

"I think, they think he did it."

"Did he?"

"No," Theresa says. "Only things Hector ever kill are bugs."

38

"Is he your husband?"

Theresa stares at her shoes.

"Lover, sí?" Tiffany hits the nail on the head.

"I get lonely being so far from home."

"Me too."

I look at Tiffany; what the hell is she talking about? She's twenty minutes away from her condo.

"It is so hard when you don't have someone you love near you." Tiffany hands over her monogrammed silk handkerchief.

"He's illegal, right?" I ask.

"Sí."

"Aren't we all in some way or another?" Tiffany must have been watching Oprah while she was sucking down her lattés.

"They won't do anything to him," I tell Theresa. "They know he's innocent."

"Should I tell him to come back?"

"How far away is he?"

"My cousins'."

"That confirms how hard they're looking for him. Tell him to lay low and I'll let you know." I keep walking, the two women slightly behind. "Tell me something, Theresa, Mr. Augustus ever walk around kinda spacey?"

"Spacey?"

"Es loco en la cabeza." Tiffany translates.

"No."

"How about drunk?"

"No."

"And his wife?"

"Drunk or loca?" Theresa wants clarification.

"You pick."

"No," Theresa says. "Mrs. Alvin too busy being mean to be drunk or dizzy."

I continue. "Would you say they made a nice couple?"

"Mr. Alvin mean, too."

"Is that about the only thing they had in common?"

"Is really not my business." Theresa is embarrassed for the second time.

"How about their kids?"

"Oh," Theresa says, "boo."

I pause.

"They treat me like servant."

"Well, isn't that par for the course?" Tiffany asks.

Although Theresa has never played golf, she gets the gist of Tiffany's question.

"What time did Alvin come home on Friday?"

"Don't know; wasn't here."

"Hector's?"

"Sí."

"She has her needs, Mister Sherlock," Tiffany informs me.

I turn back to the maid. "Whatever you do, Theresa, don't leave town."

"Sí."

Tiffany gets her handkerchief back before we leave.

———

The second-worst person in the world anyone can marry is a cop. The first is a cop who is a detective. My ex was a nice suburban girl, from a good family -- dad a welder, mom worked in the school cafeteria. At first, she thought it would be exciting married to one of Chicago's finest, but got very mad when she discovered this was not the case. The difference between my ex and the exes of most of my fellow cops was: Their wives got mad, got divorced, and moved on. Mine got mad, got divorced, and stayed mad.

In retrospect, I can't blame her for cutting me loose. My hours were awful. I'd get calls in the middle of the night and out the door I went. She was never sure if I'd come home in one piece or come home at all. My attempts to be a good husband were always interrupted by some gang war, mafia hit, or murderous crime spree. Once she started hanging around other cops' wives and ex-wives, who provided her a forum for unadulterated bitching, our marriage became as rocky as Alvin's demise.

———

We arrive at my ex and now my ex's house in Sauganash ten

minutes late. She is inside, no doubt recording my tardiness for negative fodder the next time she takes me to court for more money.

Care and Kelly are thrilled to see Tiffany, not me.

"Are we going shopping?" Kelly asks.

"No."

"What are we doing then, Daddy?" Care, my ten-year-old, asks.

"Since it is so hot, we're going someplace really cool." I tell them with a phony excitement in my voice.

"Cool, as in cool," Kelly my twelve-year-old says. "Or cool as in temperature?"

"Both."

"Don't worry," Tiffany says, "I'll take you to Saks and we'll get your make-up done."

"Now, that's cool."

"They don't need make-up," I say. "They're not even teenagers yet."

"Never too young to learn the basics of a good blush, Mister Sherlock."

We arrive at a dirty-white, oblong structure with a driveway concealed from street view. Ambulances drive in and out all day and never a siren is heard.

"What's this place, Dad?" Care asks, the more vocally inquisitive of the two.

"Trust me; it's cool." I pull the handle on the door. "You people wait in the car."

"No way," Kelly pipes up.

"Yeah, no way," Tiffany agrees.

The three females follow me through the parking area, up the ramp and into the main door. The four of us look like we're heading for dinner at TGI Friday's.

Jellyroll, an attendant I've known for years, meets us as we enter. "Doing field trips now, Sherlock?"

"Is Alvin Augustus still around?"

"Unless he stepped out when I wasn't watching," Jellyroll says.

Bad gallows humor is the norm in this place.

In the entryway, it must be sixty-five degrees, about thirty less than outside, and Tiffany's natural thermometers chart it. My older daughter stares at her chest with jealous envy. The teenage years are going to be hell.

"Alvin's been one of our more popular guests today." Jellyroll tells us as we proceed down the corridor.

"Is the slice-and-dice completed?"

"Yesterday."

"You wouldn't happen to know where a copy might be available for takeout; would you?"

"No tickee; no washee," an Asian accent from an old black man.

I motion to Tiffany with thumb rubbing my forefingers. She gets the message.

"How much for two adults and two kids under twelve?"

Kelly says, "I'm almost thirteen."

"Hundred," I answer.

Jellyroll smiles, he only charges me twenty.

Tiffany opens her Coach purse as we stop at the end of the corridor. "Is there a cash machine here or will you take a check?"

To the left is a long room with two levels of stainless-steel doors. To the right is the holding area where a number of gurneys wait with covered remains; each has a foot sticking out with a tag attached to the big toe. Just what I've always wanted my kids to see.

"Number sixteen on the right." Jellyroll points.

"You people go with Jelly and don't look at anything you're not supposed to look at."

Kelly demands. "I want to see the stiffs."

"Go."

I turn right. They turn back down the corridor and walk towards the waiting room.

I grab a pair of latex gloves on my way to number sixteen, where I flip the latch and slide Alvin out for a full view. He remains disgusting. No matter how well they clean him up, an open coffin is out of the question. I cover what is left of his face. Been there; seen that. On his torso, he has a train-track scar running from the base of his neck down past his navel where they cut him open to take inventory.

I look for needle marks on his arms, on his thighs, and

between his toes. I find one pin-prick that might even be a mosquito bite. Alvin is no needle freak. There are numerous bruises on his body, forearms, and legs, but his manicured nails have held up well. I skip his privates; some areas should remain private in life and death. He has white pasty legs and bunion-filled feet. Feet tell a lot about a person. He also stinks, not of formaldehyde, but whatever they use to stuff his veins and arteries. The entire process has taken less than fifteen minutes. I'm angry. I have seen nothing of interest, nothing that helps, nothing out of the ordinary. How shameful that I consider someone with his head bashed-in ordinary.

Tiffany and Care return with Jellyroll. I slide Alvin back into his refrigerated condo unit, take off the gloves and join them.

"Was it gross?" Care asks.

"Totally," I reply, then ask, "Where's your sister?"

Care shrugs her shoulders.

I turn to my left to see my eldest daughter in the anteroom reading toe tags like they were labels in a department store.

"Get over here."

"Just looking," she says returning. "You always say we should develop a healthy curiosity."

"You've never paid attention to any of my advice before; why start now?"

"First thing you said that ever made any sense, Dad."

I have raised an incurable wiseass.

"Anything else, Sherlock?" Jellyroll asks.

"Health records."

"Didn't have any."

"Everybody has health records," I say.

"Not Alvin," Jellyroll says. "Never spent a day in a hospital."

"Can we go get our faces done now?" Kelly asks Tiffany.

"Sure."

———

I sit in the chair reserved for the rich guy while his wife or mistress spends his money, and read the autopsy report. My two daughters sit in high chairs at the cosmetic counter with Tiffany directing the cosmeticians like Spielberg on the set of a movie.

The autopsy reports Alvin had six different drugs in his system when or before he died, not one name I recognize. The six had no correlation, except that they were all high-powered and deadly if taken in bulk. If a person is not a constant user of drugs, the substances will clear their system completely which is the reason they do random tests of athletes for steroids and growth hormones. Alvin could have been an every-so-often abuser and even his doctor wouldn't have known the difference. I make a mental note to myself to check on the amounts of each drug found in his system, because I have no clue how much would be too much. Other than six opiates found, Alvin was the picture of health. Heart, liver, lungs, kidneys all in great shape; too bad he wasn't available for parts; he would have been a goldmine.

I hardly recognized my two daughters when Tiffany brings them over. They resembled Jon Benet Ramsey, the six-year-old beauty queen of unsolved-murder fame.

"You two look like painted Barbie dolls."

"No, we don't."

"Yes, Kelly, you do."

"Barbie has breasts; we don't."

Tiffany drives us back to my apartment, where she tells the kids, "Next time I'll teach you how to shop."

I make chicken for dinner. They say it's gross, but they eat it. We watch some dumb TV show on Nickelodeon, Kelly relenting to Care for some reason I'll never know.

When the girls are with me, they sleep in my bed and I take the couch, which does wonders for my back. They were tired. I tuck them in, give them a kiss.

"Tell us a Joe and Mo, Dad," Care requests.

Whenever I was home at bedtime, when the two were young, I would tell them a story about an old geezer couple who lived in a shack by the river. Joe and Mo. I made the tales up as I went along, finishing as eyelids were closing. It was a ritual I enjoyed immensely.

Now the girls are well past story time age, but a request is a request. I sit on the edge of the bed and make up an absurd tale of Joe catching a catfish that was a spitting image of Mo and then can't tell the two apart until he plants a big kiss on the fish's lips.

In five minutes they are fast asleep.

Just when you believe your kids are growing up, they revert to hold onto a piece of their childhood. Yes, I want my kids to learn, mature, become self-confident, and do things on their own; but I never want to forget that feeling when they needed me, wanted me around and appreciated me being their dad. Exactly how I feel at this very moment.

6

Money dearest

"It was the bitch before me."

I am in a Ritz Carlton suite, twice the size of my apartment, seated in a leather chair so comfortable I could easily drift off into naptime, except for the fact that the woman across from me has the voice of a peacock.

"Bitch could never get over the fact that she got beat at her own game."

Doris Augustus refused to return to the Kenilworth house. She said bad karma still lurked within its walls. She instead booked a suite at the Ritz and was living as comfortably as she could in her time of grief.

"Doris, please..."

Doris. There is a moniker you don't hear very often any more. Too bad, I like the name, although not its namesake before me.

Mrs. Augustus is a slight woman, five-one, maybe a hundred pounds, late forty-something, trying her best to look late thirty-something. If she is bereaved, she hides it well--very little expression on her face. No doubt she's tough, stoic, unflinching in her opinions and demands. In a family argument, I can see her standing up to Alvin until he opened up his checkbook.

Tiffany sits to my left. The Ritz Carlton is her element.

"What were you doing in Palm Springs?" I ask the widow.

"Vacationing."

"In 190-plus heat?" Tiffany repeats herself from two days ago.

"It's a dry heat," Doris snaps back.

"You could cook an egg on the sidewalk," Tiffany argues.

"I don't do dairy," Doris retorts.

"Why were you there?" I try again.

"Vacationing."

"Alone?"

"Yes, alone."

I give up on hearing any valid reason for travel. "Was there anyone else besides," and I use her inflection, "that bitch second wife of his who hated your husband enough to kill him?"

"That bitch," she repeats, "and everybody else."

"Thank you for narrowing things down."

"Those guys at the Board of Trade, their job is to put the other guy into the poor house." Doris points a manicured finger my way. "Somebody takes your money, you'd hate them, too."

"But that's business," I say. "Or divorce."

"It's money," Doris says. "And money transcends all."

"Right on."

"Thank you for your input, Tiffany."

"You're welcome."

"Were you divorced before you married Alvin?" My question will surely solidify her monetary policy.

"Isn't everyone?" she replies.

I stand, mosey over to the window. The northern view from the fortieth floor is spectacular. "How long had you been in Palm Springs?"

"Two weeks."

Tiffany zeroes in on Doris with a squint each time the woman speaks.

"When was the last time you spoke with your husband?"

"Two weeks ago."

"You didn't call during your trip?"

"No. Why would I?"

"Maybe just to say, 'Hey?'"

"No."

"So, you didn't speak?"

"Only when we had to."

"How often was that?"

"I can't recall."

My ex used to give me the silent treatment for weeks and months at a time. All of a sudden she would clam up and treat me as if I wasn't in the room, driving me nuts. She wouldn't even pass the salt, if asked. Her silent treatment was the death knell of our marriage.

"So, could we say the conversational element of your marriage had fallen into disrepair?"

From what Doris answered, she and Alvin had four working

cold shoulders, night and day. They shared their distaste for one another by not speaking, unless it was absolutely necessary, which was probably when Doris was asking for more money.

I turn back from the view. "Do you know where Alvin was the night before he died?"

"No."

"Where were you?"

"In Palm Springs," she snaps back.

I raise an index finger to acknowledge my mistake. "Do you know where your husband may have been going on a Saturday morning dressed in a linen suit?"

"He always dressed to go to the office."

"On a Saturday?"

"He was funny like that."

I wait. She seemed to suddenly want to talk.

"Alvin was peculiar in some ways," Doris said in a calm tone of voice. "His idea of kicking back was a clean, pressed pair of slacks, a silk shirt, and a blue blazer. That might be a result of his upbringing, when he couldn't afford a shirt. He also didn't write checks--kept a wad of cash on him at all times. He didn't own a cell phone and didn't use a computer. His underwear had to be ironed and his shoes had to be perfectly buffed."

"Nothing the matter with that," Tiffany chimes in.

"Was that because he had bad feet?"

Doris was surprised. "How did you know that?"

"Homework."

"Besides his feet, did Alvin have any ailments?"

"No."

"Who was his doctor?"

"Didn't have one."

"Did he do a lot of cardio?" Tiffany asks.

Doris glares at Tiffany, as if she is an idiot in designer clothes.

"What was the appeal of the rock garden?" I ask.

"He'd spend hours out there, digging, designing, moving one, replacing another. I'm glad you couldn't see it from the house; embarrassing to watch a grown man playing with his pebbles."

"Did he beat you?" Tiffany asked.

"No."

I wasn't sure what direction to go next after that sudden foray.

Doris leaned towards Tiffany. There was very little movement in her face when she spoke. "When will the insurance pay out?"

"I'm not sure." Tiffany knows, but won't tell.

Doris knows Tiffany knows.

"I'm not sure the policy is ready to be disbursed," Tiffany says.

"That's my money."

"Ah," Tiffany says, "not yet."

A crack in her expression, Doris is pissed or surprised. Hard to tell which.

"Bullshit." She's pissed.

Tiffany shrugs.

"Who is in charge?" Doris asks.

"My dad." Tiffany smiles again.

I make no comment.

"His money is my money."

"Not quite," Tiffany continues the tête-à-tête, "I earned every penny. Alvin was more than a husband; he was a job."

"And when he was terminated, you got fired."

The edges of my mouth turn down and I nod slightly; Tiffany's comment amazes me.

Doris stands, walks to the door, opens it. "You can go now."

———

"Boob lift."

Tiffany and I sit in the Ritz lobby on the twelfth floor of Water Tower Place. If there is a more impeccably manicured room in the world, I'd like to see it.

"She had a boob lift."

"What?"

Tiffany demonstrates. "They pull this up to fight this falling down."

I am slightly embarrassed, staring at the young girl's flawless breasts. "You think that's why she was in Palm Springs?"

"What better time to go?" Tiffany says. "She's probably got a standing room reservation at a private hospital every year at that time."

"She's had that much work done?"

"If Doris has one more face lift, she'll be wearing a goatee."

I sip coffee from a cup of fine china. "Why does a guy like Alvin stay married to a woman like Doris?"

"He doesn't want to be bothered," Tiffany says.

"Bothered by what?"

"His house, cars, help, kids, social obligations, whatever; he's got too much else going on to worry about. He lets her do all that, 'cause she's got nothing better to do."

"She was right-on about marriage being a job?"

"All she has to do is keep the house running, keep herself looking good; so he looks good and everybody is happy."

"Think they still did it?"

"Sex?" Tiffany questions my question. "No way."

"Why not?"

"She doesn't have to anymore and he's shelling out for premium blend."

I sip my coffee. "Is there something going on with that policy, I should know about?"

"Yeah."

"What?"

"Some kind of rider."

"Ever consider mentioning that to me?"

"Not really."

"What did the rider specify?"

"I don't know."

"Tiffany, tell me."

"All I know is Daddy didn't get to be Daddy by paying out."

7
The old block's chip

Two gangbangers are found shot to death on the Red Line train at 3 am on a Tuesday night. The case falls on the rookie detective's desk.

The victims are teenagers, sporting more tattoos than a starting NBA line-up. They wore the requisite baggy shorts and skin-tight tee-shirts, but in dissimilar colors. Each had a criminal record from age thirteen and spent most of their time, doing time. Each was shot at close range, one bullet per brain. There are four witnesses who won't talk and I can't blame them. Witnesses in the projects become an immediate endangered species. The lab guys refuse to dust for prints on a subway car; can't blame them for that, either. All I have to go on are eight-by-ten glossies of the boys in deathly splendor.

I take the pictures to my cubicle, pin them up on the wall and stare at them for two hours. My fellow detectives think I am nuts. Nobody cares about gangbangers, because they are usually killed by rival gangbangers; a thinning of the criminal herd, a win-win for the citizenry. After all that staring, I finally see, amidst a slew of painted skin, one small tattoo, a replica of a handgun, is shared by the victims.

The next night two more gangbangers are shot to death beneath the Harlem "L" platform on the Westside. Again, nothing matches, except the handgun tattoo. If this is two gangs having it out, the least they can do is identify themselves. More pictures are tacked to my wall.

I go to work and question every gang squad cop to discover if they have ever seen similar tattoos. They think I am either kinky or gay. I review three years' worth of cases and find gang crimes are surprisingly boring. One kid shoots another kid and that kid's buddies shoot back, etc., etc. I visit with every gangbanger doing time in Cook County and make them take off their shirts to find a match of tats and find none. I am sure they also suspect I am gay.

I take the photos and question hookers, ER nurses, tattoo parlor artists; nobody knows or won't say a word. I keep asking questions and, although I didn't realize it at the time, what I was doing was fueling more talk on the street than a free cell phone offer.

Two nights later two more teenagers are found shot to death in an abandoned school bus; interesting transportation angle at work here. Plus, same tats.

With the total at six, the newspapers increase circulation, the local TV stations have plenty of grisly video to kick off their broadcasts and the mayor's office is screaming bloody murder, so to speak. And my wall is filling up.

The buzz on the street has grown meaner than a cocaine addict trying to free-base baking soda. Fingers are pointed, alibis are established, snitches are reeling in the money; tongues are wagging with anonymous tips and there is a massive covering of one's own ass from the top down in a number of gangs. The Insane Unknowns are blaming the Latin Kings, the Crips are ratting out the Bloods. The Blackstone Rangers say it's the Mongols and on, and on, and on.

I have no murder weapons, no stack of cash for a motive, and no connection between crimes, except six kids with one similar tattoo. All I can do is keep asking questions. I pull one leader from each gang in for questioning and put them in the same room. Although they are all in the same business, the leaders are not the type to kibbitz with their personal trade secrets or exchange favorite recipes. What happens? Stupidity rises to the surface like a fart in a swimming pool. As each blames the others, facts surface, the story takes shape, and motives are revealed.

It took me about twenty minutes to learn that six gangbangers, from rival gangs, joined forces in an attempt to start their own gang. Ah, the American dream in all its glory. Unfortunately, the upstarts didn't write a very good business plan, because once the word of their new biz got back to their respective chiefs, each was destined to pay the ultimate exit fee.

In the end we arrested nine, got great press, and I received an accommodation for a job well done. A day or two later, life was back to normal with the same amount of gang-related drug dealing, violence, and mayhem in the City of Chicago. Isn't it great to make a difference?

This case, one of my firsts, defined my career, because it taught me: 1. If you keep asking questions, somebody will eventually spill enough beans for you to make soup. 2. Newton's law of physics applies to crime. 3. Given the opportunity, people will undoubtedly become their own worst enemies. 4. Put everything you know up on a wall, because it becomes easier to see what you don't know, what you want to know, and what you should know.

———

It is late in the evening. Television is boring. You would think with all the channels they have now, something interesting would be on all the time.

I go into my kitchen and from the top cabinet I pull out a recipe box, a small, metal container. I remove the six or seven never-cooked recipes and lift out the blank three-by-five index cards. In no particular order I begin to fill in the cards with a hodgepodge of information, starting with the family.

Alvin had two sons and one daughter, Clayton, Brewster, and Christina. Clayton's mother was Alvin's second wife, Joan. Brewster's mom was Doris, the walking Botox prescription. Christina was a product of wife numero uno, Didi, who Alvin was married to for about sixty seconds and divorced even quicker.

I place the completed cards back in the box and stuff some empties into my coat pocket for later use. I call Tiffany and mention that I'm meeting Brewster Augustus after the markets close that afternoon.

At 3 pm I wait at the State Street door of the Board of Trade. On this particular piece of concrete the sun never shines. Somehow, the way it was built, direct sunlight never hits this spot. This fact should tell you a lot about life at the Board of Trade.

Tiffany arrives, dressed down, way down in a pair of used designer jeans with holes in the knees and a man's dress shirt, which could use a good pressing.

"Don't you look ravishing?"

"I don't want to be mistaken for one of those gold-diggers," she says.

Women have been known to wear wedding dresses, sexy cocktail numbers and stripper outfits to parade themselves in front of the wealthy traders and brokers on the floor. Whether this method of display has produced any marriages is anyone's guess, but it does beg the question: women's lib, where art thou?

We take the elevator to the fourteenth floor, walk down the hall to #1406 and enter a door with no name plate or identifying label.

There is a small foyer, empty of chairs, desk, or couch. If there was once a receptionist, she took everything with her when she left. We proceed into a large open room, where there are six long tables, the kind used at a VFW Hall. Computer terminals and telephones crowd onto each surface. The chairs vary, leather secretarial, folding, patio mesh, and one is the kind you need if you have a bad back. Wish I could afford one of these. All in all, a collection of what was either left by the last tenant or what was left next to the dumpster. The carpet is worn. The walls are bare, except for a few hand-drawn charts on easel-size paper stuck to the wall with push pins, and they scream for a fresh coat of paint. Empty beer cans lie next to trash baskets, having missed their mark. Four guys play baccarat; three play poker. The players range in age from thirty to sixty. Tiffany is the only woman in the room, but the boys are too busy gambling to notice.

"Excuse me," I pipe up. "Is Brewster Augustus around?"

Without looking up from his hand of cards, one player responds, "He's taking a leak."

"Good answer," Tiffany remarks.

We stand watching mini-Vegas in action until Brewster walks in the door.

"I didn't do it." This is his initial comment; his next is, "Let me get a beer."

The three of us leave the den of gambling iniquity to sit at a card table in a room not designed to house a large side-by-side refrigerator, a microwave oven, and one outdoor trash can.

"Like I told the other guys, I was at the bar with my brother." Brewster finally notices my very good-looking, so-called assistant. "Who are you?"

"Tiffany, detective in training."

I get the conversation back on track. "When was the last time you saw your father?"

"Week or so ago."

"Any special reason for the visit?"

"Usual stuff."

"When was the last time you two spoke?"

"Thursday."

"Why?"

"Usual stuff."

"Which would be?"

"Asking for money." Brewster finished his beer. "I didn't kill him."

"Why not?"

"He said yes." Brewster rose, went to the refrigerator, pulled out another beer, pops the top. "I'd offer you one, but you shouldn't drink while you're working."

"Thanks for reminding me," I say and continue, "What would your father be doing on a Saturday morning dressed in a suit out by the lake?"

"Beats me."

"Did you see him the Friday before?"

"No."

"Where were you?"

"I told you. Out with my idiot half-brother until he gets picked up and leaves me flat."

"Where?"

"Some club."

"You know where your dad was?"

"It wasn't my turn to watch him."

"Let me guess; you and daddy were not close?"

"The old man came up the hard way and wanted us to do the same, which is difficult to do when you're brought up in an eighteen-room mansion. He'd preach all this bullshit about hard work, nose to the grindstone, earning your keep; then go out and buy me a Porsche so I could keep up with the other kids at school."

"But since you have obviously followed in his footsteps, how has your relationship been since?"

"We were joined at the wallet."

I was trying desperately to find some aspect of Brewster's

personality to like, but was having no success.

"Your father an alcoholic?"

"No."

"You?" Tiffany jumps in.

"I used to be," Brewster finishes the beer. "I'm better now."

Tiffany sits up straight, as if sizing up a foe.

"Being joined at the wallet," I ask, "does that mean you worked for your father?"

"I trade off one of the seats he owns."

Traders and brokers have to own a seat to be able to trade and, since there are only so many seats to be had, they are a valuable commodity at the Board, no pun intended. Some pay rent well into five figures monthly.

"Do you pay rent?"

"No." Brewster burps.

"How much actual jail time did you end up serving?" My question surprises Tiffany as much as it surprises Brewster.

"How did you know about that?" Brewster places the beer on the table and leans forward.

"I have ways."

"The file was sealed; it was part of the court order."

"I told you; I have ways." A good detective can find out just about anything, if he wants to take the time and effort.

Brewster sits, contemplates.

Tiffany is about to speak, but I kick her under the table to keep her quiet.

Brewster tries to wait us out, but no way. "Sixty-eight days," he says, pretending to read the back of the beer can. "It wasn't my fault."

"You got drunk, you got stoned, you got in a car, and you hit a rival frat brat. What part wasn't your fault?"

"The idiot ran right in front of the car."

"Which you were driving at eighty miles per hour down a back alley at two in the morning."

This is all news to Tiffany and she soaks it in.

"If it really would have been my fault, it would have been the Marion Pen, not Cook County Jail."

"Maybe." I pause. "Was AA part of the deal?"

"Yeah."

"Didn't work, eh?" Tiffany says.

"Not a DUI since."

"Hard to believe," Tiffany says.

The rich-brat verbal battle roars back, full throttle.

"I went cold turkey."

"That ain't no O'Doul's you're drinking." Tiffany uses the double negative for effect.

"I haven't been behind the wheel in years." Brewster grins from ear to ear. "After AA, I went DA."

"Never heard of it," Tiffany admits.

"Sold the car, cleaned out the garage, and tore up the license."

"Driver's Anonymous?" I ask.

"Think of what I save on car insurance, gas, and oil," Brewster says with a smirk.

"Not to mention what you're doing for the environment," Tiffany adds without missing a beat.

I can't believe how well these two have hit it off. I get up and wander over to the microwave, which is surrounded by thousands of crumbs of every variety. "How well do you think you'll do in the settlement, Brewster?"

"I have no clue." Brewster crushes the beer can and tosses it into the trash, a two-pointer, not long enough for a three. "My father was a funny guy, not ha-ha, but peculiar. All he really loved was money, not what it could buy, but making money. Money was his booze. He was addicted to his bank account. He didn't care how he made it, who he took it from, how it got into his wallet. Money to him was the trophy, his daily validation he was alive. He once said to me, 'I'm rich, therefore I am.'"

"Why don't you trade on the floor like your daddy did?"

"Different generation."

I waited. Brewster twisted a diamond pinkie ring around and around. I sensed he was going to wrap this up.

"I'm sorry to inform you, but I didn't have anything to do with his death. I feel sorry that he died. I promise I will try to shed a few tears one of these days, but daddy wasn't much of a daddy."

"Except for being joined at the wallet?" I ask.

"Whatever." Brewster finishes his beer. "There is a slew of people who hated him a lot more than I did. Good luck hitting bingo."

One positive about Brewster Augustus, he was able to bring things down to the simplest common denominator.

———

A ringing phone at two-eighteen in the morning is a part-time dad's greatest fear.

"What?"

I shake waiting for the response.

"Get your ass out of bed," Steve Burrell says. "Get dressed and meet us at the mansion. The case just got a little more interesting."

8

Feng shui your gaydar

The Augustus house is lit up like a movie set. There are three squad cars, two fire trucks, Norbert's and Steve's sedans and now my Toyota. The front door is open; I walk right in.

"If we got to be here," Norbert says, "we thought you should, too."

"It's always nice to be remembered," I say as he leads me inside.

The den is a shambles. Drawers open and emptied onto the floor, books tossed off the shelves in no particular order, cabinets emptied, pictures and artwork off the walls.

I mill around in the mess. "A scavenger hunt gone horribly wrong?"

"Your sense of humor is hard enough for me to take when I'm awake, much less when I'm half-asleep," Steve says.

"Any other rooms get a makeover?"

"Bedroom."

I pace around the walls of the den. Two wall safes have not been touched. "Where's Theresa?"

"Night off."

I picture her lying beneath Hector, whispering sweet nothings into his ear. A tank of bug spray sits next to their bed.

"Alarm on?"

"Was."

"See anything missing?"

"Not that we can remember," Norbert says.

"Call the wife?"

"She didn't answer her phone."

"Beauty sleep," I say.

"We'll have the room dusted tomorrow," Steve says.

"Don't bother."

"Why not."

"Won't do a bit of good."

"What makes you so sure, Sherlock?"

"Because whoever did this entered, turned off the alarm, trashed the place, turned the alarm back on, and split. No one could do this much damage in the time between the alarm going off and a patrol car arriving. Nothing is missing and there is no sign of forced entry."

"Yeah, that's what I was going to say," Norbert says. "But why all the fuss?"

"They were pissed because they didn't find what they were looking for."

"Which is?"

"I don't know."

The detectives look at each other, look at their shoes and back towards me.

I yawn. I'm tired. I hate my job.

"If we assume…"

"Don't assume anything; that's my first rule of life."

Steve does not continue.

"There is a reason, and probably a bad one, for this happening," I say. "But the only thing I'm certain of is we won't be figuring it out tonight."

Steve and Norbert sigh.

"I'm going home." I turn to exit. "I got a big day tomorrow."

———

Clayton Augustus was as miserable a human being as his younger brother, but in an entirely different way.

"You talk to that half-wit, half-brother of mine?" Clayton asks as Tiffany and I sit in his renovated Lincoln Park greystone, beneath an oil painting that could double as a Rorschach test.

"He said he didn't do it."

"And you believed him?"

"So far."

"Well, I didn't kill him, either."

I look over at Tiffany. "Can I go home now?"

"No."

Tiffany was dressed junior executive, matching skirt and

jacket, white blouse and sensible, but expensive, shoes. She must have more clothes than Diane von Furstenberg. No doubt, I could fit my entire apartment into her closet and she would still have room for her winter outfits, ski equipment, and an inflated white water raft.

"How do you think you'll do in the will?"

"Like, I care?"

"I would," Tiffany says.

"The money certainly didn't do Daddy much good in the long run, now did it?"

"He had a pretty good run," I say.

Clayton puts his feet up on his coffee table and leans back onto his leather couch. He had been whisked off his exercise room treadmill to come and talk with us. The odor of sweat mixed with designer aftershave wafted from his Under Armour workout attire. He was about twenty-seven, four years older than Brewster.

"Did you ever see or talk to your father?"

"When I had to."

"And when would that be?"

"Whenever." Clayton was trying hard to act bored.

"Saturday or the Friday before he died?"

"No."

"You get this all from your father?" I ask motioning to the lavish décor or the room.

"No."

"Then, how?"

"I tap into people's greed."

"That was your major in college?" I can play his verbal game, too.

"I didn't go to college."

Tiffany removes a steno pad and pen from her purse and begins to take notes. I wonder what she could possibly find interesting in this inane conversation.

"I match people with a lot of money, with people who have ideas that can make them a lot more money and take a piece of the action from both parties. Actually, it's quite a simple business."

"If it is so simple, why doesn't everyone do it?"

"Hell if I know."

Clayton Augustus founded INCUBATE INC. when he was

twenty, to fund biotech research for the pharmaceutical industry. His business recipe was to add large parts private capital with very adept drug science, let it marinate into the promise of the next Viagra or Xanax, then sell the sizzle to the highest bidder. With a number of the biggest drug companies in the world in the Chicago area, Abbott Labs, Baxter Intl., to name two, the market was hungry. With the old money he grew up around, as well as the venture capital millions available, there was cash around to invest. And with Northwestern, University of Chicago, Children's and Rush/Presbyterian research hospitals subway distance apart, he never lacked for good ideas.

"For not caring much for your dad, you sure ended up a lot like him."

Clayton didn't appreciate my assessment. "Bullshit."

"You don't make, create, manufacture, or market any product or service. You might as well be jumping up and down at the Board of Trade."

"What I do has nothing to do with what my father did."

Tiffany stood up, breaking the tension as she sizes up the room.

Clayton watches her like a lion stalking prey.

"This room feng shui?"

"What?" I ask, wondering where that came from.

"You would have to ask my designer," Clayton answers.

"Marceau DeLeon?"

Clayton perks up at Tiffany's knowledge. "You're good."

"Marceau doesn't feng shui."

Clayton sits up, turns to face Tiffany.

"You should have it done."

I have no idea what these two are discussing.

Tiffany begins to move furniture, re-aligning the angles of the chairs and tables. "Way too much negative energy in the room."

"I didn't know I'd be getting a decorating detective, too," Clayton says, glancing my way.

"At no extra charge." Tiffany heads for the stairway. "I can't wait to see the master bedroom."

Clayton gets up to follow her.

"Ah, Clayton..."

He stops, returns, and sits. "Can we hurry this along? I have a hot chick in my bedroom."

I roll my eyes and shake my head. "Think daddy left anything for your mother?"

"No."

"She still pissed?"

"Wouldn't you be?"

The second Augustus divorce was a pit bull fight to the death. Joan claimed Alvin had been screwing around for years. Alvin countered with Joan being an unfit parent and mounted a case so strong, even Joan started believing she was a little loony. There were lawyers upon lawyers, accusing, briefing, motioning, declaring, posturing, and pleading. The legal bills could have fed a third world country for a month. The court, in the end, gave most of the money to the son, Clayton, via an executor, to dole out the dollars as he saw fit. Joan was left, not the happiest of campers.

"I was the one who took care of my mother; he didn't."

"But you did it with your father's money."

"What was I supposed to do, go out and get a paper route?"

"I had one, when I was a kid." I usually don't give personal details, but it seemed a fitting time to do so.

"Thank you, Horatio Alger."

I was surprised he knew Horatio Alger. "You spent your time between your mother's and father's homes?"

"I would go from the outhouse to the penthouse and back twice a week," Clayton shifts uncomfortably on the couch, "that was a charming experience."

"Where were you when your father died?"

"Here."

"Doing what?"

"Getting laid."

"What was her name?"

"Blond, she was blond."

"Let me guess, a special person in your life?"

"To be honest with you, she wasn't a real blond." Clayton was quite satisfied with his answer. "See, I can be a detective, too."

"And how do you suggest I go about finding this non-blond-blond?"

"Make a lot of money, drive an expensive car, hang out at the right clubs, buy a lot of drinks, and she'll come around."

"I'll get right on it, but if you happen to run across her name and number, let me know."

"I'm sure it's around here somewhere, most of them leave a calling card of sorts."

"You were out with your brother the night before his death?"

"Yeah."

"You two close?"

"No."

"Then why were you together?"

"He needed a designated driver," he pauses, "and someone to pick up his bar tab."

"Remember what club?"

"No."

"Did you have a good time?"

"I did after I picked up blond what's her name."

Tiffany comes down the stairs about as low key as Scarlett O'Hara. "I don't see you as an earth-tone kind of guy," she says to Clayton as she closes her notepad.

"What do you see me as?"

"Stripes."

Exactly what Clayton will be wearing in prison, if he's the guy who bopped his old man.

"I'll talk to my designer."

"And personal shopper," Tiffany adds.

Clayton gives Tiffany a smile, probably similar to the one he gave the non-blond blond, and turns to me. "Can I go back to my treadmill, now?"

"Whatever turns you on."

Tiffany and I leave without shaking his hand.

———

"The guy made it on his own," Tiffany says as she fires up the Lexus.

"I doubt that."

She swings out of the parking spot. "All you have to do is go through his suits. He started with Robert Talbott, moved up to Brooks Brothers, went Joseph Abboud, and finally went custom made."

"You went through his closet?"

"Guys like him never throw anything away. I think they keep their old rags to remind themselves of where they came from."

"Promise me you'll never go inside my closet, Tiffany."

"Don't worry; I'm allergic to polyester."

She makes a right on Fullerton and heads toward the lake.

"What did you think of young Clayton?"

"As a murderer or dating material?"

"You pick."

"He has a lot of negative energy. I sense a deep shade of gray aura."

"Aura?"

"His personal ethereal glow," Tiffany explains. "Mine's pink. I'm not sure about yours, Mister Sherlock; you're a tough one to read."

"What other interesting tidbits did you pick up on dear Clayton?"

"He's a Gemini, so that means he may have another personality." She takes her eyes off the road and onto me. "Don't ever date a Gemini, Mister Sherlock; ya never know what you're getting."

"You think he could drop a pile of rocks on his father's head?"

"Maybe, he's got great pecs."

We turned north on Clark. The Cubs must be in town, because it was stop and go all the way through Wrigleyville.

My cell rings with that ridiculous song. It was Norbert. The final autopsy report had been filed and they were releasing the body. If I wanted one more look, I'd better hurry. "Pass," I said and hung up.

"Do you know how to reprogram this thing so it won't sing that awful song every time I get a call?"

"Of course."

"Will you?"

"No, I like 'Breakaway.'" Tiffany sings, *"Take a chance and break-a-wayyy."*

We arrived in Uptown around four in the afternoon. We were late; hopefully Christina had waited for us.

Uptown is a gentrifying Chicago neighborhood, originally

rehabbed by the gays who could no longer afford the housing prices in Boystown, which they bought up and rehabbed a decade before. I pity gay people. They go into these decrepit, crime-filled areas, purchase old falling-apart properties, fix the places up, make the neighborhood respectable; and the straight people move in and ruin everything with their three-wheeled strollers and Starbucks coffee-klatches.

Thankfully, there still remained enough SRO hotels, drug treatment centers and Hispanic markets to keep Uptown in the up-and-coming status, instead of being recognized as the latest totally cool place to live.

The apartment was on the second floor of a brick six-flat. We rang the bell on the wrought iron gate, got buzzed inside the property, and had to perform the same task at the front door. Christina was waiting at her door when we made it up the stairs.

"Are you the insurance guy?"

"That would be us," I said a bit out of breath.

"I need you."

"In what sense?"

Christina ushered us into her large, spacious, attractive flat. Oak floors, paintings on the walls, a built-in hutch stocked with silver and china. The place was spotless; either the cleaning lady had just left or Christina was a neat freak.

I introduce myself, then Tiffany, who merely nods her head instead of shaking Christina's hand. I make a mental note to ask Tiffany if she is a germ-a-phobe.

"I've been violated," Christina says and rubs her hands together.

"I'm sure you have," Tiffany spoke up before I had a chance to ask.

"How?"

"Financially," Christina led us to an antique secretary in a small office anteroom, folded down the desktop, and slid out a laptop computer. "Somebody got into my account and cleaned me out."

I suspected my ex-wife; she was quite adept at this type of activity.

"I can't believe it," she said. "Gone, it's all gone."

To be nice, Christina wasn't a bad looking girl, or woman, if you consider anyone past thirty no longer a girl; but she did have a hard shell finish. Her hair was straight and short, her neck thicker than it should be and her arms had more bulk than needed. She wore jeans, but had the type of body that shouldn't wear jeans, one that had no shape; it started at the top and went straight down, all the way until it stopped.

"Did you call the bank?" I ask.

"Yes."

"What did they say?"

"That I should have signed up for their identity protection package." Christina hands over a number of computer printed pages with numbers and whatever. "Will my insurance cover this?"

I shrug my shoulders.

Tiffany shrugs hers, too. "I don't think my dad sells that kind of insurance."

Tiffany is obviously weak when it comes to her daddy's product lines.

"What am I supposed to do?"

I wanted to tell her it is much easier when you know who cleaned you out, but decided against adding my two cents to her injury. "I'd put a freeze on whatever other accounts I had, cancel your checking account, and pray."

"You're a detective; would you help find who did this?"

"I usually don't do this kind of work."

Christina turned a shade of pasty pale. "It was everything I had."

She had an odd vulnerability to her. You started feeling sorry for her as soon as you laid eyes on her.

"I'll do what I can," I say, not having a clue even where to start.

I smile. "Can we talk about your father?"

"Again?"

Steve and Norbert must have talked her out on the subject.

"I told the other two guys where I was, what I was doing, and that I didn't do it. Why don't you just go talk to them?"

"Yeah, why don't we do that?" Tiffany blows me away with her suggestion.

"Look," I say, "obviously you've had a bad day, but if I could just ask a few questions, I'll try to make them ones the other two guys didn't ask."

Christina peers up at me like I'm kidding.

"Do you know of anyone who may have liked your father?"

"Liked?"

"Yeah."

She has to pause to think. "No."

"No business associates, partners, charity people, chauffeur, shoe-shine guy?"

"No."

Tiffany adds, "Bartenders?"

"No, he was a lousy tipper."

"Did you ever know him to take drugs?"

"Never."

"What do you think of Alvin's current wife?"

"Hate her."

"Why?"

"She hates me."

"And the one before her?"

"Not my type."

"Duh," Tiffany says.

"Your mom still living in Boston?"

"Guess so."

"You don't know?"

"No."

Enough said on that topic. "Are you at all close with your brothers?"

"Half-brothers," she corrected. "No."

"Why not?"

"They don't like me."

"Don't take this the wrong way," I preface my next question, "but I don't sense a lot of grief at the passing of your dad."

"You don't get to pick your parents, detective."

"I'd pick mine again, if I had the chance." Tiffany perks up.

Christina gives Tiffany a look. "Daddy left while I was still in the womb. No money for years. Then, when I was a teenager, he wanted visitation, but wouldn't pay much attention to me when I was around. He did pay the tuition for college, but wouldn't chip in for clothing or rent. He let me dress like Little Orphan Annie, but had me drive around in a new car. I never understood him; but in some ways, I believe he did understand me."

"And still no grief?"

"I tried very hard to love my dad; and I tried even harder to like him, but he never made it very easy."

"I'm sorry."

"So am I."

——

In the car, I take out a three-by-five card and write that all three of Alvin's children share one common feeling and understanding: Each one hates the other two.

——

There is a rib place off Lawrence, The Gale Street Inn, which was not far from Christina's apartment. Tiffany said she needed a cosmopolitan to calm her nerves.

"Lesbians give me the creeps," she said as she sips. "You see how she was scoping me out?"

"No."

"I thought she was going to bore through my breasts with x-ray vision."

"How do you know she was a lesbian?"

"Oh, my God, is your gaydar on the blink? That hair, that body, that face; the woman was a les-bo from the get-go."

"Really?"

"What do you think that comment about the old man understanding her was all about and the mother who can't handle her being gay?"

Tiffany finishes her martini and orders a second. I was barely through half my light beer. We sit in silence for a few seconds.

"They got great ribs in this place," I tell her.

"Disgusting."

I wait until the air around her comment clears a bit. "Isn't your generation supposed to be tolerant of people of other persuasions?"

"If you'd had as many knuckle-draggers as I have had, hitting on you, you wouldn't be too tolerant, either."

The waiter comes over. I order a full slab, half-mild, half-tangy sauce. Tiffany orders a shrimp salad. Why they would have a shrimp salad in a rib joint puzzles me.

"Don't you find it interesting that no one so far has shown the least amount of remorse for the dearly departed Alvin J. Augustus?"

"No."

"All the kids have done all right, the wife is living in the Ritz; but nobody seems to care that the guy's head was squashed like a ripe melon."

"Be patient," Tiffany says. "After the dollars settle, tears will flow."

"From joy or sadness?"

"What's the difference?"

The food is served. The waiter offers me a plastic bib, which I strap around my neck. Tiffany shudders at my plebian protection, as well as the succulent pig meat in front of me."

"Have you ever seen the way pigs are raised?" she asks with a visage of disgust.

"Have you?"

"No, but I've seen pictures on TV." She picks up her fork and jostles the greens and fish around her plate. "Jews don't eat pork because it's filthy."

"They don't eat shrimp, either."

"Jews I know, do."

I slice between the bones. "Those shrimp you're eating are garbage eaters just like the little pig in front of me."

"No way."

"The scavengers of the sea."

Tiffany pushes the shellfish to the side of her plate and picks at the lettuce. "Alvin's kids aren't all that different than a lot of the kids I grew up with," she says.

I dig in with both hands, gnawing the delicious meat from the bones. In about a half a slab, I'll be messier than a finalist in a no-hands, pie-eating contest.

Tiffany continues, maybe to keep me from speaking and spraying the table with sauce, "Parents get so busy making money and being rich; they let the nannies and maids and servants raise their kids."

The waiter comes by and drops off a stack of napkins and three or four Wet-Nap packets. I take the hint and wipe myself down. "Were you raised like that?"

"My mom liked being a mom. She took us out to eat, to the park, wherever. Of course, we went in a limo while the other kids crowded into a crummy mini-van."

"You think one of Alvin's kids did him in?"

"The biggest fear people like us have is no longer being people like us."

9
Black must be the new black

The funeral was on Friday afternoon to accommodate the traders and brokers who were expected to be in the crowd.

Tiffany wore a black, Jackie Kennedy number, but with a plunging neckline. "The best places to meet men are at funerals," she explains. "If the dead one had money, so will most of his buddies and the sons of his buddies."

I notice one woman, who skirts around the church with a clipboard in hand, making hand signals and whispering orders to a number of individuals. I've heard of wedding planners, but never a funeral tactician.

We make our way up the side aisle to the front, so I can see how the mourners congregate and lay themselves out into an adult peanut gallery of sympathy and sorrow.

"The problem with funerals," Tiffany remarks as we slide into the pew, "is that -- black being the new blue -- it is really difficult to buy clothes that make you look sad." Then she adds, "Except you Mister Sherlock; your suit looks really sad."

"Thank you, Tiffany. Hearing such a fine compliment about my choice of attire makes my day complete."

"That wasn't a compliment."

This was actually a pretty good church crowd from the point of view of a guy who never spent much time in church. About sixty people were in attendance, not including the three homeless guys sleeping in the last pew. With the absence of a coffin, there was a five-foot photo of Alvin on an easel in the center aisle up by the altar, flanked by huge bouquets of flowers. I wonder what someone will do with a picture that size after the ceremony ends; it's way too big for an album or refrigerator door.

On a small table, in front of the photo, is a gold urn. Although my first rule of life is to assume nothing, I will assume here that what's inside is what's left of Alvin. The receptacle is maybe three inches wide and twelve high. It has a removable top for easy spreading or to allow a pinch or two for sprinkling purposes. There is no plaque, but I can see a metal label, the kind you sometimes see around a liquor bottle, which probably bears Alvin's name.

Doris and Brewster sit farthest upfront, indicating Doris paid for the event. Clayton and Christina sit across from them, Clayton alone; but Christina had a lithe young brunette by her side, no doubt to help her along through these troubling times. Norbert and Steve were way in the back. Theresa sat by herself. Evidently Hector took my advice and remained in hiding. There was an elderly couple seated in front, he in a tweed coat and she in one of those dresses old ladies wear after they realize they are resigned to being old ladies. The couple carries an air about them that says "We belong."

Seven or eight guys came still dressed in their trading smocks from the Board or the Merc. Smocks had to be unique and bright to be noticed by the floor managers; and these were no exception: bright blue, purple, hounds-tooth, and a black-and-white checkerboard that fit into a church about as well as a statue of Satan. Two participants no one could miss were a blond and redhead in short, tight, mini-skirts and leather jackets that accentuated their buxom figures to the max -- each kept her sunglasses on inside the church.

"Would you look at those two," Tiffany nudged me to turn around.

"Probably just stopped by from work," I say. "Afraid of a little competition?"

"You've got to be kidding," Tiffany said as she retrieved her phone from her black purse. "When they go back to work, they'll be back on their backs working."

The rest of the spectators were a smattering of business, personal, and neighborly acquaintances; although none of the Kenilworthians I interviewed were in attendance. A downtown funeral didn't fit in with busy social calendars. It would be so much easier if people had the decency to allow more lead time in scheduling their deaths.

The minister came out, made his way to the pulpit, raised his hands, and the congregation rose to its feet. If I had this kind of control at home, parenting would be much easier. He started in on a canned speech with: "Dearly beloved, we are gathered here today to pay tribute to Allen J. Augustus..."

The funeral director cleared her throat loud enough to be heard in the next county.

The minister glanced at his notes and continued. His talk droned on as he dropped in appropriate phrases about dust, valleys of death, and a most inappropriate statement, "Thou shalt not want." The only reason people were in the church was that they all wanted a piece of Alvin, but not what was left in the urn.

About halfway through the opening monologue a click-clock tapping of high heels against the marble floor made me turn to see second wife, Clayton's mama, Joan make her way up the aisle. The woman paused at Alvin's big picture, and, for a second, I thought she might put her fist through his nose. She sat down next to her son.

The minister's blah, blah, blah added a "river of life," "lilies of the field," and one more "dearly beloved" before he finally asked the congregation, "Now if anyone would like to say a few words in personal tribute to the dearly departed, please step forward."

Nobody moved. It was as if every ass in the place was glued to his or her seat. Doris elbowed Brewster and he elbowed her right back. Clayton looked to Christina, whose face was buried in the neck of her brunette.

The minister waited way too long, which made the absence of any good things to say about Alvin even more profound. When Tiffany rose to her feet and exited our pew, I feared she might give some pearls of wisdom at the pulpit, but she headed for the back of the church instead of the front.

"Okay, well, I guess," the minister stammered, "all stand for the closing prayer."

His final words were about as heartfelt and touching as the rest of the ceremony, "May he rest in the arms of the angels."

"Oh, yeah, right, that's going to happen," I whisper to myself.

Doris and Brewster strode down the aisle first, followed by the half-siblings. As Doris passed by Joan, I imagined her middle finger rising to remind the woman she replaced who ended up number one when Alvin's train left the station.

The remainder of the mourners filed out after the family. In less than three minutes the church was empty, except for a large photo of Alvin J. Augustus and a gold urn. We come into the world alone and we leave it alone. In Alvin's case he left it alone, extra crispy.

"I got 'em." Tiffany came up to me as I step out of the church, her cell phone in hand.

"Got what?" I ask, but was much more interested in Doris, Clayton, and Brewster getting into one limo and Christina and the brunette getting into another.

"I got a picture of everyone and I'm sure one of them did it, since murderers always show up to see the fruit of their labors."

"They do?"

"They do in the movies."

"Maybe I should see more movies."

"Excuse me," a rotund man in a dark blue suit said as he approached, "are you Richard Sherlock?"

"Does Richard Sherlock owe you any money?" I ask.

"No."

"Then, yes, I'm the guy."

The man pulled a business card out of his breast pocket with the stealth of a magician. "Conway Waddy, attorney at law. I'll be handling the estate."

"Lucky you," I say shaking his hand. "This is Tiffany Richmond."

"Richmond, as in Richmond Insurance?"

"That's me."

Conway is built like a barrel; he wears a pair of suspenders as well as a belt. "Where's your father?" Conway spoke with a courtroom swagger.

My dad has been dead for years, so he must be speaking to Tiffany.

"He's not here," Tiffany tells the man.

"I'm the executor of the will," he says.

"Okay," Tiffany says.

Conway's mad. "If I have to, I'll get a court order."

"Okay," she repeats.

I can sense she has no clue what's going on with this guy.

Conway sways back and forth. "I've called your father numerous times."

"He's a busy guy."

Conway speaks in his best threatening tone. "If you think you can get around me, you're wrong."

Tiffany takes a step back, peers at the man's girth. "I have a feeling you'd have trouble getting around anything."

Conway tucks the end of his tie into his pants, but it pops out the instant he moves. "The will is to be read Monday morning."

"Great," Tiffany says.

"Where is it?" Conway asks.

"You don't have a copy?" I ask.

"Not all of it."

"How can you read a will you don't have."

Conway ignores me and says to Tiffany, "Tell your old man I need the complete document."

"Okay."

"Now."

Conway Waddy waddles off.

We stand alone in front of the church.

"Whole lot of love in that guy," I say to my assistant.

"Yep."

"What does he want?"

Tiffany gets a silly look on her face. "Daddy told me it's going to be great."

"What?"

"The reading of the will."

"Why?"

"It'll be all up for grabs. Fingers will get pointed, everybody swears up a storm, the siblings start throwing punches at one another and the two wives get into a catfight. I can't wait."

"Tiffany, what's Daddy holding?" I ask.

"The rider."

"The rider he won't tell you about?"

"I would think that would be the one."

"He hasn't told you yet?"

"No."

"Why not?"

"He knows I can't keep a secret."

10
Not a good time dad

The first thing any dad does the moment he moves out or is kicked out of the house is to go out and buy a *How to be a Good Dad During the Divorce* book. There are about three hundred to choose from at your local bookstore.

They're all the same. Chapter One concerns not talking badly about your wife in front of your kids, even though your kids are quoting your wife verbatim on what a low-life their father is, or relaying messages about her need for more cash, new tires for the car, and that the garage door you fixed still needs fixing. Chapter Two is a warning about the perils of becoming a "good-time" dad. The books put this malfeasance in the same league as spilling the beans about Santa or the Easter Bunny. The good-time-daddy trap, they explain, is when your kids only look at you as the person to take them shopping, to the zoo, amusement parks, and museums, and not as the father they need in their difficult time of transition. Sooner or later, the books lecture, you will run out of *good* times and your kids will turn on you because you've become a boring, no-fun kind of a dad. The book says you should give your children a template of what life is really all about and this will prepare them to live their lives not expecting every other weekend to be whoopee from the get-go.

This is a problem I wish I had.

What has happened in our lives is the direct opposite of what the books warn. I pick the kids up on Friday night, fight traffic back to my apartment and order a pizza, because it is too late for me to whip up a culinary delight they'll refuse to eat. They eat in front of the TV on Friday, but all other nights we eat at the table as a family. On Saturday morning, while they sleep in, I get up before six, get to the "Fluff and Fold" before the crowd and do three loads. By the time I get back, they are up and back in front of the TV. I make them breakfast, which again they turn their noses up at, then we get going for our fun-filled Saturday. First stop, dry cleaners. Second, the drug store. By ten we're at the market, squeezing melons.

If you are divorced with kids, go to the market Saturday morning, for this is the time divorced-with-kids women shop. If you prefer to bump carts with single, younger women, shop in the late afternoon when the prettier of the species fill the pre-cooked, pre-packaged aisles. You can always tell a woman's marital status with one look into her cart.

Kelly and Care are a pain at the market. Each pleads for sugary cereals or those awful fruit roll-ups, which they swear are as healthy as any plum or prune. There is a constant reading of on-the-box claims of nutrition percentages, daily adult requirements, and actual fruit flavors; the conversations always end with a "Please, Dad."

"No, that stuff will rot your teeth."

"But the label says it's fortified."

"In a few years, I'm going to have to get you braces and what would be the point of putting braces on teeth that are fortified with junk?"

Unfortunately, I always concede to one or two utterly worthless food items, but that's all.

By the time we get home, unload the groceries, and have lunch, it is time to get back in the car and start driving. So far, good-time dad and his two little kids have had zero fun.

We drive and drive and drive. There are birthday parties, tryouts, lessons, bar mitzvahs, dances, study groups. These kids have a social calendar I would die for. I end up sitting in the car, waiting for one to finish or one to start or figuring out how to get Kelly to a practice and Care to a play date ten miles apart at the same time. Sure is fun for me.

On Sunday mornings I used to take them to Sunday school at a local Catholic Church. Kelly's argument of "If we have to go, you have to go" ended their formal religious training in less than six weeks. My children are pious only up to the fourth commandment.

Now on Sundays, they sleep in and I get up and clean the apartment. The TV goes off in the afternoon, when all homework must be completed. I help, but secretly fear the first algebra book coming home. We sit down together for Sunday dinner. I try to talk with them about their lives, but they are too busy complaining about what a crummy, boring weekend they have had. This is the time they remind me that when they are with their mother on weekends they get to ride their new horse and do fun things. I explain to them that that isn't what real life is all about. "Life is hard. You have to work, cook, clean, do chores, pay taxes, and be responsible."

"It isn't that way at home; Mom's got help."

"One day you two are going to thank me for teaching you all these life lessons."

"Yeah, right, Dad."

I drop them off at their mother's house at 8 pm Sunday evening. I have followed the book's instructions to the letter about not being a good-time dad. I feel so proud.

———

This weekend followed the template pretty much down the line. Pick up pizza, laundry, market, lunch, and finally to the mall, because Kelly could no longer live without a pair of bright-red Crocs, so I relented to her and also had to buy Care a pair. Thirty-six bucks for ugly, plastic shoes is outrageous.

The mail was waiting for me when we got home from the mall on Saturday afternoon. Amidst the junk, catalogs, offers to invest all the extra money I have un-invested is an envelope, letter-sized, almost square. I almost threw it away along with a timeshare offer in Boca and the chance to upgrade my computer to lightning internet speed. The envelope had been postmarked on Thursday at the main station downtown, meaning it could have come from almost anywhere in the city. It was addressed to Richard Sherlock, no Mr. and no IL, just my street address and zip-code, handwritten as if by Care when she was five, and no return address, a postal no-no.

There was one page inside, an eight by eleven, twenty-pound piece of flimsy bond paper, the kind used by Kinko's for its cheapest service. The message was printed by a computer. Who uses a typewriter in the technology age? It was folded into thirds, and folded in half. The message had no date, name, or address; this was no piece of business mail. The writing was on the top third of the page, a succinct note of brief instruction:

Don't tell any buddy about this. Call 312 555-5675 request Diane Monday.

Always nice to get personal mail.

There is some Disney musical blaring out of the TV, as I sit between my daughters and place the note and envelope in my lap.

"What is it, Dad?" Kelly asks.

"A letter."

My daughter looks at me as if I'm weird. "Nobody writes letters anymore."

"What do they do?"

"Text, email, Twitter, whatever."

I reread the note. It was written by a woman. Mid-twenties to early thirties, once a lousy student and not employed where she would use her brain over her brawn, grammatical skills a dead giveaway. She is petite. No one big writes that small, even with the opposite hand. She has some, but little, knowledge of the computer, just enough to write and print this note. She couldn't figure out how to computerize and address the envelope. I suspect she is not married, since the envelope is the kind sold with a greeting card. A married woman would never have one without the other laying around. She was nervous when she wrote and mailed the letter, due to the uneven first two folds into thirds, and then trying to make up for it with the last attempt to fold the page perfectly in half.

I pull the phone to me, dial the reverse directory, hear the command and punch in the 312 number on the letter. "The address of the number you have requested is unlisted, please try another number." I figured as much. I will assume that Monday is not Diane's last name and hang up the phone. I carefully place the page back in its envelope, place it on a stack of stuff I know I'll clean around, and ask the girls, "Tuna casserole for dinner?"

"Oh, gross."

My kid weekend ended much the way it began: boring.

I get home after dropping off the kids at about nine. I retrieve the letter and dial 312 555-5675.

If you were to dial my number and I wasn't available to answer the telephone, a lady would tell you I wasn't around, but "Please leave a message at the sound of the tone."

The exact same lady said the exact same words to me after five rings. This must be one heck of a busy woman.

"My name is Richard and I want to request Diane Monday." I say into the receiver.

My phone rings five minutes later.

"Hello."

"You called 555-5675." The male voice was deep, quick, and to the point.

"Yes."

"What can I do for you?"

"I'd like to request Diane Monday."

"Is this your home number?"

"Yes."

"What's your home address?"

I fill in the blank.

"I'll call you back in five minutes," he says and hangs up.

I wait and in exactly five minutes, the phone rings.

"Hello."

"I'm Nick."

"Nice to meet you."

"What time would you like to see Diane?"

"You pick."

"One hour or two?"

"One should be plenty."

At this point I have a pretty good idea what this is all about, and not because I've done this before.

"In or out?"

"In."

"Four o'clock." Nick's voice picks up in tempo. "Eleven thirty-eight North State. The name of the building is One State Street. Go to the front desk, tell the concierge you are Richard Sherlock and want forty-one-fourteen. He'll call, and then buzz you in. Go to the second bank of elevators, not the first. You don't want to be looking stupid wandering around the wrong elevator bank."

"I can handle that."

"Knock on the door, your hour starts at four," he hesitates, "you want anything special?"

"No, I'm kind of a non-special kind of a guy."

"It's four hundred, cash. We don't take credit cards."

"Fine."

"Where did you hear about us?" he asks.

"Ah," I hesitate.

"You see us on the net?" he says. "Escorts R us dot com?"

"No."

"In the *Reader*?"

The *Reader* is a Chicago alternative weekly newspaper, which carries "Adult Entertainment" advertising. "No."

Nick must have a sheet to record the value of his advertising dollar. "Then where did you hear about us?"

"Fan mail from some flounder."

Nick laughs, a fellow flying squirrel fan. "See you Monday."

"Thanks," I said, "can't wait."

I hang up the phone and turn on the computer. It takes forever to come on and get to the open space where I type in www.EscortsRus.com. A disclaimer comes on the screen. Is this absurd or what? I click, swear my age is over twenty-one, hit "Okay" and am sent to the menu page. What a menu. Halfway down the page are two women I last saw in church.

Off goes the computer. I pick up the phone and dial. She picks up on the sixth ring. "What?"

"I need you to bring an advance with you tomorrow morning."

"What?" Tiffany's voice is weak.

"Tiffany, are you okay?"

"I'm tired," she says, "I've been flushing my system all day. I'm sick of eating bran cereal."

"I need some cash."

"Daddy hates giving out advances. What's it for?"

"A prostitute."

"Oh, Mister Sherlock, if you're that hard up, I could fix you up with one of my friends," she stops, quickly retracts, "I mean one of my friend's mothers."

"It has to do with the case."

"I've heard a lot of excuses, Mister Sherlock."

"I'm serious."

"You're not meeting her on some street corner, are you?"

"No."

"Well, I guess that's some kind of positive."

"I'll need four-hundred bucks, plus tip."

"You're kidding?"
"Hey, nothing's cheap."
"Promise me you'll use protection."
"I promise."

11
Bored of trade

Tiffany is waiting outside Conway Waddy's door as I arrive.
"Did you bring the four hundred?"

"No."

"Why not?"

"The ATM I went to was out of money," Tiffany says. "Can you believe that?"

"You go to the bank while I do this."

"And miss the reading of the will? You have got to be kidding, Mister Sherlock. Daddy said it is going to be a blast."

"Tiffany..."

"Don't worry; I'll have the money by this afternoon when you go see your ho."

We walk inside and go directly into the conference room where all the players are present and accounted for. Brewster and Doris have taken the two seats at the head of the rectangular table, as if to say, *we're first in line*. Clayton, who said he didn't care if he got a dime, sits on the opposite side of the table, briefcase in front of him, Blackberry in his ear, spouting instructions to an unseen subordinate. Christina sits next to where she figures Conway will read the will, since there are stacks of paper, being lined up by a paralegal, three feet across the desk. I'm surprised wallets are not sitting open on the table waiting to be filled.

There is enough tension in the room to power a generator. The principals fidget, their eyes pretending to read, or they stare at their fingernails. No one is speaking. No eye contact made. Each must be imagining they are the only one at the table. I try to picture this family living in the same house together; what a sitcom that would be.

Norbert stands in the far corner of the room next to the coffee service, sampling the Danish. He is the only one who acknowledges my presence with a wave and a burp.

Conway Waddy enters the room, reading glasses precariously

balanced at the end of his nose. He carries a plastic file folder with numerous colored tabs sticking out of the side. Before sitting he hikes his pants, adjusts his suspenders, and unbuttons his suit coat. "Welcome," he says. "I'm glad you all could be here."

I can't believe anyone in this crowd cares about pleasantries at this point; it's more like *shut up and show me the money.*

Conway opens the folder to the first tab and begins to read. "Alvin J. Augustus of Kenilworth Illinois... being of sound mind, sound body..." and blah, blah, blah boilerplate of what everyone in the room knows and could care less about.

"Can we cut through the legal eagle crap?" Clayton asks during a slight pause in Conway's rendition.

"No," Christina says. "He has to put it all on the record for it to be legally binding."

"It's a reading of the will, my dear," Doris drips in sarcasm, "not a Supreme Court decision on gay marriage."

"Come on, get on with it," Brewster says. "I want to catch post time at Arlington."

The bickering Bickersons.

"By the way, dear," Doris asks Christina calmly, "that girlfriend of yours, are you her bitch or is she yours?"

"It takes one to know one, Step-mommy."

"Can we eliminate the comments, please?" Conway intervenes.

"She started it," Christina says.

"Did not," Doris snaps back.

Tiffany pokes me. "I love this stuff."

This is just like my house on a kid weekend.

"You should be thankful she's gay, Doris," Clayton says. "If she was married with kids, that's more people to have their hands in the pot."

"May I continue?" Conway asks.

"Yes, hurry up," Brewster answers.

Norbert looks over to me and shakes his head.

"The assets are as follows: home in Kenilworth, appraised at a current value of four-point-two million."

"That's all?" Clayton says it, but anyone would have asked this question.

"Current housing values have decreased substantially across the area," Conway explains, then quickly continues. "The current outstanding mortgage is four-point-three million at seven-point-three percent."

Conway couldn't have stopped the conversation in the room any quicker than if he farted. The family is stunned.

Doris recovers first. "We've been in the house more than ten years. We bought it for less than a million. I remember when the mortgage was paid off."

"The first mortgage was retired," Conway says, "but since numerous equity loans have been taken out on the property."

"I didn't see any of that money," Doris says in defense.

"Then where the hell is it?" Clayton asks.

Conway shrugs his big shoulders.

"You're telling us the house is worth less than the mortgage?" Brewster asks.

"Underwater?" Clayton adds.

"Yes." Conway points to the next section on the page and reads. "Augustus Enterprises Incorporated, which is the holding company, is currently valued at sixteen-point-nine million dollars..."

There is a collective sigh in the room.

"...with liabilities to the corporation totaling sixteen-point-three million dollars."

All breathing in the room stops. Doris' mouth drops open despite her Botox-frozen jaw. Clayton fumbles his Blackberry. Brewster scratches his privates. Christina's hand covers her mouth as if she had witnessed the first killing in a cheap horror film.

"There's more." Conway continues, attempting to be as lawyerly as possible. "Two seats on the Board of Trade have existing contracts to be sold, all stocks, bonds and securities are in the process of being liquidated and placed in receivership for outstanding debt."

Although each Augustus at the table is only half-related to one another, they have taken on exactly the same look, resembling a family of mimes with pure pasty-white skin, sunken black eyes, and drooping smiles.

"There are other odds and ends that I will not take the time to list," Conway says to fill the air with words until some of the shock wears off. "Finally, there is a life insurance policy in the amount of twelve-million dollars."

For the second time in less than five minutes all activity stops faster than in a game of freeze tag.

"To be divided between my current wife, three children, with a half share to Horace Heffelfinger and Millie Maddocks."

I make a mental note of the last two names.

"But before any disbursements are made," he pauses, "a rider to the policy demands," he reads carefully, "in the event of an unnatural death, all listed recipients of the proceeds must be cleared of any involvement of wrongdoing before their portion of the settlement is paid out."

Brewster speaks for the group. "Where the hell did that come from?"

"Your father added the rider," Conway says.

"Yep," Tiffany says and gives a slight wave to the assembled.

"You sure?" Brewster chokes out.

"It was signed and notarized in the Richmond Insurance offices," Conway explains.

"He never mentioned any rider to me," Brewster says.

"And there was no rider on the will I read," Doris' voice rises, "a month ago."

"What prompted you to do that?" I am not supposed to ask questions here, but I do.

Doris turns around in her chair to face me. "None of your damn business."

Conway takes back the floor. "Rider was dated and signed two weeks ago Thursday."

"Is it legal?" Clayton asks.

"I was the witness," Conway confesses.

I laugh. Conway was the witness to the signing of a document he wasn't allowed to read. That Alvin was a real character.

The disbelief continues at the table. No one really knows what to say.

Conway explains, "Alvin recently suffered major trading losses with the swings in commodity prices over the past months."

"No way," Clayton says. "Its been a sucker's market for weeks."

"He used to make millions when the markets took big swings," Doris says. "He'd get a hard-on on days like those."

"A little too much information," Tiffany says to me.

"I bet it was your fault." Clayton points her finger at Doris.

"Me?"

"You made Dad crazy, with your shopping and facelifts and all the crap you put him through."

"I made him nuts?" Doris screams back at her son. "Look at you."

"Me?"

"You've ruined it for all of us!" Christina yells at Doris.

"You got a lot of nerve accusing me," Doris turns to her stepdaughter. "You think he enjoyed seeing his only daughter in the arms of another woman?"

"That had nothing to do with this," Christina says.

"Did he say anything to you?" Clayton asks Brewster.

"No."

"You were trading off his seat; you had to have seen him going down."

"Were the checks still clearing he was writing to you?" Brewster surprises Clayton with this one.

This is information that will definitely end up on recipe cards.

Brewster counters, "I'd like to have half the cash he funneled into that shell corporation of yours."

"You don't know shit, so shut the hell up."

"Make me, asshole!"

Brewster and Clayton stand and slap at each other across the table like a couple of third-graders on the playground.

Norbert uses the disruption as cover to grab the last Danish on the tray and wolf it down. I fold my arms against my chest, lean back, and watch. Tiffany's hands become fists, and she acts like a woman at a prizefight, egging on the combatants.

Doris stumbles out of her chair to scream at the boys, "Sit down."

Christina comes out of her chair to scream at Doris, "Don't tell them what to do. You sit down."

"Who the hell are you to tell me what to do?" Doris squares off against Christina.

The scene at the table reminds me of one of those reality TV shows my kids make me watch, where all the fights just happen to take place in perfect lighting, with numerous camera angles, succinct dialog, and the tempo rising to a high pitch. A fight where no one gets hurt and ends at the exact last second before they break for the final commercials.

"Quiet!" Conway puts his bulk behind the order and the combatants cease their attacks. "You want to fight, do it on your own time. Pick a place away from here and go at it to your hearts' content." Conway's breathing is so hard, his suspenders pulsate upon his chest. "I suggest you all read the will in its entirety." He slings copies to each.

Doris grabs her copy, her purse, and heads for the door. Clayton tosses his in his briefcase. Brewster rolls up his like a program at a baseball game and slaps it into his bare hand. Christina sits down, staring at the pages in front of her, as if she is afraid to touch them in fear of contacting germs. The three file out in order, each giving the other plenty of space.

The Augustus family's life, as they once knew it, was now pretty much over.

"Was that great or what, Mister Sherlock?"

"Tiffany..."

"What can I say? I love drama."

"Now would you go to the bank?"

"Oh, yeah, money for the hooker."

"And meet me no later than three-forty-five," I write down the address.

"One North State," she says, seeing the address on the paper. "I've been in this building, and it sure didn't look like a brothel to me."

"Looks can be deceiving." I head out the door.

"Where are you going, Mister Sherlock?"

"To check out the last two recipients."

"Can I come?"

"No, you have to go get my money."

"Oh, yeah."

And they say you lose your memory as you age.

————

I walk a few blocks and enter the Board of Trade. I take the elevator to the fourth floor and enter the viewing room that hangs over the trading floor, which is similar to a luxury sky box at the United Center. I stand with the rest of the tourists and watch as guys jump around flashing hand signals while tearing off scraps of paper to hand to the chit collector in their respective pits. It is a particularly active day for pork bellies.

There have been a number of epidemics in the pits. One guy gets a cold, screams his lungs out, and infects all the other guys around him. From sore throats to the flu, this is one of the odder hazards of the workplace. There are few women in this line of work, due to the fact that they cannot take the physical contact of flying elbows, deadly felt pens, bad breath, and having to wear an ugly, unflattering smock to work each day. On the trading floor hundreds of thousands of dollars are changing hands in a ritual, more than one-hundred years old, based purely on honesty. Quite amazing, and mighty hard to believe in this day and age.

Once I get the feel for the place, and feel hyped up to the equivalent of three loaded cappuccinos, I make my way upstairs to the offices of Alvin J. Augustus Enterprises Incorporated.

"May I speak to the person in charge?" I ask the young, attractive girl seated at the reception desk.

"He's not available."

"When will he be in?"

"Not soon," she says. "He's dead." She takes out a small pink pad of paper, pre-printed with While You Were Out on the top. "Would you like to leave a message?"

"Wouldn't the chances of me getting an answer be pretty slim?"

She leans forward and whispers. "That's what I thought, too."

"Could I speak with the person filling in during the eternity that Alvin is away?"

"Mister Heffelfinger."

"An older guy, wears a tweed coat?" I ask.

"Tweed?"

"Patches on the elbows."

"Yeah, that's him," she says.

"Is he available?"

"No."

"Where is he?"

"I don't know."

I keep this incredible verbal repartee at the optimum level. "Is there anyone else working here I could talk to, besides you, of course?"

"Miss Millie went with Mister Heffelfinger, so we're pretty much closed."

"Millie Maddocks?"

"Yeah."

There are two large, ugly, Uzilevsky prints hanging on the walls, a couch and leather chair with a table and lamp between. Tasteful, but hardly impressive. The carpet is industrial grade.

"Mind if I wait?"

"No."

I get the impression she is glad to have some company. I sit down on the couch.

"Do you like working here?"

"It's okay; pays well," she tells me. "I want to go back to school and learn to be a dental hygienist."

"You like teeth?"

"I like mine." She flashes me a big smile.

"Was Mister Augustus a good guy to work for?"

"Mister Alvin was cool, I guess." She retrieved a nail file from the top drawer. "Since I'm out here, I'm not real close when he's back there screaming and swearing at people. He never swore at me."

"How were his teeth?"

"I don't think he ever had braces."

"Did his kids ever come here?"

"Not while I was around."

"Wife?"

"She'd pop in and walk right by me."

"How were her teeth?"

"Capped."

"Did anybody ever come in that looked scary?" This is a dumb question, but fitting for the person being asked.

"Mister Alvin had some weird friends."

"Like who?"

"I don't know; they'd walk right by me, too."

"I bet you hated that."

"Not really."

I can see celebrity magazines, *US, People, Star, Enquirer* etc., in a stack beneath her desk.

"Mind if I go back and take a look at the offices?"

"No," she shakes her head, "I don't know if that would be a good idea."

I get up from the chair. "Is there a restroom I can use?"

"Sure, it is on the left after you go through this door." She points me in the direction of the offices, then picks up the file and starts in on her pinkie finger.

I begin my non-guided tour. There are two secretarial desks in the open part of the room with four offices, one in each corner and two facing east. The doors to the offices are open. There are no nameplates.

The corner office on the right screams accountant. A calculator, adding machine, and a computer sit on the desk, perfectly positioned for the left hand to hit the adding key, the right hand the calculator, and both to work the keyboard. A stack of papers fills the in-box. I search through the loose leafs, examine a few at random and see numbers, numbers, and more numbers. On one wall there is a line-up of four-foot filing cabinets, reminding me of a library's card catalog system. On the other wall is a table, maybe three feet in width. It is covered with stack after stack of charts, graphs, papers, books, legal documents, and assorted articles that will never be read. This table of material is obviously added to often, but seldom subtracted from.

The man who occupies this enclave is totally set in his ways, stubborn, has a mind like a steel trap, a dandruff problem, worn shoes, and does not remove his suit coat while he works.

I walk behind the desk, open the drawers until I find something of interest. It pops up in the third drawer. I lift the large, three-to-a-page checkbook, page to the middle; and tear out one check that will not be immediately missed, stashing it in my pocket for safekeeping. I return the checkbook to its rightful drawer. I go through files, write down what I find to be of importance, and leave the room.

I skip the middle offices, leery of how much time I'm allowed in the men's room.

Alvin's office is twice the size of the accountant's. On a massive desk sits an empty in-box, a large desk blotter, a gold pen-

and-pencil set. It is past being neat. On the opposite wall, facing the desk, are three plasma-TV screens stacked one above the other. To the left and right of the screens are two computer desks with the largest PC monitors I have ever seen; they must be twenty-five inches in width. There are two Oriental rugs on the floor, one beneath Alvin's desk and the other under one of the computer stations in front of the TV monitors. There is one spot on the floor that needs a rug to cover the crummy carpet.

The drawers of Alvin's desk are locked. I get on my hands and knees, crawl under the desk and use my miniature Swiss Army knife to pop the lock. Locking a desk is stupid; any idiot can open a locked desk. The middle drawer holds pencils, pens, a ruler, stapler, and other assorted office accessories. The file drawers have green alphabet files, none of which hold a single sheet of paper. The drawers on the opposite side of the desk have little of interest, except the one holding a silver lock box. I could pick its lock, too; but instead lift it up and shake it. Empty, as I suspected.

I have seen enough. I go back through the office area to the reception area, where the future teeth cleaner has finished her right hand nails and is on the ring finger of her left. I pat my stomach and say, "Mexican food last night."

I have given her way too much information and she does not respond. I smile as I leave.

I take the elevator to the ground floor, walk out the back way, and proceed about half a block to the Sign of the Trader, a favorite watering hole in the financial district.

I man a barstool, order a light beer and a burger, and sit alone until 2 pm, when the losers of the day trickle in to drown their sorrows. The winners will arrive about 3:15.

"Alvin Augustus ever come in here?" I ask the bartender, a guy who looks like he could have been born in the place.

"He used to, years ago," the old guy said, "once they get rich, they don't hobnob anymore. That is," he adds, "unless they're drunks."

"You hear anything about an undercover investigation of cheating on the floor?"

My question makes him drop a glass.

"I hear everything."

I place a twenty on the table.

"But I haven't heard anything about that."

I double down.

The man turns his nose up at my bills; what he must consider chump change.

I have one ten dollar bill left in my wallet and two singles, which I will need to take the "L" to my afternoon prostitution appointment. I offer the ten up.

He eyes the fifty-dollar pot, puts his hands on the bar, the width of my shoulders and says, "Let me tell you, bud, if I had a fifty for every inside operation, sting, investigation, or bust at the Board, I wouldn't be pouring booze, I'd be drinking it."

"Anything lately?"

His nose turns up one more time. "That'll be eighteen dollars for the burger and the beer."

I rise, pull two bills from the pile, leaving the twenty all by its lonesome. "Take it out of my tab."

Boy, did I show him.

———

I am pacing the lobby when Tiffany enters One North State at eight minutes after four.

"I told you to be on time."

"I'm sorry, your needs will have to wait a few more minutes."

"Tiffany..."

"This is about the earliest I've ever been for being late."

She is dressed in a boring gray pair of easy-fit pants and a tee-shirt that says *Wrigley Field Established 1914.* Her hair is pulled back in a ponytail. She had made herself about as un-sexy as possible.

"Do you have my money?"

"I wouldn't be considering it *your* money, Mister Sherlock," she says as she pulls out a stack of bills from her back pocket. "The money is money for the case, so to speak."

I take the entire wad out of her hand. "I promise this will be well spent," and point to an empty chair in the corner of the lobby. "Wait there. I'll be less than an hour."

"I'll bet you'll be a lot less than that."

I stash the cash in my pocket, hurry over to the reception desk, and wait my turn.

"Yes?" the male receptionist/doorman says as I step up to his desk.

"Forty-one-fourteen."

The guy cracks a smarmy smile. "Name?"

"Sherlock."

"Like Sherlock Holmes, because we have a Doctor Watson on the third floor." He giggles; this must be his big thrill of the day.

"Richard Sherlock."

He takes an eternity, dialing the four numbers, knowing I'm late and every second counts.

"Second bank of elevators," he says as he buzzes open the glass door, then adds, "Have a good time."

I do my best to ignore the jerk and get to the elevator as its doors are closing. I press the button and two passengers give me a funny glare.

I go left out of the elevator, make it about two doors down before I turn and go in the opposite direction. I knock on 4114 and step back so I can be seen clearly through the peep hole in the door.

The door opens. It's the redhead from the funeral, looking as good as her picture on the internet.

"We were worried you weren't coming." She steps back from the door to allow me entrance.

It is an interesting fear she has; I wonder if it is work related. "Are you Diane?"

"I am today."

She leads me down a short but narrow hallway, past a bathroom. I have a difficult time keeping my eyes off her thin, airy chemise, which barely covers her lovely backside.

In the main room of the studio apartment, a king-size bed, neatly made with satin pillows and silk sheets is on my right. There is a huge clock on the wall. On my left is the kitchenette, a wall with a TV and a loveseat on which sits the blond, Diane's partner at the funeral service.

Two beautiful women, one king-size bed, and me, the ultimate male pipe-dream.

"I'm Alexis."

It is not her hand I want to shake.

Before I sit, I take in the view to the west. I am forty-one stories above what was once Cabrini Green, known to be one of the most despicable housing projects in the country. Amazing how close poverty and wealth once existed.

"We need you," Diane says as she sits on the edge of the bed.

"That's flattering." I sit next to Alexis, who wears a micromini, cut-off pair of denim shorts. She must have a Daisy Duke fantasy at five.

Diane says, being careful to keep her knees together, "We need you to get us our money."

"Why me?"

Alexis speaks, "You're the detective on Alvin Augustus; aren't you?"

"I'm the insurance guy, if that's what you mean."

"That's good enough," Alexis says.

"He owes us over forty-two grand."

"Forty-two-seven-fifty-five to be exact."

I bet these two really work well together.

"We'll give you ten percent of whatever you get us," Diane says.

"Fifteen," I counter.

"Ten," Diane negotiates. "Plus we'll throw in a few extras."

This is tempting. "Twelve-and-a-half and I'll let my imagination run wild in place of the extras."

"Deal."

"I suspect the money you're seeking was for services rendered?"

"Alvin was one horny son of a bitch," Alexis says.

"Why wasn't he a cash-and-carry customer?"

Diane shifts her 105 pounds a bit. "Let's just say he was a private client."

"Nick didn't get a cut?"

"No."

"How do you expect me to secure this money?"

"If we knew how, we wouldn't be hiring you; would we?" Diane might make her living on her back, but she has learned the ways of the world of business.

"Oh," Alexis says, "and we want it in cash."

"I'm not sure I can collect, much less collect cash."

"Why not?"

"Alvin was broke."

"Bullshit."

"You two are not half as surprised as his family."

"Believe me," Alexis says, "if there is one thing Alvin wasn't, he wasn't broke."

"The reading of the will was priceless, literally."

"There has to be some money. I've seen what he carries on him."

"You two have a phony business set up with a credit card account?"

"Redblond Personal Services, LLC."

"Send an invoice for the amount -- call it concierge services or whatever -- to his office in the Board of Trade, and a copy to my apartment. You won't get a dime without an invoice."

"I could have thought of that," Diane says.

"Why didn't you?" Alexis asks.

"If the invoice gets in the right pile, you may be paid out of the estate money, if and when it gets disbursed."

"When will that be?" Alexis asks.

I shrug.

She explains, "I'm kind of having a little cash-flow problem."

"I know the feeling," I tell her.

"It is a bit hard to believe Alvin has no money," Diane says.

"Yes, it is."

"We need our money, Mister Sherlock," Alexis says. "So, get it."

"I'll do my best."

Both women sit back for a few seconds.

"By the way," I say, "when was the last time either of you saw Alvin?"

Alexis speaks first. "I don't remember."

"Sure?"

"Yeah, I'm always sure when I don't remember." Alexis was never an A-student.

"We did him on Wednesday," Diane says.

"Thank God he didn't go to the grave horny," I conclude.

"Don't be too positive. Alvin was born horny," Alexis says.

"I will need a way to get a hold of you, unless you want me to chat-up Nick again."

Diane has two cell phones in her purse and Alexis has three. I immediately feel communications-deprived. We exchange numbers.

"It is best to call us a few minutes before the top of the hour," Alexis says.

"I'd hate to interfere with any business being transacted."

Diane rises and makes it clear that it is time for me to leave.

I remain seated, as does Alexis. "Did you like Alvin?"

"Not particularly," Alexis says curtly.

"Why not?"

"Don't start asking about sexual proclivities," Diane says. "We do have some respect."

Proclivities is a big word. Diane was not the one who wrote the note I received in the mail.

"Did he ever open up to you?" I pause. "I mean in a non-biblical sense?"

"They all talk," Diane says, "that's the main reason a lot of them come."

Interesting choice of words.

"Was Alvin, in the past month or so, more tense or agitated... indisposed?"

Alexis says, "Yeah, pissy."

"Did he say why?"

"It had to have been about money," Alexis says. "It was the only thing he seemed to care about."

"He ever talk about his wife?"

"They all talk about their wives."

I see Diane glance up at the clock and motion to Alexis, who gets up. She has legs that go all the way to her neck.

"You have to get to work now," Diane says.

"And get our money," Alexis tells me.

I make my way to the front door. "I'll be in touch."

In the lobby, the idiot at the reception desk gives me another dumb smile, which I ignore as I pass through the glass door.

Tiffany runs up to me, sick of waiting no doubt.

I take her by the arm, turn slightly and parade in front of the reception desk.

"How did it go?" Tiffany asks.

I speak loud enough for all to hear. "It went so well they refused to take my money."

"Oh, Mister Sherlock, you stud, you."

12
One of us deserves a night on the town

There is a parking ticket on the Lexus windshield. Tiffany removes it and places it in the glove compartment, neatly stacking it on top of the other parking tickets. "I hate carrying around quarters," she confesses.

———

Norbert and Steve are waiting in a booth in the dining room of the Skokie Country Club. On Mondays, the club allows cops and firemen from the area to play, but not eat, for free.

The detectives are laughing as we slide into the booth.

"If you could have seen the faces of that family when the lawyer told 'em Alvin was broke," Norbert says, "priceless."

The waitress replaces Norbert's and Steve's empty cocktail glasses with a fresh pair.

"I don't know why you're laughing," I say, "all we have to follow here is the money, and there isn't any."

"Family didn't know he was broke?" Steve asks.

"It seems inconceivable," I say, "that he could lose that much money and have it go unnoticed."

There is a lull in the conversation until Tiffany wonders out loud, "Maybe Alvin knew he was going to get snuffed."

"Certainly would explain the rider on the policy," Steve jumps on her thought.

"What tipped him off?" Norbert asks.

"Maybe somebody already tried," I say.

"Or he knew if he spilled the beans to the FBI, a lot of people wouldn't be real happy," Steve says.

"That wouldn't explain why he'd cut the family out first." Norbert takes a sip of his fresh cocktail.

"We're not dealing with Mister Rogers here, don't forget," I remind the group. "If everyone hated Alvin, it would only stand to reason, Alvin returned the compliment."

"Too bad he didn't commit suicide, then the policy would be invalid and we could all go home," Tiffany concludes.

"Here, here," Steve says and picks up the menu.

Norbert orders the rib-eye, Steve the filet, me the fish since I'm watching my cholesterol, and Tiffany a chicken breast with veggies on the side, no butter or oil.

"We need warrants for all Alvin's books."

"The FBI's got 'em," Steve says. "Won't give 'em up."

"We still need them."

"I got the agent's name somewhere. I'll ask again. We got some other stuff from years past, if that will help," Norbert assures me.

We go over the time of death, the lack of evidence at the crime scene, what a bitch Doris is, and that if you look up "Momma's Boy" in the dictionary, you'll see Brewster's picture.

The food arrives.

Norbert swallows a chunk of cow and says, "I got a big appetite for protein today."

"Alibis check out?" I ask.

Steve answers, "Brewster says he was with Clayton. Clayton's with a blond, Christina at a coming out party, Doris in Palm Springs."

"Tox screen come back?"

"Not yet."

"I'd like to see it," I say.

"No problem."

There is quiet as the men eat and Tiffany picks at her food, nibbling on minute bites.

Norbert and Steve order dessert.

"Any ideas on where we go from here?" Norbert asks between bites of apple pie a la mode.

"If we keep beating the bushes, something may eventually fly out," I say.

"I hate to say this boys and girls," Steve says, "but thus far, we don't have a clue."

"Literally."

"Just don't disburse any insurance money." Norbert looks at

Tiffany as he speaks.

"No problem there."

When the bill comes, Norbert hands it to Steve, who hands it to me, and I hand it to Tiffany.

"Is this what you mean about following the money?" she asks.

———

The toothy receptionist is past distraught when we enter the Augustus offices the next morning.

"What's the matter?" Tiffany asks as she rushes to comfort the poor girl.

"I've been fired."

"That's too bad." Tiffany pats her on her back.

"I thought you wanted to clean teeth?" I ask.

"I do."

The shock of getting the axe must have caused her to forget her true calling in life.

"Is Mister Heffelfinger in?"

She flips her thumb out like a hitchhiker. We take the cue and walk past her into the office area and to the corner office door.

"Knock, knock."

Heffelfinger is at his desk, wearing a tweed coat with leather patches on the elbows. His left hand pushes keys on the adding machine as his right does the calculator. "Who the hell are you?"

"Richard Sherlock. I'm the investigator from the insurance company."

"I don't have to talk to you."

"That's correct."

"Get out."

"After the reading of the will, trust me, I'm not the only guy who will be in here wanting to chat."

Heffelfinger harrumphed. "Augustus business is none of your business."

"Well, if you ever expect to see a dime of the disbursement, you might consider changing your mind."

Heffelfinger punched one key on his phone pad, waited for the connection to be made, but not a voice, "Millie get in here."

Less than ten seconds elapse. A woman, fifty-five, maybe sixty, hurries into the room. She's wearing a pair of green pants that she shouldn't be allowed to wear. She looks like a mossy stump. "Hello."

The elderly couple from the funeral is now complete. There is no doubt in my mind that these two are boinking each other.

"This is Mister Sherlock. He'd like to have a talk with us."

"Hello."

"This is my assistant, Tiffany."

Heffelfinger gives her a cursory glance.

"What can we help you with?" Millie speaks softly, as if a grandmother to her grandkids.

"We missed you at the reading of the will," I say.

"Somebody has to do some work in the family," Heffelfinger says curtly.

I get right to the point. "When did you know that Alvin was bursting faster than the dot-com bubble?"

"I tried to warn the old curmudgeon, but he wouldn't listen to me." Heffelfinger calling his boss a curmudgeon is the kettle calling the pot hot.

"When did he begin converting his holdings into cash?"

"Who said he did that?" Heffelfinger asks.

"I read the will."

"We started selling the properties about a year ago," Millie says. "Alvin thought the market had topped."

"He sell everything?" I ask.

"Why do you want to know?" Heffelfinger keeps the tension at a maximum height.

"I'm curious," I confess. "And where did the proceeds end up?"

Neither answers.

"You're his accountants..."

"We're not sure," Millie says in an apologetic voice.

Millie reminds me of my aunt from my mother's side of the family. Her name was Gladys Pleasant, a misnomer if there ever was one.

"Shall we say that Alvin took greater control of his funds during the past year or so?" I ask.

"For being so smart with money," Heffelfinger says, "the man could be a real idiot."

"Let's go into his office." I walk out the door and down the way to Alvin's corner. The three follow.

"Tell me how this all works." I stand in front of the TV screens between the computer terminals.

Millie takes the remote, and the screens come alive with lists of trading quotes, blinking changes faster than a winking eye. "Alvin would sit at his desk, watch the ticks, and tell the trader what he wanted."

"Somebody would sit and punch in the trades on these computers?"

"Yep." Millie was enjoying her financial show-and-tell. "The top screen is the S&P's, the middle are commodities, and the bottom, treasury bills."

"Alvin did this as if he were playing three hands of poker at the same time?"

"Pretty much."

"What does all this have to do with who killed him?" Mr. Curmudgeon asks.

"I don't know."

Heffelfinger coughed up some phlegm. Standing, one leg slightly bent, his right wingtip shoe was worn down on the inside of the sole. This malady undoubtedly had something to do with his choice of careers.

"When did Alvin start trading electronically?" I ask.

"It was about a year ago," Millie answers.

"Worst mistake he ever made," Heffelfinger says. "Nobody was better than him in the pits."

"So, why did he change?"

"God only knows. I tried to reason with him, but the man was hopeless."

I slow the cadence in my delivery. "How long did you work with Alvin?"

"Thirty-eight years," he says.

I look to Millie.

"Twenty-nine."

"That's both longer than I've been alive," Tiffany puts it into her perspective.

"Painful, after all that time to see the place go down in flames;

isn't it?"

"I've seen worse."

"When?"

He refuses to provide examples. "What do you want from us? I gave all the financials to the FBI."

"So, how could you be busy now?" Tiffany asks a very good question.

Her question goes unanswered.

Heffelfinger leans against Alvin's desk. "There is nothing more we can do; we've cooperated to the best of our abilities."

"We really have." Millie and Heffelfnger must have some interesting sex.

"Did you like Alvin?" I throw out.

"Of course not, nobody liked Alvin," she smirks as she speaks. "And he didn't like us," she adds.

"Did you kill him?"

"Don't be silly." Millie laughs.

"Who do you think killed him?" I ask.

"Some guy that Alvin blew off the floor, I'd guess. But what really killed him was the thinning of his wallet," Heffelfinger says.

"The most feared form of anorexia," Tiffany declares.

"He hated to lose," Millie says. "He was on a losing streak and there was nothing he could do to stop."

"All he would have to do is quit trading, right?" I ask.

"Alvin, stop?" Heffelfinger says, "Never happen."

"We tried," Millie says, "but he wouldn't listen.

"Stupid old coot," he says.

"Mister Augustus also entered into a number of business ventures that we warned him about."

Heffelfinger harrumphed again hearing Millie's disclosure.

"Such as?"

Millie didn't speak.

"What?" I pry, "Was he investing in worm farming?"

"No."

"Then what?"

No answers.

"Clayton's business?"

"I warned him about that," Heffelfinger answers.

"Brewster's trading?"

"It is difficult following in a father's footsteps," Millie says.

Heffelfinger straightens up as best as he can. "I still have work to do, as does Miss Millie."

"What?" Tiffany asks. "You're already broke."

"This meeting is finished," Heffelfinger says. "Come on, Millie."

They leave the room together.

On our way out, it didn't take a detective to see the receptionist had moved out. The stack of celebrity magazines was missing from beneath the desk. I'll bet she took the stapler, too.

——

There is a Starbucks on every corner in the financial district in downtown Chicago. We pick the closest one. I order a small coffee of the day and Tiffany orders a grandé with soy milk, no froth, loaded, flavored latté in a cup-cone or whatever. The clerk repeats her order to the coffee chef. I couldn't pronounce it, let alone remember it.

I sit, sip the coffee, and a cold chill goes up my spine.

There is always a point in any case where you feel overwhelmed, the same approximate feeling of dumping the contents of a thousand-piece jigsaw puzzle in front of you while gazing at the Jackson Pollock painting on the cover of the box.

"A penny for your thoughts, Mister Sherlock."

"This coffee is bitter. You would think with all the Starbucks in the world, they could make a cup of coffee that tastes better."

"That's how they get you to buy all the extras." Tiffany has a valid point.

"Well, not me, I'd rather suffer." I am as sour and bitter as the overpriced coffee.

"You know what I think, Mister Sherlock?"

"No."

Tiffany sips whatever is in her cup. "If it was up to me, I'd get rid of all pennies; what's their point?"

I see a bit of milk on her lip. "I thought you ordered no froth?"

Tiffany wipes her upper lip dry. "Don't tell me I'm looking like one of those "drink-your-milk" ads."

In a very strange way, Tiffany's overt fear of appearing less than perfect makes her charming.

I sit, the picture of gloom.

"You're not having any fun; are you?" she asks.

"No."

"Why not?"

"Because I hate my job."

"I think it's really fun, running all over town, seeing dead bodies, trying to unravel a mystery."

"I could do that at home playing Clue with my kids."

"Colonel Mustard, in the study, with the candlestick," Tiffany says.

"You really want to play detective?"

"I'd love to."

My mind must be turning in bizarre circles to give Tiffany an assignment.

I remove the Augustus corporate check out of my pocket. "I want you to call the bank, tell them you have a check from this account." I show her the number on the check, "For eighty-three-thousand dollars. Ask if it will clear." I hand over the check. She reads the printed name and address.

"How did you get this?"

"I lifted it the other day when I was in Alvin's office."

"You're not supposed to do that, are you?"

I ignore her question. "If the bank won't tell you, use that feminine charm of yours. I need to know if there is money in the account."

"I thought he was broke."

"First rule of life, assume nothing."

"Next," I say, "pick up what financials Norbert's got and take them over to this guy." I scribble down an address on North Ashland. "Knock on the door and if Herman's home, don't get too close, the guy is a little creepy."

"Don't worry, Mister Sherlock, I'm used to creepy."

"Then, go home, take a nap, eat a good dinner, and go out drinking at all the clubs where I'd look like an idiot. Start asking around about the two brothers. What they're like, friends, enemies, who they sleep with, the kind of money they waste. See if you can find out anything good, sleazy, or if either gets out of town on a regular basis. And if anybody saw them the Friday night before the murder."

"Why?"

"Because one of us deserves a night on the town."

"That would be me," she says, "but besides that, why?"

"I want to see if they are following in their father's footsteps."

"Why?"

"Because don't you think it is odd that nobody will tell us anything about anything? Nobody cares who killed their father, husband, employer, or business partner."

"That never entered my mind," Tiffany confesses.

"The lack of remorse in this case is frightening."

"I'll do my best, Mister Sherlock."

"There is no one better-suited for this assignment than you, Tiffany."

"I can't wait to pick out what I'm going to wear."

"And one other thing, the four hundred dollars I was going to spend on the hooker -- I'll need it for petty cash."

"You know," she says, "I forgot all about that."

I pull away from the table. "Good luck."

"Hey, if I'm on assignment, what are you going to do the rest of the day?"

"It's Tuesday, my kid day."

13
If you can't be good, be clever...

Kelly is in a snit as she steps into the Toyota.
"What's the matter with your sister?" I ask Carolyn.
"She's table-challenged."
"Shut up!" Kelly yells at her sister. "Last time I tell you anything."
"What's the problem, Kel?"
She doesn't speak, sulks instead. I know she wants to talk and only have to wait before she spills her guts. "How was your day, Care?"
"It sucked."
"Did you learn anything new at school?"
"No."
"Good, glad to hear my tax dollars are at work."
I pull the car out of the circular pickup area and head for home.
"I have a chance to sit at the better lunch table; but if I do, my friends at the old table will think I'm stuck-up like the people at the better table." Kelly has to stop and take a breath. "I want to go; but if I go and they end up not liking me, then I won't be able to go back to my old table, and I'll have to sit in a bathroom stall and eat my lunch because everybody will know I'm a loser that nobody wants to sit with."
"Where did you sit today?" I ask calmly to slow the crisis down.
"I sat with my old table, but on the edge closest to the girls at the better table."
"That was clever." I have tried to teach my girls, if you can't be good, be clever.
"But I can't do that forever, Dad."
"How long have you been in the middle of this conundrum?"
"What's a con-un-der-um?" Care, my inquisitive one, asks.
"It's like a problem you can't figure out," I explain.

"Two days," Kelly says. "The worst two days of my life."

"Oh, the horror of it all," I say with a slight chuckle.

"Dad, it's not funny."

"I'm not making light of your situation, Kel, I'm just warning you it gets a lot worse than this."

Kelly goes back into a funk.

"I take it this table of new girls is the most popular?"

"Ah, yeah."

"Why?"

"Because they are."

"I need a better reason." I pause. "Is it because more boys hang around that table?"

Kelly doesn't have to answer.

"What does your mother say to do?" I should never ask this question, but I do, because the answer usually will make my life easier.

"She says I should go for it."

"What do you think you should do?"

"I don't know."

"Do you want my advice?"

"Not really." She does, but can't admit it-a code of pre-teenage behavior.

"Do you want mine?" Care asks.

"No, twerp."

"Try sitting with the people you like and the people that like you. Better yet, sit with people you respect and respect you." I talk slowly, she might not get it right away; but if she hears it, she'll get it sooner or later. "If you have to try to be liked, you won't be yourself and one of the worst things you can ever do is not be yourself."

"Gee, Dad," Care says, "you sound like the dad on one of those *Full House* re-runs."

"My God, that show is so lame!" Kelly almost screams. "The Olsen twins are like forty and all weird-looking now."

"I like that show."

"How lame."

"You get what I'm trying to say, Kel?"

"No."

She does; she just won't admit it (keeping in code).

——

The rest of the time spent with dad goes pretty much according to plan. Snacks, TV, hating my cooking, homework, baths, more TV, and lights out.

I tuck Care in the left side of my bed and give her a kiss. On the right, I sit. "The best way to be liked by others is to like yourself. That's what Shakespeare was talking about when he said 'To thine own self be true.'" I secretly hope Care is listening in on all this, so I won't have to repeat it in a couple of years.

"Dad, seventh-graders don't study Shakespeare," Kelly informs me.

"Well, they should." I lean over and give my oldest a kiss. "And if you ever find yourself needing someone to eat lunch with, you give your old dad a call and I'll be there in no time."

"Oh, would that be hurl-worthy."

"Goodnight, Kelly. I love you."

——

Herman McFadden resembles a gnome gone wrong. He's short, maybe five-feet-four in heels, with a scraggly white beard and a patch of thinning, greasy, gray hair plastered across his head in a comb-over. Herman is one of those obese people whose eighty-or-so unneeded pounds starts sticking out at his sternum and doesn't stop until reaching his crotch. I bet he has to pee sitting down.

Herman is at his computer all day and, when he is not watching porn, he takes time to be a financial genius.

"That chick who brought over the stuff was really hot," Herman says, opening his apartment door. "Are you doing her?"

"No, Herman, I'm not."

"I'd like to."

"Fine, Herman, I'll find out if she feels the same way about you."

"And tell her if she ever wants to do any porn, I know a lot of people."

"I'm sure that fact will improve your chances of dating her."

"I don't want to date her, Sherlock. I want to have sex with her." He paused to be sure, "She is legal, isn't she?"

"Yes, Herman, but that will be the least of your problems with her."

It was over six years ago, when Herman was implicated in a case involving the kidnapping and murder of a runaway teenager, later found six-feet under in an Iowa cornfield. There was enough incriminating evidence against Herman to send him to the joint for about six life terms. Photos of the girl on his computer, emails linking him to the site where she was featured, and he had no alibi the night she disappeared from the corner she was working. There was also an eyewitness account of the girl climbing into a black Caddy, the exact year and model Herman owned.

I sat in an interrogation room questioning Herman for more than three hours, which wasn't easy because Herman smells bad. I came to the conclusion that Herman might be a truly disgusting human being, but he was no murderer. What bothered me about the case was there was too much evidence against him, all of which was unsubstantiated. I went to work, asked questions, surveyed the neighborhood, and kept asking questions. It took me about one week to figure it all out. A neighbor of Herman set him up perfectly, except for one little mistake: the dirt under his fingernails matched the dirt from the cornfield. It pays to get a manicure.

Ever since, Herman is beholding to yours truly. He even does my taxes.

The apartment is good size, two bedrooms, a full dining room, but filthy. I wish I had a pair of latex gloves to put on. "What did you find out?"

He clears a spot at the table. "Alvin was either the smartest dude on the street or the dumbest. A year ago, he's got more money than God, but in the next twelve months, goes into a tailspin that sucks every dime out of his coffers."

"Isn't that the way of the trader?"

"Not a guy who has done it for twenty years. The idiot mortgages a house he's owned free and clear with a checkbook loan, and runs it to the max in three weeks. Naw, this guy's dick ain't shooting straight."

"Interesting analogy, Herman."

"He's got all these pieces of corporations and not one of them makes any money. That's not kosher." Herman becomes more animated, he loves being able to sneak-peek into the lives of others. "He runs his credit cards to the limit, cashes out his personal IRA. He must be giving his wife cash, because she ceases to be an employee of his company."

"Doris worked for him?"

"Tax dodge."

"The oddest of all of it, Sherlock? He pays his taxes in advance."

"If he's losing all his money, why would he pay future taxes?"

"Odd, remember, I said odd."

I am perplexed. More pieces of the puzzle, yet none fit together. "Could he be stealing from himself?"

"I thought of that, too." Herman says. "But why would a guy with millions steal millions from himself?"

"Tax dodge?"

"I just told you he paid them in advance."

I sit back, the chair creaks as if it will break any second. "Could he being doing this out of spite for the rest of his family?"

"Why not just cut them off and leave them out of his will?"

"How about the accountant? Wouldn't he know all this was going on?"

Herman sits back. His chair is silent. He knows which one to sit on. "You sure would think so, wouldn't you?"

My head is spinning. There are a million questions to ask, but I can only come up with one. "Can you use that computer of yours to find out if Alvin had any offshore accounts?"

"Do you have a number?"

"Number of accounts?"

"No, the number of the account," Herman specifies.

"No."

"Then, no."

My chair creaks to its breaking point. Herman can easily see I am at my wit's end.

"How am I supposed to follow the money when there is no money?"

"A guy like Alvin, there's always money," Herman corrects me.

"You just have to find it."

I've had enough of this peculiar brilliance. I'm up and heading for the door. "Do what you can, would you, Herman?"

"For you, no problem."

Before opening the door I notice on his computer screen similar blinking numbers to those I saw in Alvin's office. "What kind of year you having, Herman?"

"Lousy, I'm only up only seven."

"Seven what?"

"You really want to know?"

"No." I'm out the door.

"Don't forget to tell Tiffany I'm the real sensitive type."

I had parked my car under an oak tree up the street, and the birds defoliated my windshield. I get in, see the clock, which is about five minutes wrong either side of the hour, and figure it is a good time to call.

"Yes," she answers on the fifth ring.

"It's Sherlock."

"I already know that."

"I really should invest in an id system for my cell phone, uh?"

She doesn't respond.

"Is this a good time to call?"

"I wouldn't have picked up if it wasn't."

Alexis' phone manner has an innocent quality. If she gets old and fat and is demoted to a phone-sex prostitute, she will still be able to make a good living.

"I have good news and bad news. Which do you want first?"

She sighs. "Good."

"Your Redblond invoice for personal services was listed for payment in Alvin's estate documents."

She waits.

"The bad news is," I sigh, "there's a lot of invoices ahead of yours."

"Is it possible he's tapped out?"

"I only know what I read in his papers."

She's angry. "How could he be broke? The guy was loaded. I fuck other guys at the Board of Trade that have lost thousands to Alvin Augustus. It can't be."

"All the financial documents spelled it out. Alvin blew off the floor and took everything down with him."

"No way."

Her breathing picked up before she spoke again. "I need that money."

There was a long spell when neither of us spoke.

"Alexis?"

"What?"

"When you used to do Alvin, did you do him in Nick's apartment?"

"Of course not."

"Then where did you do him?"

"At his place."

"You went all the way to Kenilworth?"

"No," she snaps back, as if I'm an idiot. "The condo on Astor."

"He had a place on Astor Street?"

"Sherlock, what kind of a detective are you?"

"Not a real good one, lately," I confess. "You know the address?"

"No, it was a brownstone, two doors north of Goethe."

"East or west side of the street?"

"Lake side, second floor."

"Nice?"

"The place was on Astor."

"I got to go."

"You get my money, Sherlock. Get my money."

———

Astor is well named. It is the most expensive, exclusive street in Chicago, maybe even the Midwest. One classic home next to another, refurbished and decorated with little respect for budget restraints. The accumulated wealth of the residents would tally the GNP of Angola. The archbishop of Chicago lives on Astor Street, not bad for a guy who took the vow of poverty.

On the second building from the Goethe corner, lake side of the street, there is a wrought-iron gate with a buzzer system. No name is listed for the middle, second-floor unit. I write down the names of the first and third floor residents. I step back. I try, but can't see through the leaded-glass windows. I walk around the corner, down the alley, to the back of the building, where an old car is parked in the spot labeled "No Parking." I have caught a break. There is a mop in a pail on the second-floor balcony, next to the open back door. I walk back to the front of the building and ring the buzzer.

"Jess," comes out of the small speaker.

"I need to show you extra cleaning that needs to be done."

At the word, "cleaning," the door buzzes open. I hurry through and up the stairs to the maid opening an oak door with a cut-glass window front that must have cost more than my Toyota when it was new.

"Jess?"

I flash my badge in her face the instant the door opens, "INS."

Another break, she doesn't have a heart attack.

I push inside before she has the chance to protest. "Green card?"

She may not speak English, but she knows "Green Card." Beads of sweat form on her brow.

"Get your things, *señorita*."

The woman, Mexican, Guatemalan, whatever, resigns herself to the inevitable. She picks up her cleaning supplies, places them in their proper place and comes back to stand before me. "Pleeze," she begs.

I lead her to the backdoor. "Your car?" I ask.

"Sí."

"Go," I point. "I'm only going to give you a warning this time."

She doesn't understand.

"Vámanos!"

She hurries down the stairs, into her car, and takes off faster than a tardy Domino's pizza-delivery driver.

I stand on the porch until she can no longer see me, come back inside, lock the door, and go to work.

I take a quick tour through all the rooms, taking a mental snapshot in each. Nice place, I should live so well.

The condo is the direct opposite of the house in Kenilworth. It is built and designed for comfort, with soft couches, comfortable chairs, leather right off the cow. The art on the walls is modern, fun, full of colors and shapes. The carpet is plush, ottomans rest in front of chairs. A fully stocked wet bar, refrigerators for wine are filled to capacity. Light pours through skylights, illuminating the soft colors on the walls. The dining room table is set for four with fine china. A built-in hutch stocked with Waterford everything.

There are three bedrooms, one huge, one regular, and one small. The furniture is polished, the computer screens clean, and the beds sport duvet covers and silk sheets. A cedar chest rests at the foot of each bed.

Enough sightseeing.

I pull each painting away from the wall and, on my fourth, I find a wall safe. I check the storage areas, and in the master's closet discover a floor safe, bigger than the one in the wall, but too small to hold too much cash. I go up, under and through each dresser drawer. I remove shirts, underwear, and sweaters -- all nice and expensive. In the walk-in closet there are a number of suits covered in dry cleaner plastic. The waist of the pants would fit Alvin.

Except for the bathroom where a shaving kit is in the cabinet next to the sink, the place lacks personal items. No pictures, photos, knickknacks, stationery, or notes from mother on the refrigerator door.

I search under the beds, behind the sinks, at the secretary desk, and find nothing of interest. There is no phone in the unit; but a burglar alarm that I sincerely hope the cleaning lady shut off. An antique chest is used as a coffee table in the front room to the left of the marble fireplace. Inside of it are game pieces, playing cards, a roulette pad, poker chips, and a baccarat set.

I retreat to the master bedroom. At the foot of the bed is a large, antique cedar chest. I reach down to open the chest. Locked. I nudge the edge to see if I can move it. I can't. I have found what I've been looking for.

In the kitchen I take a knife from a wooden block holder along with the long slender knife sharpener. Back in the bedroom, the lock pops open in less than a minute. Maybe I was Houdini in a past life. I raise the lid and beneath two blankets, I find the cedar chest filled with stacks of new, crisp, Benjamin Franklins.

Voila.

14
Assignment Tiffany

Money is the root of all evil; but a man needs roots.
Clean, crisp, hundred-dollar bills, stacks maybe twenty high and twenty across. I use my handkerchief to remove one of the packets. The bills have consecutive serial numbers. This is good. Uncirculated is easier to trace than circulated. They smell great. It is true you can smell new money.

There is a lot here, but not a million. A stack of a million one dollar bills would be taller than the Empire State Building. I'm figuring four- to five-hundred thousand in the chest.

In the kitchen I find brown paper, shopping bags with handles and the logo of Treasure Island Foods on their sides. I fill four with what I quickly count-out to be forty or so wrapped stacks. I pull off another full layer of the booty, and fill an additional two bags. I take the latter two bags into the second bathroom, and place rolls of toilet paper on the top to disguise the contents. I place both bags in the cabinet beneath the sink. If there is not a run on toilet paper the money should be safe.

Back in the bedroom I do my best to relock the chest where the remaining loot remains, and wipe off all fingerprints, and probably prints of others before me. The next set of hands that touches this wood will be a leading candidate for murder. I leave the rest of my fingerprints scattered around the condo as a calling card.

Exiting out the back door, I lock only the doorknob and continue quickly through the alley, around the corner, and to my car. I resemble a city shopper, trudging home with sacks of groceries. I place the bags in the trunk, hop in, fire up the Toyota, and head west on Division to Bucktown, where an old factory, redesigned as a self-storage business, offers the "First Month Free;" and where I stash my grocery bags in the smallest totally secure space available.

Tiffany is thirty minutes late for our lunch meeting at Butch McGuire's, the Northside tavern reported for years by Butch to be the first single's bar in America. She shows up wearing the darkest sunglasses ever manufactured, and a wide hat that hangs low over her face. Underneath, her skin is as pale as a peroxide blond.

Tiffany doesn't bother to greet me. She signals the waiter, and gives instructions in no uncertain terms: "A bloody, extra shot of Tabasco, extra shot of Worcestershire, lemon wedge on the side. Quicky, quicky."

"Rough night?"

"I've never worked so hard in my life, Mister Sherlock."

"Maybe you should put in for workers' comp?"

"What's that?"

Her drink arrives. She holds the waiter by his apron, sucks the drink empty like a thirsty Bedouin, saying, "another," and releases her grip.

"Maybe you should go home and rest."

"No," she gathers herself as best she can, "the case awaits and I have information."

"Do tell."

"First, if you want an excellent example of a disgusting slime-ball, Herman McFadden is the ideal candidate."

"I warned you."

"An air raid siren couldn't prepare you for that guy."

I don't bother telling her that Herman is sweet on her, or that she has a career in porn if she wants it.

"Secondly, Clayton was a lot easier to track than his brother, Brewster."

Tiffany takes a break to sip her second Bloody Mary. "I picked this place," she confesses, "because of their bloodies. Best in town."

"I'll remember that."

She twirls the drink on the table with her right hand. "Clayton is a hound."

"A hound?"

The color seeps back into her cheeks; but she seems reluctant to continue her thought.

"I don't like to say what kind. I have my morals."

"Tiffany..."

"Clayton dated Maureen Osteen."

"Okay."

"Nobody dates a ho like Mo O who isn't a cunt hound." She stops, "Whoops, damn, I didn't want to say that."

"Cunt hound?" I repeat for effect.

"I hate that word." She pulls her hat down even lower on her head. "Shhhh."

I whisper, "Hound."

"Clayton Augustus has stuck it in places, devils would fear to tread."

"I bet Clayton and Herman would get along great," I say.

Tiffany soldiers on, "Some of the people I talked to think he does it to spite his old man, sticking it in his face."

"Sticking what in his face?"

"That was a figure of speech." She places her drink on the table. "Clayton held the record for detentions in high school, picked up a number of times for drunk and disorderly, and has blown enough breathalyzers to rival Mo O."

"I checked. He hasn't been arrested once."

"Thank God for rich parents."

I glance at the menu. Butch's has great beef sandwiches. "So, Clayton thumbs it in the old man's face, but daddy is always around to bail him out of trouble."

"Rumor also has it, he has an account at the Northside Women's Clinic." The bloodies are doing their job. Tiffany is regaining her bluster and blarney. "His victims get 'no appointment necessary' treatment."

"Anything on the girl he was with the day of the murder?"

"No. Do you have any idea of how many non-blond blonds there are in this town?"

"Tell me about Brewster."

Before she begins, we order lunch. Me: roast beef, coleslaw and a cup of soup; her, a salad.

"Why don't you get something a little more substantial? It will make you feel better," I say in fatherly tones.

"I have enough sugar floating through me right now to put me on the fast track to diabetes. I need to flush it out, not stop it up."

I give up on dietary advice. "Brewster?"

"From all I could finagle, Brewster's pretty much a momma's boy. Went to Latin for the first twelve years, then to Denison on the six-year plan."

Latin is the *crème de la crème* of K-thru-12, private education in downtown Chicago. Denison University is where rich kids who couldn't get into the Ivy League end up.

"Perfected his drinking in college, did drugs, usual rich-boy education."

"Seems a little out of character being a drunk and a momma's boy, doesn't it?"

"No."

"Continue, please."

"After he got out of school, he screwed around for a few years, worked for his old man shoveling bullshit, got sick of that and went out on his own."

"Did you find out if his old man funded him?"

"He might have paid him to leave. They didn't get along in the unfriendly confines of Augustus, Incorporated."

"Women?"

"They come, they go. Mostly sluts, except mom."

"Isn't that nice."

The lunch arrived.

"Find anyone who saw them together on that Friday night?"

"No."

"Don't you think that's odd?"

"No. It's a Friday night; everybody is wasted."

I sit silent trying to process all the information.

"Your turn, Mister Sherlock, what have you found out?"

"Not much," I say, "but I do have another assignment for you."

"Does it include drinking?"

"No."

"Good, I don't know if my liver could take two nights in a row." Tiffany sighs a breath of relief.

"Stakeout."

"When?"

"Tonight."

"So, I have time for a spa treatment and massage?"

"I wouldn't schedule it any other way." I remember one last item on the agenda. "Tiffany, what about the check? Would it clear?"

"Darn," she says, "I knew I forgot something."

———

I was waiting in the Toyota, when her Lexus stopped alongside. I pull out of the parking space and she pulled in. Leaving my car running with the emergency flashers on, I went back and got in the Lexus passenger seat. Handing her the camera, I ask, "You know how to work one of these?"

"Duh."

I pointed to the Astor Street condo. "That's the place. We need to know who goes in and who goes out. It is the second floor that we care about."

"Why?"

"Neighborhood survey."

"Mister Sherlock, tell me."

"It's Alvin's home away from his home with his wife."

"Can't blame him."

"We have to see if anyone else uses the place."

"Why?"

"Thus, the object of your assignment."

"Got it."

"There is a parking spot in the back, so I want you to walk around and look down the alley once an hour. If you see a car, get the license number." I pause. "I'll be back at midnight to relieve you."

"Mister Sherlock, one question," she said a bit sheepishly. "Where do I go to the bathroom?"

"Don't you remember what Detective Norbert told you?"

"No."

"About the bladder?"

"Oh, yeah." Tiffany remembers, but not happily.

"Good luck." I open the car door. "I'll see you at midnight."

———

The spa treatment did Tiffany a world of good. Her face looks healthy, fresh, and relaxed when I find her asleep, resting in the reclined passenger seat of the Lexus. My tap, tap, tap on the window snaps her into consciousness.

"How long do you think you've been asleep?"

She rolls down the window. "Maybe a minute or two."

"All that happened a minute or two ago?" I point to the second floor of the condo where lights were blazing inside.

"Well, maybe it was a little more than two."

"You got to move your car, so I can park here. I take it you didn't take any pictures."

Tiffany stared at the unit. "I guess I kinda blew it, huh?"

"Don't worry, what goes in has to come out."

"What else can I do?" Tiffany was sincere. "I don't want to let you down."

"You can drive around back, and get the license numbers of any cars parked in their driveway."

"Will do." Tiffany got out of the car and walked around to the driver's side. I was getting back into the Toyota when she asked, "Do I have time for a pit stop?"

"If nature calls, answer it."

After parking, I fiddle with the camera until the shutter speed was set for low light. I see through the cut-glass windows, shapes move inside. There was more than one, but no way of counting an exact number. Twenty minutes go by and a cab comes down the street, stops in front of the building, waits. I roll down the window, aim the camera to get a shot of the taxi's license plate, but don't need to press the shutter. A familiar face comes out the front door. She is dressed in a sleek, black, above-the-knee dress that clings to her body as tight as a wet tee-shirt. Her hair is brushed to perfection, which is telling, as is the fact that she carries only a small handbag. She closes the door softly, bidding goodbye to no one. She steps down the stairway slowly, not making a sound with her black high heels and climbs into the back of the cab.

I snap picture after picture. Diane is a photogenic woman.

Ten minutes later, the light goes off in the front room. I ready the camera. A man exits. In the darkness it is difficult to chart his age. I have never seen him. He is fit, has a full head of brown hair, dressed in jeans and a slightly wrinkled shirt. He wears no wedding ring, but a very expensive watch. He walks south, crosses Goethe and out of my sight.

Another five minutes ticks off the clock. The hallway light in the condo goes out. I refocus the camera, aim, wait. Two minutes. Nothing. I take my eye off the lens, glance down the block to the Astor and Schiller Street intersection. A car turns left onto Astor and heads my way. I aim the camera at the front grill and wait until I have a shot at the plate. This is going to be tough at night. What looks like a new Jaguar speeds by. I snap photos, but no way will a picture develop. I try to pick up the plate with my eyes, but it's no better than a blur. Down the street, at the same intersection, another set of headlights turns left and heads my way, faster than the previous car.

It's Tiffany's Lexus. She honks her horn and waves as she goes by. I have to have a talk with that girl about being subtle.

My cell phone rings.

"Tiffany?"

"How'd you know it was me?" she asks. "You sign up for caller id?"

"What the hell are you doing?"

"I'm in pursuit of the suspect."

"Tiffany, back off. Get the license number; that's all we need."

"Oh come on, this is fun."

I can hear her car screech to a sudden stop.

"Guess where I am?"

"Tiffany..."

"I'm behind him at the light at Oak Street."

"Get down. He can see you in his rear view mirror." I scream into the tiny phone. "Get the plate number and get away from him."

"Why do you want the plate number?"

"We want to find out who it is."

"It's Brewster Augustus," she yells back.

"You sure?"

"He's going up Michigan Avenue. He's turning left."

"Don't follow."

"Why not?"

"I know where he's going."

"You do?"

"The Ritz."

"I'll follow him just to be sure, bye."

15
No baloney since Tuesday

I pick up the end of Norbert's tie and scratch off dried egg yolk. "I don't think Alvin was broke."

"Yeah?" Norbert says.

"The fact that he was under investigation, his accountant hasn't a clue, and he takes his wife off the payroll, tells me a scam was taking place, or Alvin was going to rabbit with his loot."

"I thought he was blowing off the floor?"

"I didn't say this all fits."

"So you think he was taking a powder and somebody put a stop to his travel plans?"

"Maybe." I stop. "Your turn."

"Doris is scheduled to leave the Ritz on Saturday."

"Moving back to Kenilworth with baby Brewster?" I ask.

"Don't know about the boy."

"She'll need someone to protect her against the evil spirits still haunting the hallowed walls."

Norbert burps. "I got a twist for you, Sherlock."

"I hate twists."

"Alvin's tox screen came up with trace levels of arsenic, cocaine, anti-depressants and -- get this one--Rohypnol, used for date rape."

"No self-respecting drug addict would be caught dead taking that menu of poison."

"Rohypnol's usually slipped in a mickey."

"So somebody wanted to take Alvin home and have sex with him without his permission?"

"The twist gets tighter when all the amounts come up minor; not enough of any to put him down for the count."

"That doesn't make sense."

"That's why I labeled it a twist."

"Thank you, Norbert."

"You're welcome. Your turn."

"We have another person of interest."

Norbert is silent for a second, then says, "How interesting?"

"I'm not sure."

"Who?"

"I'm not sure."

"Where did you see him?"

"On the street."

"Sounds like a real solid lead to me."

"If I can figure out how to download the photo into my computer, upload, reload so you can load it into your computer; we can both try to figure out who the guy is."

"What century you living in, Sherlock?"

———

Murder cases, more than any other, are a step-by-step process. Problem is for every step taken forward, you usually take two back. Yet another reason, I dislike this job, a lack of constant forward momentum.

Tiffany picks me up at my apartment.

"We have to go back to Kenilworth."

"We were just there."

"I know."

"If I spend too much time in a house like that, bad-decorator karma will seep into me by osmosis."

"Do you know what osmosis is, Tiffany?"

"It's like an STD, but in your brain."

I don't argue with her.

"Don't you want to know why we're going?" I ask as the Lexus turns onto Lakeshore Drive and heads north.

"Guess, I should ask that, huh?"

"We have to figure out why the window was broken."

"What window?"

———

We park behind the black-and-white in the circular driveway. The cop comes to the door a minute after we ring and swallows whatever he's eating before speaking. "Yeah?"

"Remember us?"

"No."

"Insurance investigators."

Peter Patrolman could care less. "Sure, come on in."

We follow the close-to-rookie patrolman to the den where the movie *Rush Hour* plays on the big screen TV. There is a pile of DVDs on the coffee table next to a pizza box. He hits pause on the remote. "Only got another day here, they're lifting the crime scene."

"Good chance to catch up on your reading," I remark.

Tiffany stops to watch Jackie Chan beating up a slew of bad guys in a Chinese restaurant. "I love this part," she says.

They watch TV. I work. What is wrong with this picture?

The broken window pane remains boarded up. It is the third of a vertical group of four leaded-glass panes. It will be a custom repair job.

"Did anyone find out how this got broken?" I ask.

The cop is in the lounger, Tiffany on the couch, and Chris Tucker on the screen. No one answers my question.

The view from the window is of fifty feet of lawn, a garden, and a stand of six or seven trees, with bushes behind acting as a fence. I swivel 180 degrees to a wall of books in a dark wood, built-in bookshelf, a TV console and a door to a small bathroom on the right.

Neither of the movie fans notices my exit outside, or walk to edge of the garden near the trees. Turning back to the house, I line up the broken window for the best unobstructed view into the room. Before setting a foot into the garden, I check for broken plant limbs and footprints. There are none. I back up slowly, keeping my eyes on the window. In three steps I am at the stand of trees. There is little room to move, three, maybe four feet in either direction, before it is either too thick or the bushes get in the way. I set my bearings and go back into the house.

Tiffany is now on the edge of the couch, a slice of pizza in her hand. The cop hasn't moved. Jackie and Chris are chasing the bad guys causing more vehicular damage than a demolition derby.

At the bookcase, I measure about six feet up and start to run my eyes across this height, sidestepping my feet like a slow motion dancer. I cover the entire wall in twenty minutes, then retrace left to right.

The movie is almost over when I see the indentation.

The bullet had split, literally split, between Tom Sawyer and David Copperfield. No wonder it was hard to find. I take both novels off the shelf, neither spine had ever been cracked, and place them on another shelf and stick my finger in the hole.

A bullet, rifle size, was sunk two or three inches into the hard wood.

"Excuse me," I speak up.

No answer.

"Excuse me," I repeat and get the same response. At the table I push the remote to pause.

"Hey, we're watching that," Peter Patrolman pipes up.

"Would you mind getting Steve or Norbert on your radio and ask if either could stop by?"

"Now?"

"Yeah, now?" Tiffany remotes the movie to play.

I sit down, take a piece of pizza, remove the anchovies, and take a bite. Why anyone would ruin a good pizza with those little, too-salty fish is beyond me. The movie ends the same way as it did the ten times my kids watched it. Chris and Jackie get the bad guys and live happily ever after, or until *Rush Hour 2* comes out a year later.

———

Within two hours Alvin's home is police-party-central once again.

The lab guys pull the slug from the wall. "Came from a rifle as well as a shooter who knew what gun to use when," Steve concludes after a lengthy thought process on how the shot came from the exact spot where I stood outside. I could have saved him a lot of time, but why bother?

"Professional," Steve tells Norbert.

Duh.

The lab boys search for a second shot-bullet, casing, whatever, and come up empty.

129

"You check the garage?" I ask in the frenzy of activity.

"It's like a classic car show in there," Norbert says.

We visit.

Due to the fact that a person can only drive one car at a time, isn't it overkill to own six? But, on second thought, if you have a six-car garage, you do have the responsibility to fill it up. There is a Cadillac with fins, Porsche Roadster, massive SUV, Lexus 400, a 1955 red Chevy, and a Lincoln Town Car Alvin must have used when he chauffeured in his spare time. All are meticulously maintained, as is the garage, with a floor so clean Norbert eats off it when a slice of pickle slips from his sandwich.

"You check these out?"

"I didn't," Norbert says, and then asks, "What for?"

"Explosives."

Norbert looks at me as if I'm whacked. "You're kidding, right?"

"I got a feeling."

The lab guys enter fifteen minutes later and find absolutely nothing amiss.

"Good call, Sherlock."

"Hey, nobody's perfect."

————

Northern Trust, one of the oldest banks in the nation, is located in the Rookery Building, one of the oldest buildings in the city. There are few places on earth where architecture and commerce complement each other so well.

Tiffany and I sit in the office of Vice President P. Carrington Vogel, a man who wears a pocket watch on a gold chain on his tight wool vest. He must be fifty, but there's nary a wrinkle on his face. He moves slowly. As he fingers the new Ben Franklin I provided, the man makes a snail look like Seabiscuit.

"It is really not that odd of an occurrence," he speaks with the monotone authority of, for lack of a better example, a banker. "I've had traders come in here and pull out their entire accounts as if it were an ATM."

"You keep that kind of cash in reserve?"

"I wish they never retired the thousand dollar bill."

"Me too," Tiffany agrees.

"Did Alvin make a practice of doing this?"

"Never in an amount this large; a hundred-thousand-dollar man." Vogel's hands rest on the edge of his desk, as if he was about to say grace before a meal. "He was scared, like the rest of them."

"Of what?"

"Going broke."

"Alvin was worth millions, what would he be afraid of?"

Vogel has no inflection in his voice. "Every gambler fears insolvency. The greater the fear, the better the gambler."

"When did he withdraw the four-hundred grand?"

"Two weeks ago, tomorrow."

"Did he say what it was for?" Tiffany asks.

"No, why would he?"

"Make conversation?" she replies.

"No."

I pull out the blank check I lifted from his office "This account active?"

"Frozen."

"Balance?"

"Can't say." Vogel has not moved an inch since we sat, which includes the hair on his head and the wire-rim specs resting on his nose. The man's heart rate must be around six beats a minute.

"Alvin's main account is at First Options," he says.

"That was empty," I tell him.

"Pity."

Vogel does not stand as we get up to leave, merely extends his right hand forward to push the one-hundred-dollar bill towards me.

Tiffany is barely out the door when she says, "Bet that guy is a real riot in the sack."

"Talk about a riot," I say, "let's go see Herman."

"Do we have to?"

———

I believe Herman's fifty-inch belt is going to break in excitement when he opens his door.

"Tiffany, you came back."

Herman clears periodicals and old newspapers for us to sit. Tiffany uses the latest copy of *Juggs* as protection between her butt and the stains on the couch. She crosses her legs so quickly that a breeze is created in the stuffy room.

"I need to know how he did it, Herman."

"Did what?" Herman's eyes have not moved off my junior partner.

"Made all that money."

"Have you thought about the audition?" he asks Tiffany.

"Audition?"

"Over here, Herman," I wave my hands to get his attention. "How did Alvin make his money trading? He had to have some system, didn't he?"

"No."

"What, then?"

"Can I say one thing before we get into this?" he asks, doesn't wait for a reply, and turns again to Tiffany. "I happen to know that all the producers are begging for girls who can look sixteen on camera."

Tiffany looks at him like he's nuts, which he is, in a way. "What the hell are you talking about?"

"You didn't mention it to her?" Herman asks.

"I was waiting for the right time."

"Oh."

"Herman, tell us about Alvin. How'd he do so well in the market?"

"Alvin was smart enough to know he wasn't that smart."

"Come again."

"He knew he could never predict the market."

"I'm not following."

"Every year a new crop of well-funded traders come on the floor, convinced they can call the market. They come from Harvard, MIT, Wharton, and bring charts and theories, computer programs, moon patterns, recipes, whatever. This pack of hungry wolves are convinced they can predict the S&P's, corn, wheat, gold, silver, and the winner of the Kentucky Derby. So, they get on the floor and throw around their dads' money, and guys like Alvin just sit back. When the kiddies buy, Alvin sells. When kiddies sell, Alvin buys. And in time, usually about six months to a year, Alvin has won maybe seventy-percent of the trades; and that's enough to blow these kids back to work for their daddies in plumbing supplies or sewer construction. Alvin is smart enough to know that nobody can predict the market and willing to take the money of anyone who thinks they can."

"It can't be that simple."

"In actuality, it is."

"I'm in the wrong business," I admit.

"I don't think so, Mister Sherlock."

Herman smiles at Tiffany.

"You have bologna stuck in your teeth, Mr. McFadden," she is kind enough to tell him.

"Gee," Herman says, picking at his teeth, "I haven't had baloney since Tuesday."

"What else have you found out, Herman?"

"Not much."

"Why not?"

Herman ignores me, returns his stare at Tiffany. "I'm not kidding you, girls who looks like you could climb the heights of show business in a single bound; but you'll need an agent and I am willing to take on that role."

"I don't know what you're talking about," Tiffany says, "but whatever it is, no thanks."

"Herman, anything else?"

"Well, I'm not sure, but there is a lot of shit ready to hit the fan at the Board of Trade."

16
Where truth lies

A two-bit gangbanger, by the name of Magpie Morris, waits in his orange jumpsuit for the judge to take the stand.

Tiffany sits between Steve and me in the last row of the courtroom. We have been told that Magpie has valuable information concerning the killing of Alvin Augustus, and might consider sharing his thoughts with us. But before he makes his decision, he's in court to find out how badly the deck is stacked against him.

The first witness is a seasoned gang cop named Gus, which is not his real name.

"I found the weapon in the backseat of Mr. Morris' car," Gus tells the Judge.

I whisper to Tiffany, "He's lying."

The public defender speaks up, "Judge, my client doesn't own a car."

"He's lying, too."

Tiffany turns my way, but I silence her with the raise of my index finger.

"I wasn't in no car, and I don't got no car," Magpie throws in his two cents.

"That's three lies in a row." So much of life comes in threes, and I have no idea why.

"It was a gun used in a prior killing, your honor." The prosecutor adds his lie to the total.

The judge calls the attorneys to the bench and speaks to the two in muffled tones.

"How do you know they're lying?" Tiffany wants an explanation.

"It's a courtroom; everybody lies." I explain quietly. "The cop knows this guy's a crook and the only way to get him off the street is to tie him to the weapon. The defense attorney knows he did it, or did something twice as bad; but he has to lie because that's his job. Ditto for the prosecutor."

"But weren't they all sworn to tell the truth?" Tiffany asks.

The judge waves the two barristers back to their places in the courtroom. "Now, watch what is going to happen," I whisper to her.

The judge taps his gavel. "The court rules that the evidence is to be recognized and so noted."

Tiffany nudges my arm. "What happened?"

"The judge lied. He realizes the cop is lying, the defense guy is lying, and Magpie's a criminal, so there's no doubt he's lying."

"The evidence in the case is substantial, what difference does it make whether he owned the car?" the judge asks.

The defense attorney jumps to his feet. "Objection. There are no other witnesses, no radio transcript of any arrest being made, and the arresting officer is the officer on the stand. The guy could have planted the gun as easily as ordering donuts."

The judge has had enough. "The defendant is ordered to stand trial with a charge of first-degree murder." The gavel comes down. "Next case."

Steve leans over Tiffany and says to me, "No doubt he'll want to chat with us now."

We exit the row before the next orange jump-suited criminal enters the courtroom.

"How do you know they were lying, Mister Sherlock?"

"It's a courtroom, Tiffany; everybody is a liar. That's the way the system works."

———

Magpie sits on one side of the table with his lawyer, Lou Barris, beside him. Steve and I sit opposite. Tiffany waits outside.

Shackled at hands and feet, Magpie clinks every time he moves. A young man, mid-twenties, with a nasty scar on his left cheek gives a clear indication of his upbringing. When he opens his mouth to speak, there are at least three openings where teeth used to be. With all the money made in the illegal drug trade, you would think these kids would spend some of the profit on dental work.

"I didn't kill da some-bitch," Magpie spits out.

"What difference does that make?" Steve asks rhetorically. "You'll be going to the joint anyway. It's just a matter of how long you're going to stay."

Barris is already bored with the shenanigans. "Why don't you tell us what you have to offer?"

"No, no," Steve says. "You have to tell us what you have to offer. See, we're not the ones on the way to prison."

Magpie starts to speak, but Barris shuts him up.

"My client has information on a hit-for-hire contract concerning Alvin Augustus."

"Sho' do."

"And he came across this information, how?" Steve asks, leaning back in the wooden chair.

"My client has many contacts throughout the city," Barris says, "people in a wide variety of employment."

I could speak, but Steve is playing this pretty well.

"If you got a name, date, weapon, and tell me something that only I could know, I could see if there might be a reduction to manslaughter in the cards."

"Man, I don't want no manslaughter." Magpie's clinking so much he sounds like silverware being tossed around.

"Reduction in sentence?" Barris asks.

"Maybe," Steve says, his negotiation complete.

"All right," Barris turns to his client, "Magpie, go ahead, tell 'em."

"Man, you my lawyer, ain't we supposed to discuss dis first?"

"What would be the point?"

"Dis is bull-sheet."

Barris shouts, "Magpie, shut the fuck up and talk."

Steve takes out his pad and pencil. I sit, happy not to have been a part of the discussion.

"Shoota's name was Clarence..."

Steve interrupts, "Clarence? You trying to sell us a hit man named Clarence?"

"Sho' nuf."

"I assure you my client does not have the intellectual capacity to make this up."

Magpie is not sure what that comment was all about.

"Clarence do anybody for five grand."

"Last name?"

"Clarence, man, I toll you."

"And how did Clarence Clarence go about shooting Mister Augustus."

"Wit a gun."

Steve looks to Barris.

"Magpie, you might want to be a little more specific."

Magpie rattles big as he puts his hands and arms out as if shooting skeet.

"A rifle?"

"Big rifle, big mean rifle. Blow a hole in ya head bigger than a basketball."

"Where'd he do it?"

"Don't know that."

"Who for?"

"Who fo, what?"

"Who paid for the hit, Magpie?"

"Man if I knew dat, I wouldn't be dealin' for no reducement, I'd be dealin' to get out of here."

"Okay," Steve says. "Tell us something only we would know."

"Dude, I got somethun betta than that."

"Yeah."

"Clarence missed."

"Shit," Steve pounds a fist for exclamation. "Everybody knows that."

Magpie smiles big. There is enough room between teeth to hang Christmas ornaments. "Yeah, but dey don't know Clarence missed on purpose."

17

Never buy anything that eats

The conundrum continues.

The second-most-popular girl, Lysette, at the second-most-popular table, also has aspirations of moving up in cafeteria classification. She has enlisted my daughter Kelly, who obviously did not take my advice on the matter, to join forces and go as a package deal. Thus, if they are rejected by the popular girls, they can still sit together at lunch and not become lone outcasts to the little girls' room.

"Kelly, I thought we discussed this," I say over the phone in my nightly call to the girls.

"Dad, you don't know what this means."

"I have a pretty good idea."

"How could you? You're not in the seventh grade."

"I was once."

"In another century."

Although she is calendar correct, I do not believe her argument is valid. "Some things in life never change, daughter dear."

"Dad, you don't understand."

"Kelly, what happens if the plan doesn't work? If they take Lysette and reject you?"

"We're going as a package deal."

"So, if you get in and Lysette gets bounced, you're staying with Lysette?"

Kelly hesitates. If nothing else I have her considering what she has not yet considered.

"Dad," Kelly says, "Mom wants to talk to you."

Before I can say "no" my ex-wife is on the phone.

"I need more money."

"So do I."

"The girls need clothes for school."

"So do I."

"You don't go to school."

"Because I don't have the right clothes."

"Don't argue with me, Richard."

"Why not?"

"Because you know you are going to lose."

She is correct. She knows it and I know it, but I have to put up a fight. I have principles.

"Maybe if you spent less on horses and riding lessons, they'd have a better wardrobe?"

"The girls love their horse."

"You should have never bought them anything that eats."

"They need a healthy outlet to help them get through the divorce."

"It seems to me they are handling the situation a lot better than we are."

"They need new clothes."

"And I give you money each month for you to buy them the new clothes they need."

"And it isn't enough."

"And it never will be, no matter how much it is."

"Fine, Richard," the ex cuts to the chase, "see you in court." She hangs up the phone.

It is too bad that my ex and I cannot get along "for the sake of the children." Anger can be like weeds in a garden. No matter how many you pull, it just keeps on coming.

———

Tiffany calls the next morning quite distraught. She speaks in hushed tones that are hard to decipher over a cell phone. She tells me she has either a major problem with a French flip or French tip and has to see her manicurist or her mammy before she can rendezvous with me.

"You have your priorities, Tiffany. I understand."

I take the train downtown and pop in unannounced at the Augustus' offices. The reception desk is not merely empty, but pushed to the side of the room, as if waiting for pickup. In the inner office area the other desks in the room await the same fate.

"Going so soon?" I ask Millie who comes out to greet me.

Millie has an aura of tension about her. "What do you want?"

"I want to find out who killed Alvin, then I want to go home and relax in a warm tub."

"It wasn't me."

"And it wasn't me, either," I confirm.

I hear two voices coming from Heffelfinger's office, a man and a woman; both I recognize. "Did I pick a bad time to visit?"

"Yes."

"Good."

I walk past Millie towards the accountant's lair, but pause. "Millie, before I forget, do you remember what Alvin was wearing the Friday before he died?"

She places her finger to her lips, thinks. "An ugly suit."

"Was it wrinkled?"

"Yes," she says, "matter of fact, it was."

I smile and enter the corner office to find Doris Augustus seated across from Horace Heffelfinger.

"What the hell are you doing here?" Doris asks.

"Just dropped in to see what condition my condition was in." A unique reference to the 1970's breakout hit of Kenny Rogers and his First Edition, featured in one of my favorite films, *The Big Lebowski.*

"Get out."

I take a seat next to Doris.

"I do not appreciate your intrusions into my life, Mister Sherlock," Doris says. "I have had calls from my bank, phone company, credit bureaus, and friends, telling me my accounts are being audited."

"That wasn't me."

"I don't care who it was. I want it stopped. You have no right to delve into my personal matters." Doris speaks tough.

"I don't, but the other two detectives do. They're the ones doing all the delving."

"I want it to cease immediately," she says and adds, "and I want my share of the twelve million dollars."

Heffelfinger has been quiet during Doris' and my friendly meet-and-greet. His fingers tap nervously on his adding machine.

"Why did Alvin bounce you off the payroll?" I ask Doris,

though the question is really aimed at the money-man.

"You would have to ask my husband that question," Doris says.

"He's not available," I say. "Would his accountant know?"

"There were fewer and fewer dollars available for payout." The taciturn man finally speaks.

"Did you come off the rolls, too?"

"No."

"Millie?"

"No."

"Seems you got the short end of the stick there, Doris." I face Heffelfinger. "Why?"

"Alvin's orders."

I turn back to Doris. "He was going to divorce you; wasn't he?"

"No."

"And I bet you signed one son-of-a-bitch of a prenup."

Heffelfinger answers me with his eyes.

"No, our marriage was solid," she tries to argue, "rock solid."

"Bad choice of words."

Doris agrees with me, but won't admit it.

"I bet you curse the day you signed your name to those papers."

"I'm set for life, no matter what happens," she proclaims.

"And that's why you're here this morning? Trying to get an advance to pay off your tab at the Ritz?"

Heffelfinger answers me for the second time without speaking.

"Should have gone with the junior suite instead of the master, Doris. He who will not economize will soon agonize."

Doris takes her purse, "You are a disgusting man, Mister Sherlock," and storms out of the office.

"How could anyone who quotes Confucius ever be considered disgusting?" I ask Heffelfinger who folds his arms across his chest.

He shrugs.

"I have a feeling I just did you a favor."

"What do you want?"

"I need a record of all the trades Alvin made in the past six months."

"Can't."

"He used a computer, there has to be a record."

"Gone."

"How about the clerk who made the trades?"

"Gone, too."

"Where?"

"Don't know."

"What was his name?"

"Joey Villano."

"Sounds like a character out of a TV show."

"He looks like one, too."

I sit back and try to reason with the man. "I know you have copies, why don't you just hand them over, and I'll get out of your hair?"

Heffelfinger takes my request as a personal affront as he runs his fingers over his mostly bald pate. "Can't."

"Why not?"

"Because someone already was here to claim that prize."

18
Bureau of incompetence

Standard operating procedure was that an applicant had to have earned a law degree or a CPA to get into the FBI. This is not the case any longer, but the uppity attitude the educational requirement fostered remains alive and well inside the Bureau.

There are over eight hundred FBI agents in the Chicago office, more people than an entire day shift at the Ford Assembly plant on the South Side. Must be more crime than Fords around these parts. The offices are in the Dirksen Federal Building in the Loop. I have to visit three floors before I find the correct reception area.

"Excuse me, I need to speak with the agent involved in the investigation of illegal trading at the Board of Trade." I smile at the camera photographing me as I speak to the receptionist.

"And you are?" She speaks with a lazy, distant timbre in her voice.

I show her my license.

"Are you here to sell insurance? Because, if you are, I have to tell you, we don't allow solicitation on the premises."

"No, I'm an insurance investigator."

She clicks her thumbnail back and forth on the edge of the laminated card. "How would you know, sir, that there is an agent involved in such an investigation?"

"I'm a good investigator."

"Sir," she speaks in a drone of a tone, "if there was an agent, and I'm not saying there is, in an investigation of the Board of Trade, and I'm not saying there is an investigation; but if there was it would be classified, and he or she would not be available to outsiders such as you."

I raise one finger to halt our conversation, pull out my cell phone and dial.

"No cell phones, sir, you'll have to go outside," she orders.

I keep my finger raised to keep her at bay until Norbert answers my call.

"Who's the FBI guy on the Board of Trade case?"

Norbert says, "Guy named Romo Simpson."

"Romo. Who the hell would ever name their kid Romo?"

"Mister and Mrs. Simpson," he answers.

I hang up my phone, smile again for the camera. "I'd like to speak with agent Romo Simpson."

Her voice changes not one iota. "And who should I say is calling?"

"Alvin J. Augustus."

She glances back to my license. "That is not the name on your insurance badge."

"I go by an alias, since I'm still wanted in a few states."

I wait about fifteen minutes, during which time the reception phone does not ring and no other guest arrives. This would be a perfect place for Alvin's fired receptionist, if her career as a dental hygienist doesn't pan out.

Romo Simpson comes into the lobby.

It takes me about six seconds to size him up, three of which I spend reading an old copy of *Field and Stream*. Why the FBI would subscribe to this publication is a mystery to me.

Agent Romo wears a blue suit, rep tie, and a white shirt so starched it could stand up by itself. He looks exactly like all the other agents wandering the halls. Good cover, men. He's in his mid-thirties, probably has 2.3 kids at his suburban home, and his wife drives an American made SUV. He has that nervous energy of youth bubbling out of his pores. "Mister Augustus, I presume?"

"He couldn't be here, so I came in his place. Richard Sherlock."

We shake hands. He sits down in the chair across from me and notices the magazine in my hands.

"I'm not really into this," I explain. "My idea of camping is two John Denver records in a Holiday Inn."

He remains stiffer than his shirt. "Yes?"

"I am trying to find out who killed Alvin and I thought I'd stop by and see why you were investigating his trading practices."

"Who said I was doing that?"

"You offered him immunity for turning state's evidence." I have no clue that anyone made Alvin this offer, but I throw it out to see if I can get a rise out of Romo.

"We did?"

"I'll take that as a yes," I say and quickly continue. "You needed a player who knew everybody and everything going down on the floor to make a case, so you picked Alvin."

Romo's eyelids flick twice. He should never attempt a career playing poker.

"Alvin would be the perfect squeal, except that old Alvin could have been the biggest perpetrator of the crimes being investigated, and you'd find yourself in betwixt and between."

I've struck a tender nerve. His eyelids are flapping faster than a butterfly's wings. "Come with me," he says.

I pick up my license on the way past the receptionist. "It was a pleasure, Miss."

Romo leads me into a small conference room, closes the door behind him and points me to the middle chair. I sit and immediately fondle the poorly hidden small microphone in the cup of pens and pencils in the middle of the table. "What I say isn't going to end up on one of those reality shows on TV, is it?"

Romo sits and rolls up his sleeves, cracking some of the starch in his shirt. "You think he was killed to keep him from talking?"

"I don't know. The more I dig, the more reasons and people I find that wanted poor Alvin in the grave." I fold my hands together to convey an air of innocence. "Did you figure out how he was skimming the fat off the soup?"

"We have a pretty good idea."

Yeah, right.

"I got a guy who could figure out the trading patterns in about an hour, if you want to hand over the last month or two of his records."

"I can't do that. It's classified."

"I promise I won't tell."

Romo tightens his already taut tie.

I reach into my jacket pocket and pull out a copy of the photo of the guy seen coming out of the condo on Astor Street. "You know who this is?"

He studies the picture, turns to the telephone console, pushes a button and says "Delia, could you come in here a second?"

A career secretary enters. She's about ten years from retirement, but obviously wishes she was much closer.

"Make me a copy, then put this guy through the system."

"Yes, Mister Simpson." Calling this guy Mister is a true chore for this poor woman.

"We'll find out," Romo assures me.

"Will you let me know too?"

He thinks this over. "I'll have to clear it with my supervisor."

"It seems only fair."

"What else do you have for us, Mister Sherlock?"

"Actually, the reason I came here was the reverse of that process."

"You know I can't discuss the status of an ongoing investigation."

"I'm not supposed to do that either, but seeing we're rowing in the same boat..."

"FBI policy."

"So, if I figure out how it all worked, how Alvin manipulated the market, before and after you made the deal with him and including the fact he probably scammed the Bureau in the process, you wouldn't want me to tell you?"

"I didn't say that." Romo's eyes are blinking faster than a strobe light.

"Thank you for your time, Agent Simpson, you have been more than informative."

"I have?"

"Yes, quite."

I have left poor Romo with the problem of figuring out what he has unknowingly let out of his bag. This will ruin the rest of his day.

————

In any investigation, it is often more important to find out what people don't know, than it is to find out what they do know. In this case, the FBI doesn't know how the Board of Trade is being manipulated. All they know is that cash is disappearing at an alarming rate. With no solid evidence, the FBI makes a deal to find out what they don't know. This is risky, because once the cat is out of their bag, all the rules change. They deal with Alvin, who tells them what he wants them to know -- not what he knows -- because he knows they are in no position to make a deal. The FBI is now stuck, Alvin knows they are onto him, so Alvin can change his M.O. to work around the FBI and point the finger at the other guys who don't know what he knows. Old Alvin turns out to be one sharp cookie, at least until his skull got crushed.

My rule of thumb on deal-making is: you make a deal only when you have to make a deal, unless you're a TV game show host.

Anyway, Romo's non-information assures me that Alvin was certainly not losing money hand-over-fist due to lousy gambler's luck and addiction as Heffelfinger claimed. He has also told me a clock was ticking, that there were more people involved than merely Alvin, and that we're not talking a few quarters being pilfered out of weekly milk money. Any case big enough for the FBI to put a hotshot like Romo Simpson on it is a big case.

———

It is a nice day, not too hot, not too humid, so I walk over to the Mercantile Exchange located on Riverside Drive alongside the Chicago River.

There are a number of traders loitering on the outside of the building's common area, satisfying their nicotine cravings. Smokers are the lepers of the twenty-first century.

"Market up or down today, guys?" I ask one group of three.

"What difference would it make to us?" responds the tallest guy who sucks the hardest on his Marlboro.

"Any of you ever heard of Alvin Augustus?"

"Everybody's heard of Alvin."

"Before or after he died?"

"Both."

"Who do you think did him in?"

"Paper said it was accidental," the guy in the middle says.

The tall guy lights up a second cigarette. "It coulda been that wacky kid of his."

"The trader?"

The shortest one of the three speaks, "Not much of a trader."

"Doesn't have the genes?"

"Doesn't have the balls," the third guy who wears a hideous pink smock says, laughing. "Who the hell are you?"

"Insurance guy," I say, "I hear that Alvin figured out a way to beat the system."

"Everybody got a way to beat the system," the first guy says.

"By cheating?"

The three boys, as if coached by a director off stage, grind out their smokes with their shoes and bid me farewell. "We got to get back on the floor."

"Would anybody be interested in a universal life policy?"

Not one of the three responds to my query, so I call out, "Or have any friends who need lifetime protection with a cash value for their golden years?"

The three traders disappear into the building.

There is a concrete ledge to my right, so I take a seat. On the ground is a mound of cigarette butts. This is disgusting. If it were up to me, smoking would be outlawed along with a lot of other stuff including snuff, chewing gum, and Bluetooth phones worn on your ear.

I run over everything in my head, starting with the way Alvin died, all the way up to hotshot Romo Simpson. I get a headache. I should take two aspirin and lie down, but opt for a cold beer at the Sign of the Trader.

The lunch crowd is gone. It is that two-hour window between cheeseburgers and the close of the market. The bartender pretends not to recognize me from before. "What'll ya have?"

"I have a headache; what would you suggest?"

"Gin martini."

"Make it a light beer."

He draws a beer from the tap with way too much head and slides it in front of me. "Four bucks."

I give him a five and he keeps the change. If I have the time, I will report him to the bartender's union, if one exists.

My cell phone rings. I hate that song.

"Hello."

"It's Tiffany," the voice says. "I have a surprise for you."

"Please, do tell."

"Where are you?"

"The Sign of the Trader."

"That dump?"

"Yes."

"Stay there." The phone disconnects.

I sit. I sip.

I'm lost. I feel dumb. I'm a middle-aged guy who has nothing better to do than be in a bar in the middle of an afternoon, drinking an overpriced draft beer. All the information I've gathered since the death covers me like the stones covering Alvin. It is all a big jumbled mess weighing heavily on my head. What few connections there are have disconnected. There is no straight through-line anywhere in the case. What nags at me the most is the fact that I still have not met one person who cared, in the least, for poor, pitiful Alvin.

Lo and behold, Tiffany walks into the Sign of the Trader with Clayton Augustus.

"There you are," Tiffany says coming right at me. "Mister Sherlock, you look like a real loser sitting there. My God, the least you could do is wait for happy hour."

Tiffany turns to Clayton. "You remember, Clayton?"

Young Augustus wears a thousand-dollar suit, two-hundred-dollar tie, and a pair of dark glasses. His body language tells me he's not happy about being here.

"You two become an item?" I ask.

Tiffany gives me her evil eye.

Clayton does not offer a hand to shake. "We have to talk; there's a booth in the back."

Clayton leads the way. Tiffany and I follow side by side.

"He called me about an hour ago."

"Lucky you."

We slide into the booth, Tiffany in the middle. Clayton is about to speak, but the idiot bartender saunters over, wiping off his hands on the bar towel wrapped around his waist.

"What'll ya have?"

Clayton pulls out a ten-spot, hands it to the man, and says, "We want to be left alone."

"Coming right up," the barkeep says and walks away.

This guy makes a lot of money for not doing much.

"I know who killed my father."

"You do?"

"Christina's bitch."

"Who?" I ask.

"Lizzy the Lesbian."

"Really?"

"I thought Christina was her bitch?" Tiffany is confused.

I pull up the picture in my head of Christina weeping on the shoulder of her partner during Alvin's funeral service. "Why her?"

"She's the only one who could have done it."

I repeat half of my last phrase, "Why?"

"She works for an architect. She'd be the only one who'd know how to rig the rocks, so when Dad walked by, they'd let loose and bury him."

"Did you see her at the house, in the backyard, playing around with the rock garden?"

"No, but that doesn't mean she didn't."

His theory is far from fetching at this point.

"Lizzy hated the old man."

I interrupt. "No offense, but I haven't found too many people so far that held your father in high regard."

"Not like her. She was trying to get Christina to sue him for insufficient support, or a spot in the company."

Tiffany asks, "Was Lizzy the one who wore the work boots in that family?"

"The chick is a bull dyke with horns. She leads half-sister around by the short hairs."

"There's an image I could have done without." Tiffany throws both hands over her eyes.

"The woman hates men and my father was at the top of her list. Her and the old man used to get into it. She was like Christina's muscle. I wouldn't put anything past the bitch." Clayton sits back; he's said what he came to say.

"Never underestimate the power of a lesbian, Mister Sherlock."

"Thank you, Tiffany, quite well put."

"You're welcome."

I wish a beer was in front of me, so I would have something to do with my hands. "Well, Clayton," I say, "that is certainly an interesting theory you have, one I will take the time to investigate thoroughly."

"Good."

"And I applaud the change of heart you have had in helping with the investigation, but I have to tell you that what you've said presents itself more as an opinion than a theory based on actual evidence."

"You got nothing better to go on right now, do you?"

"No."

"Then I'd say it's about time you got into that bitch, opened her up and see what makes her stink."

Tiffany's eyes go to the ceiling.

"Just so you know, Lizzy and Christina were together both the Friday night and the Saturday morning of the event." I tell Clayton.

"She could have rigged the rocks to tumble when he walked by. Don't put that past her."

I face Clayton. "Did your father ever give Christina money to start a business?"

The question comes at Clayton from left field, the exact place I want it to come from.

"Not that I know of."

"Are you sure?"

"What the hell does that have to do with Lizzy the Lezzy?"

"I don't know. I just wondered if Alvin did for Christina what he did for you?"

"What the hell are you talking about?" Clayton stammers.

"Was your father an investor or a actual stockholder in your firm?"

"It's a private corporation."

"That doesn't answer the question."

Clayton adjusts his tie. He's stalling, so I push the envelope.

"Voting shares or common shares?"

"My father and I had an agreement," he says. "There was an initial investment on his part, but that was the extent of it."

"You ever pay him back?"

He hesitates. "I tried."

Clayton is not thrilled with the direction the conversation has taken.

I press on. "I have this feeling that not only did dear old dad bankroll the start-up of your company, at times he acted as its personal banker."

Clayton attempts to get the bartender's attention, but the man is busy earning his ten bucks.

"And Alvin was hardly the type of guy who would hand over that much cash, not without at least a little say-so about what's going on."

Clayton remains silent.

"Was he exerting a little too much authority for your taste?" I ask, not expecting an answer. "He was leading you through a steaming pile a crap, wasn't he?"

Clayton gives up the fight. "How did you know?"

"You took the bait." I give him a sympathetic smile.

"Son-of-a-bitch."

"Tell me about it."

Clayton picks at his polished nails then begins, "Initially, I needed start-up cash and I needed him behind me to make me respectable. It was the ultimate raft of shit, I had to endure."

"Some shadows never lift."

"He would squeeze me under his thumb, the same way he squeezed the buffalo on every nickel he ever made."

"How many people were aware of this arrangement?"

"Two, me and him."

"That, I surely doubt."

Tiffany has sat watching the verbal repartee as if at center court at Wimbledon. Her neck will be sore later tonight.

"Hey," Clayton says, "compared to Brewster I barely got a dime. He must have spent millions bailing out his trades."

I decide to try a more nurturing tact. "There's nothing the matter with accepting the help of your father."

"There is if there are strings attached."

"When it comes to money, there are always strings attached," I pronounce.

"I never knew what he had on me until he started yanking my chain."

"How?"

"He took access to my funds," Clayton is embarrassed to say. "An investor with a checkbook is not a good investor."

"Did he make a withdrawal?"

"A number of them."

"Without asking?"

"Or telling."

"A little difficult to run a business that way, isn't it?"

"Quite."

"I know how it feels," Tiffany says. "My sister used to get into my piggy bank without asking."

"When was that?" I ask.

"Before credit cards," she says. "I think I was about nine."

"How far down did he take you?" I ask.

Clayton looks flushed. The truth can be exhausting.

"Congratulations," I tell him.

"What did I do?"

"Catapulted yourself into the number one position for the person most likely to have killed their father."

"Bullshit."

"You have motive, access, a lousy alibi, and a business the old man was taking into the toilet."

"I wouldn't kill my dad."

"Even if he was bleeding you dry, ruining your business, and making life unbearable, as only he could do?"

"You are out of your mind." He becomes angry, animated and quite sweaty. "It was that muff-diving, bitch of my half-sister."

"If you say so."

"I didn't kill him."

"Everything you've told us so far has been, if not exactly a lie, pretty close to being untrue. That doesn't put you in our highest regard."

"I hated him, but I didn't kill him."

"How could you hate your father?" Tiffany asks. "He was your dad."

Clayton gets up from the table. "I came here to help and this is what I get."

We watch as Clayton hurries out of the Sign.

"Weren't you supposed to tell him not to leave town?" Tiffany asks.

"Only cops can tell suspects that; and I'm no longer a cop."

"Do you think he did it?"

"He could have."

"Really, you mean I was sitting next to an actual murderer?"

She giggles. "How exciting."

"The only thing that bothers me is that I'm not sure he's bright enough."

19
A Clarence in a Bird house

Since my girls were old enough to spit up, I have stressed that there is no such thing as an unloaded gun. I pray to God, they have listened.

I hate guns. Coming from a cop that may be hard to believe, but I do hate guns. There are more than 270 million guns in America, almost one for every man, woman, and child. Worse yet, the majority of guns are handguns. Absolutely absurd, this is more guns than were used in World War II.

What is the purpose of a handgun? You don't hunt, shoot skeet, or compete with one. No, their purpose, and only purpose, is to shoot people. All the millions of handguns in our country are for the distinct purpose of shooting another person.

As a cop, I hated toting one around. Not only can they hurt others, they can hurt you. Hence the term, "shooting oneself in the foot." Guns are heavy, uncomfortable, need holsters, and are horribly unfashionable. They do not fit on a belt, under a suit coat; nor can they be hidden anywhere on a normal person's body. Herman might get away with stashing one in a fat fold, but not me.

If it were up to me, all handguns would be illegal. I'm not advocating the end of your right to bear arms. You want a gun, get a rifle, but no handguns or automatic weapons. Those are more ridiculous than handguns, if that's possible. The USA would be a much nicer place without these elements of destruction.

I've kept my service revolver. In my line of work it is a necessary evil; but it seldom sees the light of day from the locked, upper kitchen cabinet where it is kept.

I strap on my gun. Where I am off to tonight, I might need it.

The sun is down; a full moon is up. It is a perfect night for trolling the mean streets. I take the Dan Ryan south and get off on 35th, close to Sox Park. It's quiet. The team must be on a road trip. I travel east, past the projects. The usual idiots are hanging out, smokin', chuckin' and jivin' on street corners, dealing weed and crack. They all eye me going by; but how much money could a guy driving an old Toyota be worth?

I turn onto a residential street where all the tree trunks in the parkway are painted white. This denotes a block club, where the neighbors take turns watching the street for gangbangers up to no good, a very effective brand of protection.

Two more blocks up is a line of small factories, each protected by circular lengths of razor wire and high iron gates locked up tight for the night. The factory owners have added bright florescent lights to ward off evildoers, which not only complement the city streetlights, but provide an illuminating glow to the streetwalkers working the block.

I pull up to the first ho dressed, or almost dressed, in a pair of diamond-sparkled hot pants. I wonder where she shops. "Babala, how you doing, girl?"

Babala started out ten years ago as a fifty-dollar whore and remains the same today. What she needs is an understanding of inflation, besides better teeth, deodorant, and to maybe lose forty pounds.

She flips the hair from her bad wig aside as she leans onto the passenger side window. "Sherlock, man, where the hell you been?"

"They threw me off the force."

"Oh, man, if that ain't shit, I don't know what is."

"Bennie come around yet?"

"He been here twice, already; bizness bad when the Sox outta town."

"Tell him I'm hanging at the screw."

"No problem, Missa S."

I wave goodbye and drive up the street to the Snyder Screw Corporation, seemingly a perfect name for a business on this block. I park in the driveway and wait.

Bennie Jackson has been a street hustler and pimp going on twenty years. Get past his choices of profession and he's actually a pretty nice guy. He can talk Chicago White Sox fluently, is buddies with every alderman in a three-district area, and has a working knowledge of the mean streets like no other. Bennie is smarter than your average pimp. He knows where the lines are drawn, when to cross and when to stay put. He keeps his business away from the homes in the hood out of respect, and has an innate sense to keep on everyone's good side -- good guys as well as bad. More criminals out there should be like Bennie.

It must be going on ten years now that a rookie cop arrested Bennie on a pandering charge, brought him in and locked him up. Bennie's one phone call was to me. I had him back on the street in a matter of hours, complete with an apology from the cop.

A brand-new black Chrysler pulls up behind my Toyota. I get out of my car and head back to his. As a guest in their neighborhood, you always visit in their living room.

"Bennie, how you doing?"

"Sherlock, I miss ya."

"Business good?"

"Problem with this business, Sherlock, you just can't get away. I haven't been on vacation since you been off the force."

"Hey, you got to do it."

"Tell me about it."

"How's it hangin' wit you?"

"Could be better, Bennie. Could be better."

"I can hear ya."

I settle into the plush leather seat. I wish my Toyota had seats this comfortable.

"What do ya need?" Bennie's never been a man to beat around the bush.

"I got to find a shooter named Clarence."

"Clarence?"

"Yeah."

"Who told you 'bout him?"

"Magpie Morris."

"Ah, man," Bennie shakes his head. "Magpie is dumber than dog shit."

"Told you things were bad. See who I got to deal with?"

"You lookin' to shoot this shooter?"

"No."

"Arrest him?"

"No."

"You want him to join your weekly poker game?"

"Something like that."

Bennie thinks it over for a few seconds. "I don't know him, but I know someone who would."

"I only want to chat."

"These dudes ain't the kind that give out interviews."

"I'm kinda stuck, Bennie; I need this one."

Bennie pulls on the extra flesh on his jowls. There is plenty to yank. "You go, drive to Leon's and wait in the parking lot." Bennie puts my cell phone number in his phone, then puts out a hand as big as a tennis racket to shake. "Next time you got to hit somebody, you call Bennie, okay."

He is referring to the end of my police career. "I will."

Good friends are hard to find.

———

Leon's is a takeout rib joint on the South Side. Ribs so good, white folks come and stand in line on summer nights. Success brought Leon money, a standing in the community, and more guys trying to rob him than all of Robin Hood's Merry Men. It got so bad that criminals would buy a giant bucket of rib tips, sit in their cars and, while eating, count the customers going in and out. After reaching a total equal to their fingers and toes, the slimeballs throw on a ski mask, pull out a Glock, and rob the place; then back to the car for Leon's peach cobbler dessert.

Poor Leon tried everything: security guards, home delivery, paying off cops, mafia thugs; but nothing worked until he devised a bulletproof glass, lazy-susan window. Necessity was the mother of that invention. A customer orders, puts his money on a spinning circular tray, which sticks out from under a thick piece of plate glass. The clerk inside unlocks the glass, swings the wheel a one-eighty, makes change and adds a receipt with a pickup number, and swings it back to the customer. Ten to fifteen minutes later, the clerk calls out the number and the food slides down a pickup window shoot. The delivery system worked like a charm. Leon's crime rate plummeted. Only problem remaining was the number of bullets stuck in the thick glass from thieves who couldn't believe a system could be that foolproof.

My cell rang three minutes after I arrived. I was glad no one but me was around to hear "Breakaway" coming out of the tiny cell speaker. "Hello."

It was Bennie. "Is there a big-ass, black Mercedes parked near you?"

"There's two of them."

"Go between 'em. Whatever door opens up, get in that one."

"Thanks Bennie."

"Come by more often; I miss ya."

I flip the safety off my gun and place it loosely in my shoulder holster. I make a very slow trek across two lines of parked cars (Leon was having a big night) and stop behind the bumpers of the two Mercedes, whose windows were almost opaque from their custom tint. The rear door on the car on my right opens. I take two more steps forward and climb in.

Two guys are seated in the back, chewing on ribs. One small, one huge, both with Bozo-the-Clown smiles from the amount of sauce on their faces.

"You didn't get no ribs?" the smaller guy says, tossing a perfectly clean rib bone into a cardboard bucket on the floor. It was obvious he's the one who does the talking.

"I have to watch my cholesterol."

"Hell, that's no fun."

"Tell me about it."

"Bennie says you looking for Clarence."

"Yeah."

"His name ain't Clarence."

"Lucky for him."

"You realize there are guys cheaper."

"I'm into referrals."

"Whose?"

"I'm embarrassed to say," but I have no choice. "Magpie Morris."

"That fool?"

"He's on his way to the joint." The big guy can actually speak.

"I didn't say it was a good referral."

"You used to be a cop, right?" the man asks bluntly.

"Used to be."

"Got retired, I hear?"

"You could put it that way."

He's checked me out, which is good.

"You the guy that cold-cocked that D.A.?"

He is referring to a slight bit of temper on my part. Hearing that my district attorney made a deal with Jerry "The Tooth," Lombardo to turn state's evidence on some bullshit theft, after I had spent nine months building a case against Jerry and most of his immediate family, I got a bit perturbed. One crummy punch got me kicked off the force sixteen days before my twenty-year anniversary, a major financial plateau for lifelong benefits. Ouch, the punch hurt me a lot more than it hurt the D.A.

"What are you doing now?" the little man asks.

"Make a living checking out insurance claims."

"Bet that's a shit job."

I like this guy and I can tell he likes me.

"This kinda info don't come cheap."

"I know."

Little man takes another rib, bites off the meat on one side. "You want his cell or his email?"

"Cell, I'm not very good on the computer."

"You don't got a I-Phone?"

"Sorry."

"Man, you got to get with the times."

"Yeah, yeah."

I hand over my phone and he punches in the number, leaving sauce on the key pad. "Here."

"What can I do for you?" I ask.

"Nothing right now, but you know, there's always something around the next corner." The man gives me a wink as I exit.

"We could use another bucket of tips." The big guy speaks for the second time.

I pull out a twenty and leave it next to the bone bucket. "Bon appétit."

——

It is amazing what someone with access can discover, using a database with all the cell phone numbers in the country. Clarence wasn't Clarence. The phone number was registered to a Preston Bird. He lived in East Chicago, Indiana, in a small bungalow in a neighborhood of steel mill laborers.

East Chicago is actually southeast of Chicago and why it wanted to call itself East Chicago, with the big Chicago being so close, was anyone's guess. Seemed stupid to me. It was, is, and always will be a soot-laden town that has not, and will not, see better days. One two-bedroom, one bath houses, one after another, with small backyards and one-car garages standing on block after block, each with a clear view of the U.S. Steel smokestacks pumping effluent into their air. The bad news about the smoke was it would be the death of all of them; the good news was when the stacks were all puffing away, everybody who wanted a job had a job.

The Bird house was in the middle of the block. It had burglar bars on all the windows, a plexiglas screen door, a four-foot chain-link fence and a walkway of cracked concrete. No makeover could make this house any better.

My first pass-by gave me no indication of anyone being home. No doors or windows open for ventilation, no lights on, or flicker from a TV set. My second pass, which was much slower than my first, told me the front windows were being blocked by thick curtains or blankets. The lawn of weeds was cropped, no mail hung out of the box, and the throwaway newspapers and advertising flyers were blown against the outside of the fence, not the inside. I wouldn't put the place in a "pride of ownership" category, but whoever lived there cared.

I drove through the alley and immediately wished I had counted which house the Bird house would be, because each garage was a spitting image of the garage next door. I drove back around to the front and parked on the opposite side of the street, one door up.

A kid, about ten, came up to the car, looking inside as if I were a penguin behind the glass at the zoo. "Hey, you a cop?"

"No."

"Sheriff?"

I rolled down the window. "A sheriff is a cop."

The kid didn't care. "Repo man?"

"No."

"Then what you doin'?"

"Why do I have to be doing something? Couldn't I just be here enjoying the neighborhood?"

"No."

"Why not?"

"You're white."

He had a point.

"I'm trying to find a guy named Bird."

"Yeah?"

"Yeah."

"He live right there."

I pull a five dollar bill out of my pocket. "Go up and tell him a guy named Clarence is here to talk to him."

The kid tries to grab the bill, but I hold it back. "You get paid on completion, not hiring." I tear the bill and give him half.

"I can't spend this."

"I'll give you the other half after you get Bird."

The kid runs off, enters the yard, up the six stairs, and rings the bell. As the door opens, I can't hear what is said, but a man about forty steps out onto the small porch, looks to where the kid points and nods his head.

I get out of the car, lock it, and make my way onto the property. I fork over the other half of the bill to the kid. "Nice doing business with ya."

The man hasn't moved from the spot on the porch. "You Clarence?" he asks.

"No," I say, "I think you are."

He holds the screen door open and I go inside.

Preston Bird wears a Bulls Three-peat tee-shirt which sports stains from all the major food groups. The neckband sags. There is a small hole on the shirt's bottom that reveals a soft belly, the result of too many beers during Bulls, Sox, and Bear games. The pair of jeans he wears covers his butt crack, for which I am thankful.

"You a cop?" he asks.

"No."

"You want a beer then?"

"No thanks."

The room is dominated by a four-foot-wide plasma TV, which is worth more than the accumulated value of the couch, chair, coffee table, side table, so-called art, lamps, and knickknacks. Two black boxers are on the screen, beating the crap out of each other.

"I've been referred to you," I say after he sits down.

"By who?"

"A little guy in a Mercedes who likes ribs."

"Leon's?"

"Yeah."

"Man, those are good ribs."

The bell rings, the round ends, but one fighter sucker punches the other, jumps on top of his opponent, and wails away.

"Boxin' getting more like professional wrestling every day." Preston Bird tells me.

"I hate that."

We watch as a brawl breaks out in the ring with cornermen, managers, and one fighter's mother throwing haymakers.

"No women, no kids," he says, "so if you here about a wife, I can't help you."

The guy at ringside dings the bell so fast it sounds like school recess, but does little to stop the melee. Preston punches the sound way down with the remote.

"How's business?"

"You think I'd be living here if business was good?" He lifts beer cans off the table until he finds one with liquid inside. "Competition is a bitch. You got all these kids out there that'll pull the trigger for a rock of crack."

I shake my head to add sympathy to his plight.

"Man, them drugs are destroying our society."

On the TV the brawlers have run out of gas and reduced to a bunch of tired old folks pushing and shoving each other. The scene switches to a commercial with a skinny lady asking, "Do you have too much body fat?"

"I want you to know," I say. "I could care less about you."

He finishes the beer, adds the empty to the others. "What the hell is that supposed to mean?"

"It means if it isn't you doing this job, it is going to be somebody else getting it done, so you make little difference to me."

"Who the hell are you?"

"My name is Richard Sherlock."

"Sherlock?"

Bird reaches over to a side table, opens the drawer, and pulls out a gun. "Hey man, you sure you're not a cop, 'cause if you are I got to shoot you, clean it up, wrap you up, cart you away, and bury your sorry ass. And right now I don't feel like doing all that. Sox game comes on in an hour."

"All you got to do is tell me one thing."

Bird shakes his head, points the gun at my head.

"Why did you miss Alvin Augustus? You had a clean shot at him. You could have made that hit in your sleep."

"Damn right."

"So why the hell you miss?"

"Deal was twenty-five hundred in advance and twenty-five on the way out. I show up and the envelope has a grand in and a note that says fifteen hundred after. Bullshit. Nobody cuts Clarence's price except Clarence."

"You want to tell me who it was?"

"No."

"Want to put your gun down?"

Preston lowers his gun, resting it in his lap. "You try to make a deal based on a handshake and this what you get."

"I hate that, too." I am trying to get on his good side, if he has one. "Sure would make my life easier if you told me who."

"Word get around I do that, I got no business."

"I see your point. I apologize for asking."

I drop two twenties on the table.

He points the gun back at me. "Sure you don't want a beer?"

———

Traffic was horrible coming back north into the city, an accident near the interchange. I get off on Congress, wind my way through the Loop and Near North until I'm back on Astor, two doors away from Alvin's condo. I wait four hours for someone to come in or out. Nothing. What an exciting life I lead.

———

At home, I put it all down on a three-by-five card and place it in the recipe box. The box is filling.

Someone paid Clarence to kill Alvin. There are plenty to choose from: wife Doris, ex-wife Joan, sons Clayton and Brewster, daughter Christina, daughter's partner Lizzy; and we can't forget Hefelfinger the accountant, little Millie, couple of hookers, plus all the guys in the pits who Alvin put into the poorhouse. Fun bunch.

In most cases the suspects narrow; this case they multiply.

At two-thirty-two in the morning, the phone rings. I wake petrified. "Hello."

"Guess who just got busted for drugs?"

"Barack Obama?"

"Brewster Augustus," Norbert says.

"Bet that made his day."

"It gets better," Norbert hesitates. "Rohypnol."

"Little Brewster?"

"Mom's bailing him out right now," Norbert says. "I figured you'd want to go down and see for yourself since you live so close."

"It's two-thirty, Norbert."

"It might be fun."

"Goodnight, Norbert."

"Goodnight, Sherlock."

20
The Carlo cover-up

"Do you miss Theresa?"
"Sí."
"She misses you, too."
"Sí."

Hector Elondiso had killed the bugs, replanted the backyard garden, weeded the lawn, and put in a very attractive sandstone walkway between the garage and the backdoor at Theresa's cousin's house.

I allowed Tiffany one last question before I stepped in.

"Who do you miss more, your wife or Theresa?"

Hector doesn't answer.

My turn.

"I love what you did to the Augustus garden."

"Gracias, señor."

Pleasantries over. "When was the last time you saw Mr. Augustus?"

He shrugs.

"Friday?"

"Yo no sé."

"Do you remember how he was dressed?"

"No."

Tiffany jumps in. "Was it a wrinkled suit?"

Hector shrugs again.

Tiffany crunches up a handful of my sport coat. "Wrinkled?"

Third shrug.

"Hector," I ask, "do you remember anything different about the rock garden that day?"

"No."

"You like the rocks?"

"Estupido."

"Did you see anyone else in the garden during the week?"

"No."

I'm sure glad we fought the morning traffic and took the time to drive out to this very nice Hispanic neighborhood on the west side. I get particular enjoyment in the colorful graffiti and gang tagging displayed on almost every garage door and wall, giving it a certain "criminal outdoor museum" vibe.

"Is there anything you want to tell us about Alvin?"

"No."

I sit down on the step to the small patio in the back of the postage-stamp-sized yard. Tiffany stands with Hector. Both watch me think.

"He isn't helping, is he?" Tiffany says.

"No."

"Too bad I can't speak gardener Spanish as well as I speak housekeeper Spanish."

"Tis a pity."

I look back to Hector. "Was Mrs. Augustus home Friday night?"

"No."

"You're sure?"

"Sí."

"Alvin ever take walks around the property?"

Hector doesn't understand the question, so Tiffany mimics a walk and uses her finger to draw imaginary circles.

"No."

"He ever move the rocks around himself?"

This is a much more difficult pantomime for Tiffany, but Hector finally gets it.

"Sí."

"Did he spend a lot of time in the garden?"

"Mas o menos."

"Hector," I say getting to my feet, "you are a man of few words."

"Sí."

"Come on, Tiffany."

"Un momento," Hector says.

"Sí?"

"Meester Alvin owe me mucho dinero."

"Get in line, Hector."

As Tiffany hands her keys to the valet at the Ritz, she warns me, "Unless you want another family, Mr. Sherlock, keep away from those Hispanics. They're breeders."

"Are Hispanic Gemini women the most fertile?"

"I wouldn't be a bit surprised."

We meet Brewster and Doris on the twelfth floor. They are seated at the bar.

"He didn't do it," Doris says pointing at my assistant, dispensing with the usual greetings.

"Didn't do what?"

"I didn't buy any dope," Brewster says. "It was planted on me."

"Planted?" My thought is of Hector adding a few pansies.

"Yeah."

Brewster has had one too many, and it is not even lunch time.

"And how do you suspect the perpetrator performed this bout of chicanery?"

My use of the English language throws him.

"What?"

"He was set up, Sherlock," Doris says. "They must have followed him in, slipped it in his pocket, then alerted the narc to bust him."

"Who?"

"We don't know," she says, "that's why we called you."

"A Bloody Mary," Tiffany tells the bartender. "And a lunch menu."

Her interruption does little to calm Brewster.

"I told those cops to dust the dope for prints and they'd see I never touched the stuff."

"Those things never happen," I tell him.

"You have to find these guys, bring them to justice, let 'em suffer the same indignities as I did last night." Brewster is wound up tighter than a new Slinky.

"Me?"

"You're a detective," Doris says, "aren't you?"

"You're hiring me?"

"Yes."

"Do you really think it's a good idea to put the guy who is investigating the both of you for murder on your personal payroll?"

"Dad says the best business always comes from referrals, Mister Sherlock."

"Thank you, Tiffany."

"I was set up." Brewster takes the Bloody Mary arriving for Tiffany and drinks half. "Whoever it is, they're trying to frame me."

"How?"

"By planting that drug on him," Doris explains, as if I were a third-grader.

"The Ryphonal?" My rhetorical question.

"Whatever it was."

Tiffany orders a round of drinks for the three. "Maybe someone wanted to have sex with you?" she asks.

"What?"

"That's what the drug is used for."

"Nobody wants to have sex with Brewster." Doris gives not the most ringing of endorsements.

"Now that I think of it," Tiffany says, "you have to put it in a drink, not a pocket."

I ask, "Where did it happen?"

"The River Shannon."

A neighborhood bar on Armitage; place has been there forever.

"What were you doing there?"

"Drinking."

"Were you drunk?"

"What do you think?" Doris says.

"I'm walking out of the place and all of a sudden I'm on the ground with two gorillas holding me down, putting the cuffs on me."

"You've had plenty of practice at that; haven't you, Brewster?" Tiffany asks.

The chances of Brewster and Tiffany becoming an item are diminishing rapidly.

"Just find the guy, Sherlock."

"Okay," I say, "but I'll need a retainer."

"I don't have any money," Brewster says.

"Not until daddy of "dearie" over there releases the insurance settlement," Doris says.

"No can do," Tiffany says.

"It is amazing that I can secure two jobs from one of the wealthiest families in Chicago and I can't get a dime in advance." I get up from my barstool. "I'll see what I can do."

Before leaving, I remember a question I wrote down on one of my recipe cards. "Hey Brewster, besides you, who else trades off your dad's seats?"

"What?"

"Your dad's seats at the Exchange, who uses those?"

"Couple guys. I forget what their names are," he says. "But who the hell cares? You got bigger fish to catch, Sherlock."

"Just looking for bait." I turn to my assistant who hasn't left her stool. "Are you staying for lunch, Tiffany?"

"Their walnut salad is divine, Mister Sherlock."

"I wouldn't know."

———

I have a large painting hanging in my living room. It has a bright yellow sky for a background, with a brown barn or farmhouse with a red roof in the foreground. There are weeds in the painting and a set of four mailboxes in the left-hand corner. Why one farmhouse or barn would need four mailboxes only adds to the intrigue of this masterful work of art. The work is an original, signed by the artist, CARLO. I bought the piece on the last day of a sidewalk art show, just before it closed. I paid eight dollars, which included the frame. I consider my *Original Carlo*, a work of art so bad, it's good.

———

It's Tuesday. I have picked up the girls from school. Kelly goes on and on about how her star would rise after being seated at the number-one table at school. Care talks of the upcoming horse show, in which she and her sister are entered. I listen to each, toss in one "I see," one "yeah," three "reallys?" and two "bet you can't waits." I am having a difficult time concentrating on anything besides my confusion in the case.

After a meatloaf, made with ground turkey instead of beef they didn't eat, the girls open up their backpacks. They complain that the TV stays on at their mother's house while they do their homework, but not at mine.

"If you have the TV on, it will distract you from your assignments," I use as my argument.

"But if we have to block out the TV to concentrate," Kelly argues, "it will make our brains stronger."

"I'm not buying it," is my final answer.

While the two girls slave away at social studies and math, I retrieve my recipe box and empty the cards on our combination kitchen-dining-room table. I page through the three-by-five cards, read each one, and lay them into neat rows. I finish with six rows across and eight down.

"What are you doing, Dad?" Care asks.

"Trying to make sense out of nonsense."

"Dad," Kelly asks, "are you losing it?"

"Yes, and it was because I watched TV while doing my homework as a kid."

"Did they have TV when you were a kid?" Care asks.

"Yes."

"Cable?"

"No."

"Direct TV?"

"Finish your homework."

I find a box of pushpins in my desk drawer and place them on the arm of the couch. I pick a card, labeled "ALVIN BITES ROCK," and tack it up into the top left-hand corner of the *Original Carlo*. Below that card, I push in the card with numerous scribblings about the rock garden, path, and blood stains. Beneath it, I push in a card saying, "BIG ROCK, BIG HEAD, BIG HURT."

I hear the sounds of two schoolbooks slamming shut.

"I want to help," Kelly says.

"Me, too," Care quickly adds.

"I asked first."

I hand Kelly a card. "Put this on the top in the second row." I hand Care a card. "Move the second card in the first row and insert this one."

It takes forty minutes of mixing, matching, switching, ordering and reordering to cover the *Original Carlo* with index cards.

"Dad," Kelly asks, holding a card, "shouldn't we put the gunshot in the den before the actual murder?"

"And the stuff in the office with that Heffelfingered guy," Care points, "should go over here."

I lean against the back of the couch, dead center, in front of the index-card-filled painting. "Right now, they're in the order of discovery."

"I think we should rearrange..."

"We?" I interrupt Kelly.

"The cards, in the timeline of the crime," Care finishes for her sister.

"Thank you, Dora the Explorer."

"Dad, I am like so over that show," Care says.

Kelly comes over and leans on me. "I think Brewster did it," she says.

"You do, why?"

"Come on, Dad," she says. "They named him Brewster. That would make anyone want to kill their parents."

"I think it was the lesbian," Care says.

"Do you know what a lesbian is?" I ask.

"Ah, duh."

"She probably is one."

"Shut up, Kelly."

"Enough." I see the clock, and it is past their bedtime. "It's time for bed. Get in there and brush your teeth."

"Maybe if I tell the number-one lunch table that I'm helping to solve a big murder case, they'd want me to sit with them." Kelly says.

"No, don't, and don't tell your mother, either."

"Why not?"

"Because kids aren't supposed to be subjected to people getting their heads smashed in with rocks. It's not considered good parenting."

"If mom asks," Care says, "do you want us to lie?"

"No."

"Then what should we say if the topic comes up?"

"And why would the topic ever come up?"

"Ah, you know," Kelly says, "if Care says 'Gee Mom, did you hear about anyone getting murdered lately?'"

"Go to bed."

I hurry my daughters into the bathroom, wait for them to change into their PJs, and go in to kiss them goodnight.

Care says after her smooch, "Dad, what if I figure out who did it?"

"You can leave a message on my cell."

I kiss Kelly.

"I'm still leaning toward Brewster. He did it to prove he wasn't a wimpy son."

"Goodnight."

The kids were almost asleep as I shut the door to the room. All that thinking can be exhausting.

I go to our small closet, grab what's available and return to the couch. I spread a sheet, blanket, and sit staring at the tacked-up cards for what seems to be an eternity. I play, replay, figure and reconfigure every possible scenario until my eyes close, sometime past two in the morning. I was hoping that if I thought hard enough, my brain would work on its electrical impulses while I slept and I would awaken with the whole thing figured out.

It didn't happen.

———

The next two days I flounder around chasing bad ideas, misplaced thoughts, poorly suspected plans, and uncovered leads. I come up with more questions and no answers. Tiffany tags along both days until she gets bored and makes up a lousy excuse to go to the spa, gym, nail salon, special sale on Oak Street, or wherever. I can't blame her for taking a powder. I'm in a lousy mood. I'm as frustrated as a diabetic with a sweet tooth.

I did receive a few phone calls.

Christina called to ask if I had any luck finding out who

pilfered her account. Since I hadn't thought about her problem since I left her apartment, I told her, "My investigation is in process."

"I'm broke, Mister Sherlock."

"I know the feeling," I try to console her. "What I'd like to do is bring in a specialist in these matters to consult."

"Who?"

"His name is Herman McFadden."

If nothing else, Herman might know someone in the lesbian porn business, especially if he thinks Christina's photogenic.

Both hookers, or escorts as they like to be referred to, called and asked about their money. I don't know why they're so itchy. They are the only ones bringing in any cash. I don't bother returning either of their calls.

Doris was the last to call and tell me that Brewster was going before an arraignment judge on Friday. "Do you have anything we can use?"

"Not yet."

"When?"

"I'm not sure."

"Did you get hold of the idiot cop who arrested him?"

"I put in a call," I lied. "He hasn't called me back."

"What should we do?"

"Get a good lawyer."

"We can't afford one."

"Find one that takes American Express."

"I tried."

"Word gets around fast, huh?"

"What should we do, Sherlock? I'm worried."

These are the first words from Doris that do not ring with sarcasm and evil.

"Plead 'not guilty,' claim innocence, and don't admit to any wrongdoing."

"And if they ask us to explain?" she asks.

"Lie."

"Lie?"

"Make up a whopper, the more absurd the better. The judge will have no choice but to delay the matter to a later date. A good lie can always buy you time."

She was silent for a moment, then said, "This is not the type of advice I believed we were paying for."

"You haven't paid me, yet."

———

Each evening I move the recipe cards around on the *Original Carlo* so many times that the painting now sports more holes than a pin cushion. I tried my daughter's advice and rearranged the cards into a timeline, but that didn't work. I arranged by suspect, but too much overlapped. Worse yet, I found myself asking more questions and adding more cards to the mix. By midnight the second night, so many cards are overlapped that you can barely tell the sky in the painting is bright yellow.

I am almost to the point of giving up when I remove one card, read the question I had written upon it, pick up the phone, and call Norbert.

"When Alvin was rock-uncovered, was there money in one of his pockets?"

"What?"

"His wife told me he always carried a wad of cash."

"Sherlock, it is one-thirty in the morning."

I look at my digital clock. "It's one-thirty-two actually."

"Couldn't this have waited until the morning?"

"Probably."

There is a pause.

"So, did you find any money in his pockets?"

"No," Norbert says. "No money and no watch, either."

"Did he wear a watch?"

"Rolex."

"Maybe it was a random killing, some murderer liked his wrinkled suit, crushed his skull, and took off with his money and watch?"

Norbert's not happy. "A mugging, in Kenilworth, in his own backyard, on a Saturday morning?"

"Well, it was just a thought," I admit to the detective. "I haven't been getting a lot of sleep lately."

"I was doing quite well in that capacity before you called."

I wait a few seconds. "You do the pawnshops, yet?"

"Yes, Sherlock."

"Find the watch?"

"No." Norbert is breathing deeper and deeper into the receiver.

"One more question."

"Sherlock, I want to go back to bed."

"Please, it's a two-part question."

He sighs. "Go ahead."

"Who was Franklin Pierce's vice president and how did he die?"

There is a long pause. "Goodnight, Sherlock."

"Goodnight, Norbert."

———

A number of corporations in Chicago allow their employees to leave at noon on Fridays during the late spring and summer months. I am told they do this because it fosters a positive attitude between labor and management; but in truth they do it because they know nobody does a lick of work on a sunny Friday afternoon.

Tiffany, after an exhausting lunch, is ready to go home for a revitalizing nap before venturing out to dinner and a night of frivolity. She is dropping me off at my apartment when "Breakaway" blasts out of my cell phone.

"Hello."

"Sherlock."

It's Norbert, and I can tell by the inflection that he is not in a joyous mood. "Why didn't you tell us about the place on Astor?"

"What place on Astor?"

"The one where the cleaning lady described you as an immigration agent."

"She did, huh?"

"I could have you arrested."

"For impersonating an INS Agent?"

"That would be the least of the charges," Norbert says.

Tiffany follows half of the conversation closely.

"Better get your ass over here, Sherlock. You got a lot of explaining to do."

"I'm on my way."

I flip the phone closed.

"What?" Tiffany asks.

"I got to go back downtown."

"Why?"

"They found the condo on Astor."

"Alvin's hideaway?"

I look at Tiffany. "You make it sound like someplace Jesse James would hole up."

"I'm going with you."

"I thought you had plans tonight."

"I have plans every night, Mister Sherlock. What do you think I am, some kind of a loser?" Tiffany puts the car in reverse and backs into the street.

"I got to get my kids," I tell her. "It's my weekend."

"I thought last week was your weekend?"

"We switched."

———

"Are we going shopping?" Kelly asks the moment she climbs inside Tiffany's Lexus.

"Not right away," I tell them.

We fight traffic back into the city, which is worse than the traffic going out-a new phenomena referred to as the reverse commute. Care talks about school, the horse, junk food and how dumb boys are.

"They don't change much," Tiffany tells her.

"Tiffany," Kelly asks, "when you were in junior high, did you sit at the number-one lunch table."

"No."

Kelly is shocked. "You didn't?"

"The number-one lunch table is only number one to the people not sitting at that table. I was way above that."

"Isn't that what I told you, Kelly?" I say.

She ignores me and says to Tiffany, "You weren't with the

popular kids?"

"I didn't sit with them," Tiffany says. "They sat with me."

Kelly is lost in thought the remainder of the trip.

We arrive at the condo on Astor. Tiffany double parks in line with a squad car, ambulance, Norbert and Steve's car, and a few other government-issued vehicles.

"This doesn't look like Nordstrom's," Kelly says.

"You people wait in the car."

There is a cacophony of "No way."

Inside, the condo is buzzing with activity. Fingerprint guys dust, photographer snaps, evidence techs place little numbered markers around and about.

"So good of you to join us, Sherlock," Norbert says as we enter the foyer. "And you brought the family along. How nice."

I give a slight wave and "hey" to the cleaning lady who stands beside Steve Burrell, pointing her finger my way.

Kelly and Care notice the quality of the surroundings. "This is really neat," Care says. "Why can't we live like this, Dad?"

"Ask your mother."

The doors and windows are wide open, allowing the lake breeze to sweep through the place; but there is a distinct odor present, one I am familiar with.

"How long have you known about the place, Sherlock?" Norbert asks.

"Few days."

"It was Alvin's hideaway," Tiffany informs the detective.

"Hideaway?"

"Told you that was a bad term," I say.

"How about erotic, secret lair?" Tiffany suggests.

"Works for me."

A young CPD detective named Jonas Jones joins Norbert, Steve, and I as we stand in the dining room. Jonas' first question is: "Are you the guy who cold-cocked the D.A?"

"My reputation remains intact, I see."

"Start talking, Sherlock," Steve says.

I go through my initial visit to the place, my introduction to the cleaning lady, tell them where to find the wall safes and floor safe in the closet. I tell them about the stakeout, Tiffany's nap and my disappointment of not discovering more.

"How did you find out about the place?"

"His hooker," Tiffany whispers out of earshot of my kids. "I try to help him meet a nice lady, but he won't listen."

"You should be ashamed, Sherlock."

"By the way, did you find out the identity of the mystery man? Out front is where I snapped his picture."

"I think Romo might know," Norbert says, "but he won't tell us until he has the chance to ruin any good evidence we would get out of it."

Out of the corner of my ear, I hear Kelly admonish Care about touching things and leaving fingerprints. "They'll think you did it and lock you up."

"You guys find something I didn't find?" I ask.

"Oh, yeah," Steve says.

"Let's get on with this," Jonas says and leads me into the bedroom of the condo. The odor is much stronger.

He goes straight for the chest, unlatches the hasp. "Ready?"

"Wait," I say and turn to my assistant. "Tiffany, take the girls into the other room." The tone of my voice convinces her not to argue.

"We'll replicate the exact moment of our discovery, so you can benefit from the exact same experience as us," Steve says. "Lean in...real close."

The lid is flipped open and a waft of death fills the air. Some poor schmuck has been folded in half and stuffed inside the trunk. His head comes up slowly as he graciously sits up, so we can meet and greet him in a proper manner.

I push my dirty handkerchief to my face to block the odor. He's young, chubby, has a dark complexion, a full head of black hair, and is clean-shaven. Dressed business casual, no spilled blood.

"You got any idea of who it is?" Jonas asks.

"Yeah."

"Who?"

"Joey Villano."

21

A couple rolls in reserve

"**P**ersonal friend of yours?"

"I've been waiting for him to pop up," I say. "He was Alvin's trader, one of the few people who could have known how Alvin was ripping off the securities markets."

I creep closer and look down into the chest to see if Joey sits on stacks of money. Nope. "He worked with Alvin in his office above the Board of Trade after he got off the floor."

"You ever meet him?"

"No, Heffelfinger told me about him."

"Kill the perpetrator, kill the witness," Steve says.

"Maybe, maybe not," I say.

"Excuse me, Mister Sherlock." Tiffany is at the doorway to the room, making sure my daughters are kept at bay. "Could we switch spots so I can come in and see, too?"

"Sure, I'd hate to have you miss this."

The three detectives follow me out of the room where I meet my daughters.

"Who farted, Dad?" Care asks.

"You don't want to know."

Jonas motions to the techs. The crime scene is now theirs for the taking. He is last in line to follow the rest of us through the kitchen and outside.

I take my girls by their hands.

"Another stiff, huh, Dad?" Kelly asks.

The three detectives, me, my girls, and finally Tiffany, who remarks, "Man that guy has certainly smelled better days," sit on the back patio deck around a glass table.

"You talk to Romo?" I ask.

"I called, assistant said he couldn't talk," Norbert says, "maybe his necktie was tied too tight."

"Who's Romo?" Jonas asks.

"FBI guy," Steve tells him.

"My God," Jonas says, "everybody is in on this one."

"We should meet next time at ChuckE. Cheese."

"Cool," Care says.

We sit back in our chairs, attempting to get comfortable.

"Theories?" One of us was going to ask, it might as well be me.

Steve starts. "I'm leaning toward the mob angle or some group that needs to cover its ass in a securities fraud."

Jonas asks, "No self-respecting mob guy would ever stuff a guy in a trunk."

Norbert takes his turn. "Although I don't see her physically doing it, wife Doris has the clearest motive."

"I'm still going with Brewster," Kelly says, surprising everyone at the table. "There's drugs in Alvin, Brewster getting busted for drugs and both murders were blows to the head. It follows a pattern."

"Chip off the old block there, Sherlock?" Norbert asks.

"She does have a point." I turn to my daughter. "Thank you, Nancy Drew."

Kelly beams.

"Who's Nancy Drew?" Care asks.

"I have a question."

"Yes, Tiffany?"

"Why here?" She leans forward for effect. "If they want to get rid of him, why didn't they whack and dump him in the lake? I would think they'd want us to keep looking for the guy."

"Too much trouble dumping a body in the lake," Norbert says. "Ya got to get a boat, weights, weather to deal with."

"Someone is making a point?" Jonas asks.

I know why; but I'm not saying.

"The big boys are letting it be known," Steve says, "if anyone talks, the same fate awaits."

"I'm not sure the murders are connected," I change the subject slightly.

"You have got to be kidding," Steve snaps at me.

"At least not in the traditional sense."

Care looks over to ask me, "What's traditional sense?"

The other detectives may not like me, but they want to hear what I have to say.

"Maybe, Joey in there is a result of the plan taking a u-turn?

Something could have happened, someone could have panicked, a clue got dropped that wasn't supposed to get dropped, or maybe someone is starting another case to throw us off the first one." I pause, take a breath. I have their attention. "The biggest problem I see is there are too many motives, too many suspects, too many reasons to kill old Alvin. I mean, have any of us run across any human that liked the guy? He was a cheating spouse, liar, gambler, manipulator, and thief. His business enemies number in the hundreds. Both sons he had by their business shorthairs, his daughter's kept on a budget, and his employees are standing in the unemployment line. He's fired his wife and has a couple of ex-wives who aren't too fond of him, either."

"What a guy," Tiffany says.

"Somebody wanted Alvin six feet under, and they were willing to shoot him, blow him up, poison, or trap him in an avalanche."

"We," Jonas says, "have a world of possibilities at our fingertips."

"I'm still leaning toward Brewster," Kelly says.

I get out of my chair. "Come on, girls, we should go; you need some food in you."

"I thought we were going shopping, Dad?"

"No, you never shop on an empty stomach. Right, Tiffany?"

"Or after seeing a corpse." Her agreement is not exactly the positive reinforcement I desired. "Come on," she says, "I'll take you to dinner."

Before leaving, I tell the girls, "Go to the bathroom before we go."

Tiffany, Care, and Kelly go to the little girls' room together. When they return, I say, "My turn."

I lock the bathroom door behind me, go straight to the sink and look underneath. I'm relieved. I next relieve myself the usual way, flush, wash my hands and return to the three detectives, carrying the two shopping bags with toilet paper sticking out of the tops.

"Can I ask a favor of you guys?"

"What, Sherlock?"

"I haven't had a chance to get to the store this week and I'm all out at home. Mind if I take this with me?"

Before they can say no, I add, "My girls go through toilet

paper like water."

"Sherlock, you have hit a new low," Steve says.

"Okay with you, Jonas?" Norbert asks the detective who is officially in charge of the crime scene.

"Sure, I got daughters of my own."

Norbert grabs a couple of rolls off the top as I pass by. "Always good to keep a couple in reserve," he says, as I lead my crew out of the condo.

———

If it were up to me, I'd do the drive-thru at Superdawg for hot dogs and curly fries; but Tiffany opts for a health food noodle place off Lincoln near Belmont. The kids eat their dinner only because Tiffany eats hers. They want to be cool.

"Where do we go from here, Mister Sherlock?"

"Home. The kids are tired."

"I mean in the case."

"I think we have to divide to conquer," I answer.

"What does that mean?" Care asks.

"Yeah," Tiffany says, "what does that mean?"

"Don't you see it as a bit strange that almost everyone in this case has a partner?"

"They do?"

"Brewster and Doris, Christina and Lizzy, Heffelfinger and Millie, even Clayton and his mother."

"And," Tiffany blurts out, "the two hookers."

Kelly perks up at Tiffany's addition to my list and Care follows suit. "Hookers."

"I didn't think we had to mention everyone."

"Oh, darn," Tiffany says, seeing my daughters have stopped eating.

"Tell me about the hookers," Kelly pleads.

"No."

"What's a hooker?" Care asks.

"I'll tell you later," I say, and glare at Tiffany.

"When?"

"In a few years."

"Don't worry, Care, I'll tell you when we get home," Kelly says to her sister. "Come on, Dad, this is getting good."

"Sorry about that, Mister Sherlock," Tiffany says in apologetic remorse.

"Eat your dinner, girls; we're going home."

"Gee, Dad, you're no fun."

"Yeah, but at least I'm consistent."

22
A crack in the case

Judge Anton Berle gavels one case to a close and begins another. "Next case."

The Clerk of the Court calls out: "Brewster Alvin Augustus."

As the accused, mom, and an attorney in a suit with stripes as wide as a railroad track walk to the bench, I start to stand; but Tiffany pulls me back down, "Are you going to get up there and lie, Mister Sherlock?"

"Tiffany, you're learning."

I walk to the front of the courtroom. I have already talked to the arresting officer and now only have to convince the judge.

"May I approach the bench, your honor?"

The judge smiles at my familiar face. "Haven't seen you in a while."

"I come, I go, and sometimes I come back."

Brewster and Doris are surprised to see me.

"I've missed you, Sherlock."

"And I too, judge, have missed the pleasure of your company. Would it be possible to see you in chambers?"

"Concerning this case or are you going to try to sell me magazine subscriptions?"

"I've fallen, but not that far."

The judge speaks to his bailiff, "Is the arresting officer present?"

"No, Judge Berle."

The judge leans closer so only I can hear, "You head him off at the pass?"

"I would never consider such a thing, judge."

Judge Berle rises and I and the prosecutor follow him through the back door. We are in his little office only a few minutes. Coming back in the courtroom I pass by Brewster and say, "Do what he tells you," and return to my seat next to Tiffany.

"Was it a real whopper?"

"Shush."

The judge speaks. "Due to the arresting officer's absence, the court will permit personal recognizance and continue this case for one month. During that time if the accused is willing to wear a monitor and attend a series of AA meetings, bail will be dropped." Judge Berle pauses, stares at Brewster. "Yes?"

Brewster looks at the judge, then to me.

I nod my head.

"Yes, your honor," Brewster speaks softly.

"So ordered." The gavel comes down. "Call the next case."

I wave goodbye to the judge before leaving.

Mom and attorney meet me and Tiffany outside in the hallway. Brewster is off being fitted for his bracelet.

"Great job in there, counselor," I congratulate the attorney and add, "and I love the suit."

Doris slips the man a hundred dollar bill and he makes his way back to taxicab court. "Why didn't you tell us?"

"I had to buy off the arresting officer first," I lie.

"How much?"

"It will be on your bill."

"What happens now?" Doris asks.

"Brewster will be wearing an attractive ankle bracelet. Don't let him leave town and have him start attending AA meetings. If he's a good boy, in a month the charges will be dropped."

Doris is at a loss for words.

"You should say 'thank you' to Mister Sherlock," Tiffany tells her.

"I don't thank my employees," Doris says to my assistant, "I pay them."

"That's music to my ears."

"In due time," Doris adds. "I had to borrow that hundred to pay off that awful attorney."

I give the woman a slight smile. "Funny, I would have thought you'd use some of the cash you pulled out of the joint account a week before Alvin's death. There certainly was plenty to pull from."

Doris stops breathing for a nanosecond. I have caught her at an opportune moment for me, but not for her.

"How would you know?" she asks abruptly.

"I have ways."

As usual her face shows little emotion. Her chin takes a rest on her chest.

"That kind of money could have taken you a lot further than Palm Springs."

She looks up.

"Sure you were in Palm Springs, Doris? Because we searched far and wide and can't find a hotel with your name on the guest list."

Her facial expression does not change, probably because it can't, but beads of sweat form on her forehead.

"I stayed in a private home."

"Name?"

"They were friends of a friend who is a broker."

"Nice to have friends, too bad your husband didn't."

"If you don't believe me, call the airline and they will confirm I was on the flight back," Doris says.

"I'll add it to the list of my homework assignments."

Brewster approaches, walking a bit funny. Doris clutches her Coach purse and bids a "good day, Mister Sherlock." She pulls Brewster along towards the elevators.

Tiffany and I are left by our lonesome. "How'd you know she wasn't in Palm Springs?"

"I didn't, but I do now."

"How?"

"I planted a seed, added water, fertilized, and watched it grow. Then I shook the tree."

"What came out?"

"Fear."

Tiffany admits, "I didn't see any."

"Her story is starting to crack, but she doesn't know how big of a fissure."

"What's a fissure?" Tiffany says, sounding like my daughter Care.

"The size of the crack."

Tiffany walks beside me as we make our way out of the court's lobby. "How big is her crack?"

"It's not how big it is; it's how we can make it bigger."

———

The same afternoon, the Lexus parks in front of hit man Clarence's house. We sit.

"I trust you are enjoying the ambience of the neighborhood?"

"If I lived here, Mister Sherlock, I'd move."

As we wait, I take the file of photographs Tiffany has printed from her computer and mix in pictures of Martin Luther King and two Queens: Mother from England and Latifah from Hollywood.

"Got two tens?"

Tiffany reaches into her purse, pulls out her wallet and extracts two bills from the many and hands them to me. "What's this for?"

"A snitch."

Finally, the brat kid comes by and taps on my window. "You back?"

I roll down my window. "Want to make another ten bucks?"

"No," he says, "I want to make twenty."

"Get in."

Tiffany hits the button, the door locks pop up and the kid takes a seat in the back.

"This is our snitch?" Tiffany asks.

"For this kind of money, what would you expect?"

The kid sits back, luxuriating into the soft leather. "Dis is a cool ride."

"Maybe if you work hard, you can afford one too some day," I do my best to counsel the boy.

"How much crack you sell to get one of these?"

"I wasn't referring to selling illegal substances."

"She your ho?" he asks of my driver.

"No."

"Then how else you get a ride like this?"

"Her father gave it to her," I say, tiring quickly of the conversation.

"Wish I had one a them."

"Father or a car?" Tiffany asks.

"Car."

"You're not old enough to drive," Tiffany says.

He shrugs as if to say that fact isn't much of a problem.

I take the folder of photos, hand the kid ten bucks. "You tell me if you've seen any of these people hanging around here."

The pictures Tiffany snapped at the funeral with her camera phone weren't very clear, but that didn't seem to bother the boy. I watch him closely. He pauses for a second look at Queen Latifah. "This one looks familiar."

"Great," I roll my eyes. "Keep going."

He also pauses at Joan's picture, one of the traders who attended and one homeless guy who slept in the back pew.

"Anybody?"

He shakes his head.

"Take a look at this one again." I page back to the picture of Martin Luther King. "You ever see this guy before?"

"Don't ring no bell."

"How about her?" Tiffany says, showing him Doris one more time.

"Not sure."

"So far, he's a pretty lousy snitch," Tiffany says.

"Who you talkin' 'bout, bitch?"

I place the pictures of Doris and Joan side by side. "Mister Bird ever get white women visiting him?"

He picks up both photos, gives them one last look. "Maybe. Can I have da other ten bucks now?"

"No."

"Why not?"

"Who said you were getting another ten bucks?"

"I ain't leavin' till I get another ten bucks," he says, sitting deeper into the seat.

"Tell me more."

"I didn't say there was no white woman, especially no old white woman bitch hangin' 'round here."

"Start the car, Tiffany," I say, roll down my window and hang the bill outside. "Come and get it."

The kid comes out of the backseat, up the side of the car, and snatches the bill out of my hand.

"Go."

I can faintly hear the boy yell, "Come back if you need some weed," as we drive off.

In a few seconds Tiffany asks, "Was that worth twenty bucks?"

"It was to me."

"Why?"

"Because it was your money."

———

Tiffany wastes no time getting out of this part of Dodge. She breaks every speed limit to the Dan Ryan Expressway. "Why don't you tell me what you're doing with the suspects, then maybe I could be more help."

"I would, but I don't know myself."

"Then how am I supposed to learn from somebody who doesn't know what he's doing?"

"Thank God, Tiffany, that is your problem and not mine."

The skyline of the city reflects the afternoon sunlight. Chicago is beautiful in a phoenix-rising-out-of-the-ashes kind of way.

"Where are we going next?"

"I'm not sure," I say, "but head North."

We get caught in lunchtime traffic just before the interchange. I get out my cell and dial.

"Hello, Nick... Richard Sherlock... I'm calling from my cell... Does Alexis have any time open this afternoon?"

Nick calls back in five minutes.

"I knew you'd be back," he says, consulting her schedule, "For you, she's available."

"Good, I'll be there at four." I flip my phone closed.

"Now what are you doing?" Tiffany says.

"Return trip to the escort."

"Again?" Tiffany asks. "You turning into some kind of sex maniac, Mister Sherlock?"

We continue north.

———

It is no secret that architects don't make a lot of money. They are considered more artists than businessmen. Architects probably have mixed feelings about this. So, it only stands to reason that an architect's assistant wouldn't be pulling in the big bucks, either.

The building we arrive at, just past 2 pm, is no designated landmark. The offices of Frued and Associates are not going to win any design awards. Our person of interest sits at the front desk in the one office, office. There must not be a lot of associates associated with Frued.

"Are you Lizzy?" I ask the somewhat attractive, under thirty, thin, but slightly weathered brunette.

"Only to my friends," she says as if she knows who I am.

"Richard Sherlock," I put out my hand to shake.

She pushes back in her chair. "Christina told me about you."

"Anything good?"

"You're supposed to be helping her get her money back; but instead you send over this disgusting beast of a man."

Herman must have made a house call.

"Who are you?"

Tiffany matches Lizzy's level of politeness. "His assistant."

"Do you mind if we ask you a few questions?"

"You already have," Lizzy says.

I sit in the chair. Tiffany prefers to stand.

"You didn't get along too well with Christina's daddy, I understand?"

"No."

"Why not?"

"He was a tight-assed, cheap son-of-a-bitch that Christina could have done a hell of a lot better without."

"Please," I say in all modesty, "don't hold back."

"Alvin didn't do shit for her. He sinks tons of money into those idiot half-brothers; but she has to fight for every dime she gets. She should be part of the corporation, drive a company car, get expenses, health insurance and a salary, as well as that miniscule trust fund she had to wait five years to collect on."

"Do you also act as her de facto business manager?"

"I try."

"That's big of you," Tiffany says.

"How about the mother?" I ask.

"Never met her, either."

"Never met Doris?"

"Oh yeah, her," Lizzy says, "is she a piece of work or what?"

I sit back in the chair, in an attempt to allow the venom in the room to dissipate a bit. "Who do you think killed him?"

"I don't care."

"That wasn't the question," Tiffany corrects.

"Does it matter?" Lizzy asks.

"Yeah," Tiffany says.

"All I know is it wasn't Christina. We were together the night before and that Saturday. Plus, she doesn't have an evil bone in her body."

"Being a product of Alvin's genes, that doesn't seem possible; does it?"

"Believe me, a more loving, trusting, gentle human being doesn't exist," Lizzy says.

"Must take after her real mother," I conclude. "You know her?"

"I've never been to Boston."

"How did you two meet?" Tiffany asks, as she decides to sit in the chair next to mine.

"In a bar."

"Which one?"

"I don't remember."

"Was it a lesbian bar?" Tiffany keeps it all in staccato.

"Probably."

"Which one? There's not that many."

"Girl Bar, maybe."

"Don't know it."

"Why would you?" Lizzy asks.

"Some of my best friends are lesbians," Tiffany says in obvious false admission.

"Name one."

Tiffany hesitates, caught in a game of her own making.

I take back the questioning. "Were you ever at the house in Kenilworth?"

"No. I wasn't welcome."

"Your and Christina's picture was in the den," I say.

"No, it wasn't."

Lizzy is either calling my bluff or was lying on the previous question.

"How long have you two been a couple?"

"Six, eight months."

"Love her?"

"Of course I love her."

Lizzy shuffles papers on her desk. "I got to get back to work. And that fat slob you sent over, what a treat."

I stand. "Herman might be a beast, but he's a genius when it comes to anything money."

"Your buddy embodies everything disgusting about men."

Lizzy may have a point.

———

We get into the Lexus and head back downtown. "You feel okay?" I ask.

"Fine."

"What did you glean from our visit with Lizzy?"

Tiffany says, "I wouldn't want her in the audience if I was doing stand-up."

"I don't see the two of them together," I say.

"For every fem, there's a dyke."

"They just don't fit."

We drive down Western Avenue, past car dealer after car dealer. Each one offers better financing options than the last. Something is wrong, but I don't know what.

"Sure nothing is bothering you?"

"Yes," she says.

"Good."

We pass a bank.

"Don't forget to stop at an ATM. I'm going to need cash for my appointment with Alexis."

———

Same idiot works the concierge desk. He makes another "Enjoy" comment as I pass through the inner doors.

Instead of 4114, I knock on 4116 directly across the hall. There is a short wait until Alexis opens the door. She is dressed in a tight black mini-skirt and flowered blouse.

"I'm surprised to see you," she says, as I enter the condo almost identical to the one I visited before.

"I try to be a surprising kind of a guy whenever possible."

"So this is regular business?"

"Whatever."

We sit. She offers champagne. I decline. She crosses her legs and smiles. I am perfectly still. She watches me and I watch her. Alexis leans forward, places her hand on my knee. Smiles again. I cannot imagine a situation less sensual or sexy.

"I didn't come for sex."

"You called Nick."

"I wanted to see you alone."

"Why?" She removes her hand from my knee.

"Numbers don't add up." I cross my arms on my chest. "Even at five hundred bucks a pop, you two would have had to have done Alvin over eighty times to run up such a tab. Alvin would have keeled over weeks ago from the fluid loss."

Alexis stares at her shoes.

"So, I conclude it was a family type operation. You did Alvin, Clayton, Brewster, maybe an uncle, a distant cousin... business partners when they were in town?"

Alexis bites her lip, "I only did Alvin."

"Diane do the rest?"

"Brewster."

"Really?" *And they said he didn't have the balls.*

I pace around the small room. "Was it just you or was Diane also in the condo the night before Alvin died?"

"We weren't there."

I stop. "Dumb to lie now; don't you think?"

"Both of us," she says.

"You do Alvin that night?"

"Yeah."

"What time did you leave?"

"Around one."

"That jives with the cab." I never checked with the cab company, but said this anyway to make myself seem a little more professional. "Leave alone?"

"I had another appointment. Fridays are prime time in this business."

"Alvin promised to pay what he owed you that night, didn't he?"

"How'd you know?"

"I'm real smart," I say. "Why didn't he?"

"He was in such a surly mood, that asking him would have been suicide."

I pause to consider a number of questions.

"Was there an old guy there, about sixty, probably wearing a tweed sport coat, limping a bit?"

"His accountant."

"You ever see him before?"

"Oh, yeah."

"Fun guy?"

"Swell, just swell."

"Diane hang around after you left?"

"Yeah."

"How'd she get out of working for Nick that Friday?"

"Monthly excuse."

At times being a woman has its rewards.

"Could Diane have gotten paid and not you?"

"Certainly hope not."

I walk over to look out the window at the city beneath. "Were there guys at the party you had never seen?"

"One."

"A guy named Joey Villano?" I ask, wait...see the name doesn't register and add, "Italian, dark hair, maybe thirty, pudgy, maybe a bit on the nerdy side?"

"Yeah."

"Anyone else?"

"No."

"Small party, eh?"

"Intimate," she says.

I check my watch. Tiffany is, no doubt, downstairs wondering how I have managed to last so long.

"Do you have my money, Sherlock?"

I flip two Ben Franklins on the coffee table. "I have what you'll need to pay Nick for my time." I wait for her to pick up the bills. "I hate to inform you, Alexis, but I'm not sure Diane and you were equal partners."

"Why not?"

I'm not only fishing, but I'm casting way, way out. "I get these hunches. I can't explain them.

Alexis asks, "Would you trust her if you were me?"

"She makes her living screwing people."

"So do I."

23
Exfoliate. You'll feel better

I sit in front of what is now a wall of recipe cards. The *Original Carlo* is totally covered. I remind myself that lives are a series of patterns.

Mine, for example, is a series of failed female relationships. To say I don't do well with women is an understatement. My third grade, sixth grade, and junior year girlfriends dumped me for jocks. No wonder I'm not much of a sports fan. In college, the women I liked didn't like me; and the ones that liked me, I didn't much care for. My ex and I fell in love and our love resulted in a pregnancy. Pregnancy begat marriage. Marriage made for a life of diapers, credit card bills, and complaints, mostly about my job. In our first six months, we had less and less time together, and less and less love. After Kelly was born, the descent continued. To break the negative pattern, we took our first "weekend away," which was meant to rekindle the love-lust my wife and I once thought we had for one another. The only success over that weekend was to get pregnant again, which doubled the daughters, diapers, bills and complaints. The only thing worse than my marriage was my divorce. Not only was I taken to the cleaners, but taken back repeatedly each time a wrinkle was discovered.

Now, in the middle of the night, I search the cards for patterns and see none. I am at the point of asking all the suspects to line up and take off all their clothes so I can see if each has a similar tattoo.

———

Joan Augustus lived in one of those highrise one-bedroom condos that, in my estimation, would have been considered a cramped, boring, non-descript apartment until the downtown condo conversion boom of the 1990s turned these units into chic, urban enclaves. For Joan's sake, I hope her condo holds its value as well as she's held the grudge against her ex-husband.

"I should have killed him," she tells me. "I thought about it about a million times. I planned it, plotted it, and watched it play out in my head over and over. There is a window in the bank building across the street with a perfect line of sight to the front door of the Board of Trade. I was going to sneak up there, do a Lee Harvey Oswald, blasting him with a high-powered rifle the second he stepped out of that revolving door." She pauses, reflecting, "Would that be a fitting end or what, his blood staining the spot of concrete where the sun never shines?"

"Certainly would have been poetic. Why didn't you do it?"

"Somebody beat me to it."

"Too bad," I say, "would have made my life a lot easier."

Joan sips coffee, seated at a small table pushed against the one wall in her kitchen. "I hated him. He made my life a living hell. I had every reason in the world to kill him and I should have; I don't deny it."

With each word, Joan rises rapidly upward on the list of *The Most Likely*.

"You wouldn't have gotten anything out of it."

"Satisfaction."

"Pretty big risk for something you can't take to the bank."

"Probably why I never got around to doing it."

"Any other reason?"

"Clayton."

"Really? Because I don't get the feeling he was all that enamored with his daddy, either."

"As horrible as Alvin was, he was the father of my son."

"Clayton is Alvin's son?" I have no idea why I ask this question. It pops out of my mouth without forethought.

"Yes."

"Sure?"

"Of course, I'm sure," Joan shouts. "What kind of a person do you think I am?"

"You were just waxing nostalgic about putting a slug though his heart as he's leaving work."

"That's different."

"Of course, silly me."

Joan has no job, no business or career; and I suspect few friends. She must hang around this place all day, reading bodice-ripper paperbacks, such as the one open on the kitchen counter with a Fabio look-alike on the cover.

"Those two detectives tell you where I was when Alvin was killed?"

"I didn't ask."

"Isn't that your job?"

"Yeah, I guess so," I say, "but I never said I was good at it."

"You want to know?"

"Not really."

I see on her refrigerator a number of magnets, but no pictures, notes, or lists being held in place. "You could have paid somebody to kill him."

"Why would I do that?"

"Remember, 'he made your life a living hell?'"

"I don't think so," she says.

"Did you know someone took a shot at him?"

"When?"

"A week or two before he died."

"Too bad they missed."

My back hurts. All the time sitting up nights, staring at recipe cards on the wall is taking its toll on my lumbar region.

I cut to the chase. "Who do you think killed Alvin?"

"No doubt about it, Doris whacked him."

———

Tiffany refuses to visit Herman alone. I have to meet her at his apartment and we go in together.

"What did you find out?"

Herman removes the toothpick from his mouth, tucks it into the greasy hair behind his ear for future use, and says, "It had to be an inside job."

"Why?"

"They didn't touch her credit cards. Whoever did Christina got her password, pin numbers, and merely transferred all her money from her account to a number of his accounts all within a few hours."

"How much?"

"Two hundred grand."

"The lesbo kept two hundred grand in her checking account?" Tiffany asks rhetorically. "Even I wouldn't be that stupid."

"Her last trust fund payment kicked in a week before."

"She tell you all this, Herman?" I ask.

"No." Herman rubs his ample stomach. "You guys want some cheese?"

"No thanks."

"Pass," Tiffany adds.

"How did you find out?" I ask.

"I'm sneaky," he says.

Herman struggles out of the non-squeaking chair, goes to the refrigerator and removes a baggie from the crisper drawer. He finds a filthy Swiss Army knife in the sink and returns to his seat, where he removes the hunk of bluish cheese from the plastic, opens the knife blade and begins to shave the mold off the sides. "Ya always got to be careful not to let anyone see you put your pin number in the machine at the grocery store," he tells Tiffany.

"I have my groceries delivered," she explains.

"Where did Christina's money end up?"

"The never-ending black hole known as cyberspace." Herman whittles down the cheese as if he's carving a duck decoy.

"Did you have any luck reviewing Alvin?"

"Nope." Herman bites into the cheese, which I thought was Roquefort, but with the mold off, it is actually Muenster. "Thought I would, but nope."

"Doesn't sound like you tried very hard."

Herman chews a hunk of cheese in the side of his mouth as if it were a wad of tobacco. "They didn't send me a lot to go on, but something's funny about how he did it all."

"Explain, Herman."

"I can't until I see his trades."

Tiffany begins to turn pale from the smell of Herman's cheese-tainted breath. I better get my assistant out of there before she passes out. "We got to be going, Herman, keep being sneaky."

"Oh, I will," he says. "Want some cheese for the road?"

"I'm going to get you his trades to look at," I tell him. "You figure it out."

"Yeah, whatever." Herman is more interested in watching Tiffany's backside as she heads for the door. "Ya know, Tiffany, you don't always have to bring Mister Boring along when you come over to visit."

"Oh, yes I do."

Outside, as we head for her car, Tiffany says, "I feel like I should go home and take a shower. Herman's bad breath has soaked though my clothes and is laying on my skin like a cheese fungus."

"Herman does have that effect on people."

Tiffany drops me off in the Jefferson Park neighborhood, not far from the Harlem "L" stop. "Go home, exfoliate, you'll feel better," I tell her.

The house is a small Chicago bungalow. There is a FOR SALE sign on its front lawn. On the sign is a picture of the broker, Honest Abe Benershevski, in an Uncle Sam outfit, finger pointing out with the slogan underneath reading: *I Want You in a New Home.*

I knock.

She sees me through the front drapes, then unlatches two deadbolts and opens the door.

"How did you know where I lived?" Millie asks as two cats scurry out of sight.

"I'm a detective, remember?" I stand on her doorstep. "May I come in?"

"The house is a mess."

"Not compared to where I've just been."

I step inside and am hit with the distinctive odor of well-used cat litter. "Nice place."

"Thanks."

"Is Mister Heffelfinger here?"

"No," she says. "Why would he be?"

"Just wondered."

She leads me to the front room, points to where I should sit, but another cat is stretched out on the cushion. "Sit over there," she says, motioning.

"I won't take a lot of your time."

Millie sits next to the cat.

"Moving?"

"I have a sister that lives in Florida."

I take a little time before I begin. "Millie, do you know how much Alvin was getting in rent for his trading seats at the Board?"

"He used to get eight thousand."

"Used to?"

"I don't know anymore since he was taking the money in cash."

"From whom?"

"The company was called Nivla or Nivia or something like that."

"Wouldn't you have to know the name for the license renewals and whatever?"

"I was supposed to."

"But you didn't?"

"Alvin said he'd handle it."

"Why?"

"I think Alvin was using the rent as his walking around money."

"He'd walk around with eight grand in his pocket?"

"He had a big bulge."

A line I wasn't going to touch.

"Do you know where this Nivia or Nivlia had offices?"

"No."

"Did you know when he put the seats up for sale?"

"No," she said, "but that could be why he said he'd handle the paperwork."

"Was Alvin good at paperwork?"

"Terrible."

"Do you think he was going to pocket the money for the seats, too?"

"That would be hard to do with all the regulations."

"If Alvin was losing all this money in trade after trade, and his account was in arrears, wouldn't the Board hold up a sale until all trades were complete?"

"Yes."

I was about to ask my next question when a knock came on the door.

"Excuse me." Millie gets up goes to the door and ushers in Honest Abe, who left his Uncle Sam hat at home.

"We have a showing, Millie," he tells her.

"Oh, I forgot."

Abe begins to open up doors and windows. "It's not going to sell if it smells like a cat kennel."

I wait for Abe to rush off to another part of the house. "One last question?"

"Fine," she says.

"Was Alvin a crook?"

"You mean, did he cheat?" she asks.

"Yeah."

"Lots of people cheat."

"Did Alvin?"

"If he did, he had his own system, because it is tough to do when it's all done electronically."

"Easier to cheat if you trade on the floor?"

"Oh, yeah, they use the honor system on the floor."

"Thank you for your time." Walking towards the front door, I see Honest Abe emptying cat litter into a garbage bag.

"Good luck with the house."

Before I leave, I sneak in one last question, "Do you know where I can find Mister Heffelfinger? I've been unable to reach him in the last few days."

"He's out of town. I don't know where."

"Well, then, meow."

She smiles at my goodbye.

I pass the prospective couple on their way into the showing. I hope they are cat lovers.

———

I walk six blocks to the "L" station and ride the Red Line, transfer to the Brown at Fullerton, and get off at the Board of Trade stop.

I head inside to the administration office and flash my license at the clerk.

"Yeah, what?"

"I'm looking for a company or individual names Nivlia or

Nivia or a sounds-like."

"Good for you," the clerk, a middle-aged man, who obviously doesn't like his job, or doesn't like me - or both, says.

"Could you help me?"

"I could."

Out of my wallet I pull out a ten and slide it towards him. His fingers snap up the bill like a lizard tongue finding lunch.

"Hey, Bruno," the clerk says to the janitor emptying wastepaper baskets behind him. "This guy wants to see the Nivla office."

Bruno stops his collection process. "Another one?"

"Bruno don't come cheap, either," the clerk informs me.

I pull out another ten-spot and follow Bruno to the service elevator.

"I'm not allowed to use the regular elevator," Bruno says as he hits the number-twenty-three button.

"Why did you say 'another one' when the clerk mentioned Nivla?"

"You're the third guy to want to get in."

"You make ten bucks each time?"

"The last guy gave me a twenty."

The elevator jerks to a stop and we walk down the hall to the last door before the one marked MEN. On the spot where the company plaque should be is a small piece of paper with the name NIVLA CORP. Scotched-taped in its place. "Classy," I remark.

"People here are too busy making dough to be classy," Bruno says as he pulls out a key ring with about a thousand keys. He picks one right out of the middle, slides it into the lock and opens the door.

"You don't knock?"

He looks at me like I'm nuts.

One room, long and narrow with one desk, one chair, one phone. I pick up the receiver, no dial-tone, and place it back down in its cradle. I hear a slight whooshing sound.

Bruno hears it, too. "You can hear the toilet flush," he says.

"Quaint."

"Not the urinal, just the toilet."

"Thank God for small favors."

I pace around the room to the one window and look down on

the alley below. "Tell me about the other guys who came and saw the place."

"No."

I hand him another ten-dollar bill.

"The first guy was like one of those muscle-head guys," Bruno says and puffs up his chest like Charles Atlas. "The other guy was old."

"Did he have a tweed sport coat?"

"Yeah, but he wasn't from England. He was a Jew."

"Work in the building?"

Bruno nods.

"The other guy about thirty, dark hair, about this tall," I raise my hand a little less than my height, "dressed to impress the ladies?"

"Not my kind of ladies."

"He's the one who gave you the twenty?"

"Yeah, how'd you know?"

"I'm smart."

There is one whooshing sound, then another.

"It always picks up after lunch," Bruno says.

———

I am hardly euphoric, but I have made a connection; my first in the case. I can't wait to go home and rearrange the index cards on the *Original Carlo*.

24
Bare witness

The elevator doors open on the lobby level. I step out and find myself in a sea of look-alikes. Each man is in a blue plastic jacket, white shirt, and tightly-tied, striped tie. They flood into the building like a swarm of Smurfs, flashing their badges high for identification. The well-dressed platoon is led by none other than Agent Romo Simpson.

Commoners, such as I, are caught in the lobby during the rush, parting like the Red Sea, allowing the squad to commandeer the elevators.

Romo picks me out of the crowd. "What are you doing here?"

"Just visiting."

"Well, you're in the middle of an official FBI operation," he says, as he waves cohorts into an elevator.

"I would have never guessed."

Next, through the front doors come a gaggle of TV news crews, one from each of the stations. All have lights blazing, video cameras recording, and reporters announcing into microphones that they are "live at the scene."

I wonder who tipped them off?

"By the way, did you ever find out who that guy was in the picture?" I ask Romo.

"I am not at liberty to say," he says, and crowds into the car as if he were the last man jumping on a boat leaving the dock.

Figuring I will see all this on the news, I decide not to hang around. I have better things to do.

———

Tuesday night's feast is macaroni surprise. Kelly and Care are not only not surprised, but not too thrilled as it sits in front of them at the table.

"This is gross."

"It's good, if you just taste it," I say. "You can't judge a book by its cover."

Care asks, "You got this out of a cookbook?"

"Dad, this looks like one of those flesh-eating diseases," Kelly says.

Maybe mixing tomato tuna casserole with mac and cheese wasn't the best menu choice, but I am thinking nutrition for my girls.

"All four basic food groups are represented," I tell them and take a bite to back up my "try it you'll like it" argument. The ploy doesn't work, so I add a cup-and-a-half of guilt. "You know people that are starving in Africa would die for a dinner this nutritious."

"Then let's put it in a baggie and send it to them," Kelly suggests.

I boil the girls tube steaks, aka hot dogs, which they devour. They may have been right about the surprise; it was pretty bad.

"How is the number-one table, Kel?"

"How did you know I got picked?"

"Your dad's a detective."

"Did you tell him, Care?"

"No."

"I knew because you didn't tell me," I explain to my eldest. "Teenage avoidance is always a great clue."

"See," Care says, pretending to understand.

"So far, it's awesome," Kelly says.

"Why?

"Because it just is. Everybody in school sees me sitting there."

"And?"

"That's awesome."

"You should have known that, Dad," Care says. "You're a detective."

"How long has it been?"

"One day."

"Well, don't be surprised if the glow fades fast."

"It won't," Kelly argues.

"I don't want my daughters getting their self-respect from the way others view them," I lecture. "You should get your self-esteem from the way you view yourself."

"Like in a mirror?" Care asks.

"No. Self-worth should come from within," I speak slowly, fatherly. "If you are proud and happy about yourself, you won't care what others think."

"Dad," Kelly says, "I'm beginning to understand why you don't date."

———

The BOARD OF TRADE RAIDED BY FEDS headline in the *Sun Times* is twice the size of the *Tribune's* BOARD OF TRADE INVESTIGATED. Romo Simpson's picture isn't on either cover. You have to go all the way to page twenty-three and thirty-one, respectively, to see him in all his glory. Pity. The corresponding story in each is mostly flash and trash on how the FBI has been secretly recording conversations, and about their going undercover to weed out the dastardly criminals taking advantage of the honor policy on the trading floor.

Once, when I was still with the CPD, there was an investigation of illegal dog breeding in a number of kennels. At the Monday morning detective's meeting I offered to go undercover as a cocker spaniel to help bust the bad breeders. My offer was refused.

———

In a day or two the RAID will disappear from the media, a few low-level doofusses will be charged and OPERATION FUNNY MONEY will fade into the FBI files of yore. It is obvious that Agent Romo spent months of taxpayer money and found little malfeasance. Failing in his investigation he does the next best thing, which is to stage a big bust, get on TV, get his name in the newspapers, and hopefully be promoted for his quick-thinking actions. If anyone has the audacity to see through his cleverly press-agented scam, and make a case of it, Romo will claim it was all done to put the fear of God into anyone trying to manipulate the hollowed tradition of the Board of Trade's honor system. I can picture Agent Romo on TV, saying, "Future prevention is just as important as past indiscretion."

———

I meet Steve and Norbert at Al's Italian Beef on Wells Street. We sit at an outdoor table.

"So what do you know, Sherlock?" Steve asks.

"It's not what I know at this point, it's what I don't know."

Steve says, "You sound like a game show host."

Norbert finishes one sandwich; but before starting on his next, says, "I got this feeling you got a list."

Norbert is correct. *What a sleuth.*

Every good detective I have ever met or worked with is an incessant list-maker. To-do, What's Missing, Don't Understand, Doesn't Fit, Probables, Improbables, Longshots, People, Places, Things -- lists, lists, and more lists. On each you'll see cross-outs, additions, notes, memory floggers, arrows, phone numbers, directions, reminders, whatever. Lists are the only way to keep it all straight. I keep most of my lists in my head, a scary place no doubt; but with my memory, it works. Most other dicks keep them on their pocket writing tablets or on one of those yellow legal pads, although the latter is a pain to carry around all day. I guess you could put a list into one of those Blackberry or iPhone things, but I can barely figure out the phone part, much less the rest of their high-tech applications. My memory works. Why not use it?

Steve pushes his plate to the side, takes out his tablet and pen. "What do you need?"

"I still need the identity of the mystery man in the photo."

Norbert speaks through a mouthful of fries, "Sent out a copy to every major department in the country, somebody has got to recognize the guy sooner or later."

"I think Romo knows who it is," I tell them.

"Romo doesn't know his ass from his elbow," Steve says.

"Anything on the two escorts who were servicing the family?"

"Nothing yet," Steve says, "I got a friend in Vice who said he'd help."

"Those two are hooked into this somehow," I say. "Pardon the pun." I eye the fries on my plate, but decide against grease, and push them toward Norbert. "Heffelfinger is gone, I suspect out of the country. Can you find out where?"

"No."

Norbert follows his partner's answer with, "You know how long that would take?"

"Just check the flights to bank account islands," I say. "Bahamas, Aruba, Cayman, wherever; he's visiting one of 'em."

"You're sure Alvin's money's there?"

"It's got to be somewhere."

"You don't think he was broke?"

"I know he wasn't broke." I don't want to get into a discussion of how I know, so I quickly say, "I want you to run a history on Christina's partner, Lizzy."

"You're stretching."

"There is something about her that isn't Kosher."

"Sherlock, you're being homophobic and possibly anti-Semitic."

"Not I, not I."

"By the way where is the lovely junior detective?" Norbert asks.

"On assignment."

"You were right about the kid in the chest," Steve says.

"Joey Villano, the trader Alvin used."

"Drunk, bopped on the noggin and stuffed in the trunk. What a way to go."

"Do you think he was killed in the condo?"

"I don't," Steve says. "Norbert does."

Norbert lifts one finger, as if to cast his vote. "Carpet fibers on his body," he says, taking another bite of barbeque.

"There were too many fibers on his clothing. I think he was dragged in," Steve says

"Fits with Alvin." I surprise my colleagues with this thought.

"It does?" Steve asks for the two of them.

"I'm next to positive he was killed then dragged to the rock garden."

"The coroner said a rock did him in."

"I'm not debating that," I say.

"You don't think the final blow was part of the avalanche?"

"No. It seems that was more of an exclamation point."

"Then why bother doing it?"

"Got me." I pause. "The more I get into this case, the more screwed up I get. I don't know how Alvin was scamming the Board, or even if he was. Or why the two sons hated their father who was bankrolling each in business. He has a wife he hates, ex-wives that hate him, a daughter he treats as a second class citizen, two accountants who have to know what the hell he was doing, a couple of hookers he refuses to pay, major cash withdrawals the week before his death ... and why anyone would wear a linen suit on a Saturday morning in the summer is beyond me."

Norbert eats my fries during my litany. "You guys going to have dessert?" he asks after I conclude.

Steve ignores Norbert. "Conway Waddy, the lawyer called yesterday."

"He wants the insurance money released?"

"Immediately."

"Good luck on that," I say. "Old man Richmond will hold out until their lawsuits grow mold."

"Could Joey Villano have killed him?" Steve asks. "Then somebody kills him?"

"Downward spiral theory?" Norbert asks his partner.

"I'm not even sure Joey knew what was going on," I admit, "and he was in the office with Alvin every day."

"So were Millie and Heffelfinger," Steve says. "A lot of good they've done us."

"Just as I thought we were getting somewhere," I say, "we're back to floating around in detective netherworld."

"We're running out of time," Steve says.

I'm not sure what he means.

"I got an idea," Norbert says before scooping his vanilla ice cream. "Let's shake the tree."

"How?"

"Announce a break in the case."

"Do you have one?" I ask.

"No."

"You got an idea for one?" I ask again.

"Not yet," Norbert says, "but we're smart guys; we should be able to come up with something."

———

"I sat at that desk over eight hours, Mister Sherlock," Tiffany informs me. "The last thing I want to get out of this case is secretarial spread."

"What did you find out?"

"Nothing."

"Nothing?"

"I didn't find one clue. I checked every property, account, trust, investment, car, house, gold bar, and piggy bank; and each and every one was held in the Alvin Augustus Revocable Trust. And every one was either broke or disappeared in the last six months."

"That's good."

"Didn't we already know that?" she asks.

"Yeah."

"I called every hotel, medical clinic, plastic surgeon and boob doctor in Palm Springs and Palm Desert. I checked personal physicians, dermatologists, personal trainers, even yoga instructors, and nobody has ever heard of a Doris Augustus."

"She's probably using another name."

"I didn't think of that," Tiffany says.

"How about the boys?"

"I got a slew of paperwork on Clayton -- numbers, tax stuff, corporate junk. My eyes were going blue going over that crap."

"And?"

"Clayton's leveraged."

I'm impressed at a business acumen that I didn't believe she possessed. "Please, do tell."

"Well, you know, leveraged."

"You know what leveraged means?"

"Not really."

"You got your dad to help you?"

"I certainly wasn't going to ask Herman."

"How leveraged is he?"

"My dad says he's a house of cards waiting to be blown away."

"Brewster?"

"Coming from me, this might sound a bit strange, but after talking to a number of Brewster's schoolmates, so-called friends, enemies, and hangers-on, I'd say Brewster isn't the sharpest dresser on the runway. And momma chokes him daily with her apron strings."

"And the sister?"

"The best thing I can say about Christina is that, even for a lesbian, she's past dull. She likes to read, go antiquing, takes night classes in foreign languages, drives a Chrysler Le Baron and is a member of the Audubon Society. Totally boring."

"Tiffany," I say, "you did good."

"But I didn't find out anything that could crack the case."

"And neither have I, so don't feel bad."

"What happens next, Mister Sherlock?"

"A witness is going to come forward and blow the case apart."

"You're kidding," Tiffany perks up, "that's fantastic."

"Yeah, I'm making him up right now."

25

Pity there's no school for scoundrels

Norbert leaked the info to a friend of mine at the *Sun Times* in exchange for getting on page three as the lead story.

The story read like a promo for one of those over-plotted, too-many-twists, caper movies that star Julia Roberts or George Clooney. It mentioned a non-identified witness to the murder of Alvin Augustus, the Friday raid at the Board of Trade, missing funds, Clayton, Brewster, Doris, Joan, Joey, sex, drugs, and rock-and-roll. It actually didn't mention music; but it would a have a perfect spot for hyping a hip urban soundtrack available for download tomorrow.

No actual name mentioned, but the mystery man who came forward had valuable information, which could break the case wide open. His statement would be heard by the Grand Jury as soon as his story could be thoroughly investigated by the Chicago PD, Kenilworth detectives and agents from the FBI. Rumor has it, the article said, the witness may be testifying in exchange for immunity from prosecution. The item ended with: "Police had been waiting for a break in the case and now may have the information needed to move toward arrests."

Any cop or criminal worth his salt would read the article and conclude "it was a bunch of crap." But one thing a good detective always keeps in mind is that most criminals are stupid. The vast majority are totally uneducated in the business of wrongdoing. Why? Because colleges don't offer curriculums in fraud, classes in money-laundering or night school degrees in pimping and prostitution. Unless you're from a crime family, you pretty much have to learn the business by yourself. And that can be tough. The stuff seen on TV rarely helps, because no crime gets planned, executed, and resolved within one hour, with timeouts for commercials. There is quite a bit of 'true crime" non-fiction out there to study, but most criminals are either too lazy or just not the *reading* types.

Criminals, for the most part, are either plain stupid or rank amateurs when it comes to malfeasance. Not only do they all believe they can get away with it, but think they are above and beyond all those other run-of-the-mill felons. Operating on this ill-advised thought pattern is not a strong basis for the carrying out of successful illegal endeavors. They make mistakes, plan poorly, don't synchronize watches, tell lousy lies, vary from their original plan and, more often than not, panic at the first bump in the road.

A good detective will always operate on the basis that the criminal mind is beneath his. Sounds easy, but actually it can be tricky because sometimes it is difficult to think *that* dumb.

Consider the guy who placed a 911 call, frantically screaming a robbery was taking place in Fifth Avenue liquor store, when in actuality the robbery was happening in a Twenty-second Avenue liquor store -- a clever ruse to get the cops three miles away, while his buddies "did the deed." Problem was the guy who came up with this plan forgot to disable the caller i.d. on his phone when he made the call and the police arrived just as his buddies were returning with six-hundred in cash and three bottles of Chivas Regal. Most would believe that anyone couldn't be that dumb, but there is no underestimating the idiocy of the common criminal.

To take this all one step further, the difference between a good detective and a great detective is: the latter finds ways of unleashing the idiocy of the criminal so that he or she will inevitably do something so dumb that they will virtually handcuff themselves on their way into the slammer.

This was the whole point of releasing bogus information in the *Sun Times* article.

———

"I'm getting good at this, Mister Sherlock," Tiffany tells me as I climb into her parked Lexus.

"And your reasoning behind this revelation of self-worth?"

"I did exactly what you told me, as soon as Heffelfinger got off the plane, I followed him here."

We sit in her car, watching the house. A newer bigger sign with Abe's picture has been added to the front lawn.

"You know where here is?"

"No, do you?"

"At Millie's house."

"You're kidding?"

"Remember, you dropped me off here?"

"Oh, yeah," she says. "Heffelfinger must have gotten really horny on his trip."

"I have an odd feeling that Heffelfinger's personal needs are not the primary purpose of his visit."

We hear a row taking place inside the home. Millie is especially vocal.

"Told ya," Tiffany says, "little accounting lady is quite the screamer."

"Sound effects are assumptions, Tiffany."

"They're doing it."

"I don't think so."

"Mister Sherlock, I had this boyfriend once, who'd be gone for only three days and become an animal when he got back into town."

"What happened to that one?"

"First time he came home and wasn't chomping on the bit, I knew he'd been playing around."

"Damned if we do, damned if we don't."

A cab drives up and parks a few spaces in front of my Toyota, honks its horn, and waits.

The front door of the bungalow opens. Heffelfinger steps out. He and Millie continue their heated discussion. Tiffany and I watch through the car's tinted windows.

"See, after-sex pillow talk, Mister Sherlock."

"She's pissed because he didn't come back with any of Alvin's money; and he's pissed because he's heard of a witness popping up and spilling a lot of beans. At least that's a good guess."

"My guess is," Tiffany says, "there ain't no fury like the fury of a granny scorned."

Heffelfinger wheels his overnight bag behind him on the way to the cab.

"Where do you think he's going?" Tiffany asks.

"He's going to see Doris."

"One woman not enough for him?"

"Not in this case."

"Maybe he took Viagra and has one of those four-hour erections, and he's visiting all the women he knows," Tiffany concludes.

The cab takes off.

"He's getting away. You want me to give chase?"

"No, Tiffany. You've earned a spa treatment."

"I agree, Mister Sherlock."

———

Agent Romo Simpson is much more conducive to meeting with me than he was before.

"You release all the guys you captured?" I ask.

"Yesterday."

"Your boss come down on you yet?"

"Yesterday."

"You have no clue how Alvin did it; do you?"

Romo twirls his coffee cup around and around. "None."

"Don't feel bad."

"We went over every trade made, traced money, watched every movement for a month, and I had every MBA in the FBI on this thing. We come up with bupkis and still millions disappeared, vanished into thin air."

"You picked the wrong guy to cut a deal with."

He looks up at me for the first time. "Now you tell me."

Nothing worse than knowing you got sucked in, suckered, and skewered on the way out. I do feel a bit sorry for the upstart G-man, but my feeling will pass.

"You want in on this investigation or are you going to continue to be a lone wolf?"

"I can't jeopardize the Bureau's investigation."

"You just admitted you know nothing."

"All right," Romo says, "I'm in. What do I got to do?" Romo is at least smart enough to realize that to get into the club he's going to have to pay a few dues.

I hand over a list of serial numbers. "If any of these Ben Franklins show up in bulk, do your best to get a description of who cashed them in."

"That's next to impossible," he says.

I continue my list. "Take whatever you pulled on Alvin's trading habits, take them over to this guy's house and put your heads together." I hand him Herman's address and phone number.

He has no idea of the amount of dues he's about to pay in order to get into our little club.

"I have to know who the guy was, leaving the condo that Friday night."

"We've run the picture through every database we have and nothing comes up."

"Keep trying."

Romo writes it all down, making his own list.

"Breakaway" blasts out of my phone. "Hello."

It is rude to talk on a cell phone in front of another; but it's Romo, so it is easy to make an exception.

"How did you know Heffelfinger would be here?" Norbert asks.

"I'm smart," I answer. "How many times do I have to tell you?"

Norbert is in his car, probably eating a donut, in front of the Augustus mansion in Kenilworth. "The little mice are starting to scurry, Sherlock."

"I thought they would."

There is a pause for Norbert to swallow. "Guess what?"

"They found the shooter on the grassy knoll?"

"Lizzy doesn't exist past two years ago."

"Ah, now that's interesting."

"We traced her back to Massachusetts and then she falls off the radar screen."

"Any way you can pick up some prints on her?"

"Not without asking."

"More on Joey?"

"No."

"Have you tapped Doris' phone yet?"

"It's been tapped for weeks. We got nothing."

"Steve working Clayton?"

"As we speak."

"If you talk to him, tell him to check our little entrepreneur's credit line."

"Why?"

"I believe it has run aground in a sea of red ink."

I hang up Norbert. I look over and see Romo has written down notes on my conversation. "Want to get filled in?" I ask.

"Please."

———

I obey the rule of the FBI receptionist and make my next call outside on the sidewalk.

"Yes, boss," Tiffany answers.

"Before you get to the spa, I need you to do something."

"I'm your girl."

"Jonas needs a set of Lizzy's fingerprints."

"Okay."

"I want you to get them."

"How?"

"Find something she's touched."

"Christina?"

"Something a little less animated."

"I'm on it, Mister Sherlock, I'm on it."

I return home a little after seven. The only thing in the house to eat is a box of Fruit Loops. I sit on the couch, eat cold cereal, and stare at the index cards on the *Original Carlo*.

———

Horse shows rank right up there with watching paint dry, standing in line at the DMV, and waiting for your turn in the emergency ward. Painful boredom at its best.

It is Saturday morning at nine a.m. I sit in the last row of spectators in a huge, hot, humidity-filled barn which reeks of horse manure. There are hundreds of kids, ninety-nine percent of whom are girls seven to twelve years old, all dressed in jodhpurs, black boots, white blouses, blue blazers, and black riding helmets.

The three or four boys in the group are dressed in similar garb and might as well be singing show tunes and signing up for a subscription to the *Advocate*. In the middle of the arena is one hefty women, she's the Judge Judy of the horsey set. To my left, on a slight riser, is a table with one woman announcing the different events, horse names, and corresponding riders. One woman shuffles papers, trying to keep it all straight, and one woman is filling out the winner's name on the back of cheap red, white, and blue ribbons.

The events, which began at a little after seven a.m., are strikingly similar. Sets of eight riders, weighing somewhere between forty and eighty pounds each, sit upon horses ten times their size. They line up, nose to butt (the horses, not the riders) and march in excruciatingly slow motion down one side of the arena, turn around, and march back from where they started.

I can see absolutely no difference between one rider and the next. The horses -- many of which are stable nags who repeat the same thing over and over with different riders -- obviously share the absolute monotony. At the end of each event, Judge Judy hands a note to a semi-Pony Express rider who gallops the results to the announcer's table, so the winners can be blared over the tinny loudspeaker system.

In the spectator section where I sit, very well-dressed moms (husbands must be on the golf course) sip coffee, fiddle with video cameras, scratch, fidget, or talk on their cell phones so all around them can hear their innermost thoughts. They share the traits of being wealthy, polished, Northshore folk who pride themselves in being members of an exclusive, thoroughbred set of individuals, who can afford a hobby where the plaything eats more than the player. The aspect I find most fascinating about this group is that these neat, clean, manicured women have no problem whatsoever with a horse defecating a steaming, stream of crap, a few feet before their very eyes. They don't gag at the smell, and oftentimes walk right through it without the least bit of hesitation. These are the same women who pay people to walk their purebred dogs.

My ex-wife has become, or at least is trying to become, one of the chosen few, "horse mother" women. She wears her boots and equestrian garb proudly, straddles a fence with the best of them, and yells encouragement to the girls with comments like "Give 'em a lot of leg." Why my ex-wife would ever want my daughters involved in such an insipid, so-called sport, as well as the vaulted social strata, is beyond my imagination. Not only is it boring and obviously rigged, I have yet to see one kid break into a smile while on a horse. They are either too frightened, or having fun is prohibited in the rules of the road -- or path in this case. Worst of all, it is hardly a fair competition. Some kids ride their personal ponies while others are stuck with beat-up stable horses who have "been there done that" way, way too many times. The sport's management, the people that run these shows and pick the winners and losers, are older, fat, unmarried females who obviously consider horses a much better choice of companion than the opposite sex. These women are in a constant heaping-praise mode to all the young riders, whether the kids are any good or not. They never quit patting backs, rubbing helmets, and hugging the girls as if they were the little ones they never had.

Little League, where art thou?

Before the lunch break at noon, where the barn barbeque sells five-dollar hot dogs and eight-dollar energy drinks, Kelly has ridden in two competitions and garnered one white ribbon. Care hasn't been so lucky. She is zero for three. In her last event, one kid fell off her horse and got third place, but my Care got nothing. She is in tears as she greets me.

"I lost."

"No, you didn't, you were great."

"You're just saying that," she says through her tears.

"You were as good as anyone else out there -- actually better." I try to reassure her.

"It isn't fair."

"Nor is life, Care."

"I want to win."

"So, do I."

"What should I do, Dad?"

Not being of the horsey mind set, I'm not sure what to say. "What did your mother say?"

"I'm not giving Rascal enough crop."

I have no clue what this means, so I merely tell my daughter, "try your best, Care, if you always do your best, you'll always be a winner."

Kelly comments on my comment. "That is so corny, Dad."

We move up in the line to sample the overpriced fare, it's funny how the kids leave their mother and come to see me when they're hungry.

Care asks, "Dad, what do you think of our horse?"

"He looks like he's had a lot of practice at these shows." I try to keep the sarcasm out of my tone. "A real, seasoned professional."

I look to my left and see the Judge Judy lady retrieving something from a horse trailer hooked up to an SUV that should be named The Terminator. I give Kelly a twenty, leave the line and approach the woman. "Hello," I say, "I'm Officer Sherlock. My girls are in the horse show."

"How are you?" she says suspiciously.

"My daughter's a bit disappointed. The last event she was in, the kid who got the ribbon fell off the horse and still beat her."

"That'll happen," she says, trying to busy herself with a bridle or some such thing.

I place my foot on the bumper of her trailer stopping her activity. "I see your registration is not current and the brake lights don't seem to conform to legal specifications."

"I didn't know that."

"Hate to see you get pulled over, before you get a chance to fix all that. Ticket could be as expensive as the repairs."

Judge Judy asks, "What did you say your daughter's name was?"

The afternoon events, which were scheduled to stretch far into the night, were slightly different than the morning's marches. Three, two-foot jumps were placed on the path, and the riders would have to maneuver over the obstacles both to and fro. At the speed the horses travelled, this could hardly be called a jump, more like a step up.

It seems a bit inconceivable to me that a fifty-pound girl would have the strength to get a twelve-hundred-pound horse to jump. There must be a lot of faith within show jumping.

It is the same series of eight horses in a row, with Judge Judy in charge of picking the winners and losers. Over and over and over, one flight is as slow and plodding as the last. The excitement being generated would challenge anyone with a weak heart.

Care's first flight goes on a little after 2 pm. She's tentative, a bit unsure of herself, and barely slaps the horse with her black riding whip, sending Rascal over the jumps with the enthusiasm of a criminal returning to solitary confinement. The event, which lasts less than two minutes, takes about as much athletic ability as drinking a beer at a Cub game. I can see no difference between the riders.

A few minutes after the event ends, the announcement is made: "And the blue ribbon goes to Carolyn Sherlock."

I see my youngest daughter jump for joy into the arms of her mother. I promise myself I will wait at least twenty years before, or if ever, I tell her the truth.

"Mister Sherlock..."

I hear, and a few seconds later feel a tap on my shoulder. "Mister Sherlock."

"Tiffany."

"Hi."

"What are you doing here?"

"Somebody tried to kill Brewster."

"Who?"

"I don't know."

"When?"

"An hour ago."

"Why didn't you call me?"

"I did," she says. "You must have turned your phone off."

"Oh yeah," I say. "They ask you to do that so you don't spook the horses."

I get up out of my chair. "I got to say goodbye to my girls."

"Say hello for me, would you?" Tiffany sees the girls across a well-traveled horse path. "I'm not risking six-hundred-dollar Manolos with this much horseshit lying around."

"I can't say I blame you."

I make my way over to the girls who stand with their mother. "Congratulations, Care. Told you if you just did your best it would all work out."

"I won; I won." Care shows me her ribbon.

"I'm proud of you."

Her mother clears her throat to get my attention.

I don't give it to her. "Girls, I have to go."

"Why, Dad?" Kelly asks.

"One of my clients just got shot."

"Can I come?" Kelly asks.

"No."

"Why not?"

"Because you're in the middle of this exhilarating and exciting competition."

"I'd rather see somebody bleeding."

I give the girls each a kiss and almost get away; but I hear my ex say, "the babies still need shoes."

"And their mother needs priorities."

She says, "See me now or see me later."

I ignore the orange-level threat. "You girls do your best, sorry I got to go. Love ya."

I give last hugs and walk off toward where Tiffany waits. I hear in the background, "Is that your dad's girlfriend?"

——

"This is the third Saturday in a row I've had to work, Sherlock," Norbert informs me as I arrive. "I hate that."

"Where's the victim?"

"Inside. The boy's still shaking."

The police techs are once again out and about in Alvin's back forty. It has got to be easier for them this time, since it is a return appearance.

"How many shots?"

"He remembers four," Norbert says, "so I'm figuring maybe two."

"Pull any slugs?"

"Two from the garage wall."

"A foot or two above his head?" I ask.

"How'd you know?"

"I'm smart."

Tiffany follows as I walk off into the wooded border of the property, which would be the line of sight to the back of the garage.

"What was little Brewster doing out here?" I ask my assistant.

224

"Taking out the trash."

"Brewster does chores?"

"Theresa's day off."

"Hector's probably busy shooting a few of his own bullets."

I move into the bushes, see exactly where the shooter stood. "Tell the techs to search here for shell casings, although they won't find any."

"Mister Sherlock, you're beginning to sound like me."

Tiffany's right, I better start thinking before I speak.

"Are we going to walk all over the lawn like we did last time?" She asks with definite lack of enthusiasm.

"Nay, nay," I sound like I'm still at the horse show.

Tiffany and I go inside.

Brewster sits uncomfortably on the uncomfortable couch. His feet are up on a chair from the dining room set, saving the glass coffee table a smudge. He has an icepack on his forehead, his skin color is bright white, and the wet spot on the front of his pants is nearly dry.

"Fun day, Brewster?" I ask.

"He could have been killed out there." Doris interjects. "Where is the police protection in this town?"

Norbert shrugs his shoulders.

"This is a conspiracy against my family," she yells at poor Norbert. "I could be next."

A certain selfish element always seems to surface in the Augustus family at the most inappropriate times.

"Did you see him, Brewster?" I ask.

"Of course, he didn't see him," Doris says. "The killer was laying in wait."

"That's amazing," I say.

"What?" Doris continues to yell.

I focus on the boy. "I didn't see your lips move once when you said that, Brewster."

Brewster moans.

"Your attitude, with my son's life hanging in the balance, leaves much to be desired, Mister Sherlock."

"By the way, Missus Augustus, any progress on my retainer?"

"I'd be more than happy to pay, but a certain little chickie won't release my money."

Tiffany smiles and says, "That would be me."

I sit on the couch next to Brewster. "Almost enough to get you to give up drinking?" I ask before I see an open can of beer tucked between cushion and his thigh.

"It isn't funny," he tells me.

"What happened?"

"I'm walking back toward the house and all of a sudden this machine gun opens fire. I hit the ground, cover my head and crawl to cover while the bullets fly around me like I'm in the middle of some Middle-East war."

"They only found two slugs in the wall," I inform him.

"Tell them to look harder," he orders me.

"Do you usually take out the trash?"

"No."

"Mom ask you?"

"What the hell kind of question is that?" Doris asks.

"Good one, I hope."

"Somebody just tried to kill me, Sherlock," Brewster says.

Tiffany interrupts, "Excuse me, but did you see your whole life pass before your very eyes when it happened?"

The question stops everyone cold.

"I saw this TV show about near-death experiences and I wondered if one happened to you?" she asks.

"No."

"Darn."

I ask, "Why would anyone want to kill you, Brewster?"

"I told you," Doris answers. "It is a conspiracy."

"Damn, if your lips didn't move again, Brewster."

"To get my portion of the twelve million, why else?" Brewster says.

"So it would have to be one of the people on the money list? Three of which are related to you."

"I was in the kitchen when it happened," Doris tosses in.

"Congratulations, Doris," Tiffany says, "you're off the hook."

"That brings the total down to two." I conclude. "Which one should we send Norbert out to arrest?"

"The one who did it," Brewster says.

"Norbert will get right on it."

"No problem," Norbert says.

I get up and off the couch. "Sorry to leave you in such a state, but we have a stop to make on the South Side before it gets too dark."

I wonder if the comment will get a rise out of Doris, but the best she does is blink twice, which is hard to constitute as a reaction since her face is rock solid.

———

The traffic is light going down the expressway. Tiffany has question after question.

"Did somebody really try to kill Brewster?"

"I doubt it."

"Then why did he get shot at?"

"I don't know."

"Did it have anything to do with him getting busted for dope?"

"I doubt it."

"Maybe drug dealers scaring him into paying up?"

"Tiffany, you watch too much TV."

We arrive at Clarence's house in an hour. My little friend must be busy with some other type of illicit activity, because he doesn't run up to the car with his hand out for cash.

"I'll be right back."

"You're going to leave me here in the car, all alone in this neighborhood?"

"Yes."

"How can you do that, Mister Sherlock?"

"What would you rather do, talk to a guy who has killed hundreds of people? Or stay here and listen to the radio?"

"Don't be long, okay?"

Clarence peers out the corner of the thick blanket he has covering the front windows before he opens the door.

"What?"

"I came to pay back a favor," I say as he unlatches the heavy chain lock on the door.

I step inside. The Sox are on his big TV. They're losing eleven to four in the sixth.

"You get hundred dollar bills for your last gig?"

Clarence gives me an odd look. It is as good as an answer.

"Careful where you spend them."

"Why's that?"

"I'm not positive; but if they are out of a certain stack, the serial numbers are on watch. Anybody laying down two or three in a bank is going to be pulled in for questioning."

Clarence, aka Preston Bird, contemplates the problem. "Sure wouldn't like that."

"They're warm and getting warmer." I pause and give some advice. "And if you got a place to go, it wouldn't be a bad time for a vacation."

Clarence watches the third out of the inning, "Thanks."

I turn to leave. "You missed twice?"

"Don't tell anyone, bizness bad enough."

26
You'd be surprised, it happens

"She likes me, Sherlock."
"Herman, she's gay."
"Yeah, but I bet I could turn her."
I hang my head and shake it slowly back and forth, pretending I didn't hear what I just heard.
"Did you figure out where all Christina's money went?"
"No and never will."
"Why not?"
"Because whoever stole it, got her password; and once you got a password, it's pretty much lights out."
"Did you tell her?"
"Not yet," Herman says as he pulls on a number of his double chins. "I figure she's good for a couple more visits to my place before I have to come clean."
"Interesting choice of terms, Herman."
"I need a little more time than most guys to show her my suave side."
"And your review of Agent Romo Simpson?"
"One star. The boy has no second act."
"Did he give you the stuff on Alvin?"
"It's over there." Herman points to a stack of papers a foot high, resting on his couch. "I asked him to score me some of that FBI confiscated porn."
"Good for you, Herman."
"Told him I was working an alternate angle on the case."
"You figure out how Alvin scammed the Board yet?"
"I'm not sure he did."
"Herman..."
"I can't find any trades, especially losers, although his account at First Options was in arrears." Herman pauses. "Sounds gay doesn't it?"
"What sounds gay?"

"Arrears."

"You going to figure out how he did it?"

"If I can."

I take out one sheet of paper from my coat pocket. "I got one more guy for you to run numbers on."

"What do I look like, a laptop?"

"No, you look like a walrus with a three-day beard."

"You don't have to be mean." Herman reads what I wrote on the paper, "Horace Heffelfinger?"

"I know he was skimming, find out how much."

"How did you get his social security number?"

"I stole it when I went through his desk."

"What a guy." Herman's face scrunches a tiny bit; he leans his body to the left, resting his bulk on one butt cheek, and emits a long stream of thunderous, undiluted flatulence.

"I love pigs in a blanket, but they don't love me."

———

I never worked vice. I avoided it like the plague. It is the purgatory of a police department.

Vice cops have the most difficult job of any detective on the force, because they not only have to catch the bad guys and girls, but have to decide what's bad enough to be considered a crime. This is much more difficult than it seems, because cops have feelings, too.

Some poor sucker wants an hour of escape from his lousy life, so he books a hooker who is more than willing to help him relieve a very human pressure. A couple of hundred bucks are exchanged; the deed is done in less than an hour. Everybody leaves happy, but the vice cop's job is to bust all involved.

What's the point? If the cop does his job, the poor jerk gets busted, hauled in, mug shots are taken, and from that point on he is vilified as a degenerate. The hooker gets tossed in the clink for a few hours, is bailed out, goes in front of the judge, promises not to do it again, and is forced to come up with a viable excuse to reschedule her regulars. It's pointless.

If it was up to me, prostitution would be: "Don't ask, don't tell." Heck, if it works for gays in the military, how can it not work for horny guys and willing women? Or make it legal like liquor, cigarettes, and state lotteries that ruin lives -- and tax it to the max, although it might be difficult securing the tax dollars.

Jonas, the CPD detective has set me up with Ernie Shevers, one of the more seasoned vice cops on the street.

"You ever get the urge, Ernie?" I ask as we enter the lobby of Chicago's famous Hancock Building.

"Oh, sure. Some of these women are past gorgeous."

Ernie is mid-forties, hair thinning, muscles sagging, body mass relocating from chest to stomach. He flashes his badge at the doorman and we are buzzed through the glass door to the elevator bank.

People assume that Chicago's second-tallest building is a mass of offices for an insurance company. Not true. The basement and first couple floors are restaurants and retail, then forty floors of ad agencies, real estate firms, lawyers, and whatever. The forty-fifth floor is the concierge floor complete with party room for rent and the most expensive grocery store on the planet, nine dollars for a can of peanuts. There is also a health club, pool, and a lobby where the wealthy tenants hang out when they have nothing better to do, which for a lot of them is most of the time. The next forty-nine floors are overpriced condominiums until the Ninety-Fifth Floor restaurant. On floor number ninety-six is the observation deck where "you can see three states on a clear day." If you want to avoid paying the price of observatory entrance, merely go to the bar at the Ninety-Fifth and buy a couple of drinks; the view comes along free of charge.

"Business has changed a lot in the last few years," Ernie tells me on the way upward. "Used to be down-on-their-luck girls trying to make a few bucks, but now they're the college sweethearts who can make five grand a weekend, and spend the rest of the week working on their acting skills or their tans."

"And this is a good thing?" I ask.

"Girls don't consider sex sacred anymore. With all the porn and skin out there, you can see why."

I immediately think of my daughters and say a silent prayer.

We get off on the eighty-seventh floor. "Nick's not a bad guy, he pays his taxes."

Ernie knocks on 8713. It takes a while, but the door opens.

"This is a surprise," Nick says.

"Surprise is part of my job." Ernie enters without being asked. "Nick, meet Sherlock."

We shake hands. He is not what I expected.

Nick eyes me suspiciously. "We talk before?"

"I'm only human."

"I thought so."

Nick is a dolt, the kind of guy who never had a date in high school and hasn't had too many more since. He's maybe five-nine, twenty pounds too many, acne scars, no wedding ring, maybe forty, but could pass for fifty. A headset, with the wire that plugs into a computer/phone system dangles down his left side.

The telephone rings in the room down the hall. "Got to get this," he says and we follow him into a second bedroom, converted office. "Check-in time."

The view is straight south; I can see smoke rising from the U.S. Steel stacks in Gary.

Nick plugs his cord into the port on his computer/phone terminal. "He showed up?" Pause. "Relax, he's harmless," Nick speaks into the headset. "And get the money up-front." He pauses, "And no second cups of coffee without another two hundred." Nick clicks off the connection.

Ernie and I sit on a couch behind Nick's desk and computer screen and wait until he turns back around.

"New girl?" Ernie asks.

"You wouldn't think a porn star would get nervous," he says.

"Who is she?" Ernie asks.

"Melinda Bad Manners."

I make a note to ask Herman for a review of the starlet.

Nick leans back, crosses one leg over the other. "I have a feeling this isn't a social call."

"My friend Sherlock needs a little information on a couple of your girls."

"Do I have a choice?" Nick asks.

"No," Ernie answers.

"Diane and Alexis," I say.

"She's a pain in the ass," is Nick's immediate reaction.

"Which one?"

"My ass."

"Which girl?"

"Diane. She's constantly late, complains about the quality of the men, only wants to work days, and has more periods than a short story."

"And Alexis?"

"She's not as bad, but she's learning from Diane." Nick sees a call come in on his computer screen, but doesn't answer.

"Real names?"

"Those are trade secrets in my business."

"Make an exception, Nick," Ernie says.

Nick pulls up a different screen on the computer. "Clair Elise Robbins of Elkhart, Indiana, and Donna Epson of Downers Grove, Illinois."

"Hometown girls?"

"Good solid, Midwestern stock," Nick says. "Alexis is always worried she's going to have to do some guy who sits in front of her in church."

I give him a skeptical look.

"You'd be surprised, it happens."

"And when it does?"

"The guy usually can't wait to come back for more."

"How long they been working for you?"

"Diane's been here over two years; Alexis, maybe a year. I'm sure both were in the business before me."

"They do well?"

"They'd do better if they'd quit complaining and just lie down and do their job."

I lean toward the screen and write down the information. "These really their social security numbers?"

"I report them as independent contractors, so I really don't care." Nick says. "No offense, Ernie, but the IRS is scarier than you."

"No offense taken."

"These girls ever freelance?"

"They're not supposed to," Nick says, then asks, "You know something I don't?"

"Hope so," I say, then ask, "Was Alvin Augustus a client of yours?"

233

"Come on, guys, let's not play that game."

"He's dead," I tell him. "He won't care, anymore."

Nick takes a deep breath. "Was."

"And his boys?"

Ernie gives me an odd look.

"Sons," I say, a little better put.

"Was."

"When did they quit?"

"About six months ago," Nick says. "I was sorry to see them go."

I finish copying down the information on the screen. "One more question."

Nick waits.

"Did either of them go out on a job the night before Alvin died?"

"Friday, the eighteenth," Ernie says.

Nick pulls up the calendar on the computer. "Diane was off, big surprise, but Alexis had two calls."

"Alvin's?"

"No."

"Thanks."

Ernie is up out of his chair.

"You like your job?" I ask for the hell of it, as his phone rings.

"Believe it or not, it's lonely sitting up here in the clouds all day, hooking people up."

"Then why do you do it?"

"I have a strong aversion to real work."

———

Norbert, Steve, Jonas, and I sit in the back booth of the Red Lion Pub on Lincoln. It is a Monday night. Colin, the Irish owner, stocks a case of Guinness in the cooler and Jose, the Mexican cook, removes a box of sausages from the freezer. There are a few regulars at the bar, sipping light beers. Except for the London phone booth and the greasy bangers and mash, the place is refreshingly Chicago, with the Cubs on TV and photos of the two Daley mayors adorning the walls.

Tiffany joins us late, wearing a pair of latex gloves, carrying an office trash can, desk lamp, and computer keyboard. "Here," she says, laying the bounty on the table.

"Scavenger hunt?" Norbert asks.

"I hid in the hallway until the cleaning lady went into the other office, and made my move. A good set of prints has to be on something here."

"Whose?" Jonas asks.

"Lizzy."

"Christina's partner," I explain.

"Why?"

"Lizzy isn't a Lizzy and maybe not a lesbian," I tell the Chicago detective.

"Which way are you leaning?" Jonas asks.

"Straight."

"They didn't look too straight at the funeral."

"Yeah, but Tiffany's gaydar didn't go up when we talked to her, so Lizzy's maybe a lesbian in name only."

"You know you're right, Mister Sherlock," Tiffany says. "I didn't get all weirded out when I met her."

"Voilá."

Colin comes over to take our order, breaking the conversation. When he finishes it seems like a good time to play: Who do you think did it?

Norbert goes first. "The last wife, Doris, she had the most to lose."

"Heffelfinger, the accountant," Steve says.

"I'm still with Brewster," Tiffany says and adds her reasoning, "Them momma's boys are always a little screwed up."

I finish up the round. "I have no clue."

"We're no farther along than we were the day we found Alvin's body." Steve makes the point for all.

"I hate that," Jonas says.

Statistically, if a crime isn't solved in the first seventy-two hours, the odds against success skyrocket, as well as the amount of time that is going to be put in to bring it all to a conclusion. The three detectives have no desire to work this case the rest of their careers.

"Can't put the puzzle together until you have all the pieces," I say.

"What's missing?" Our Chicago colleague plays a good devil's advocate.

"Plenty."

Jonas takes out his list. "The two wall safes in the condo were empty, nothing on the murder weapon used to kill Joey Villano, the trader who worked for Alvin. The condo was too trashed to give us anything good, and no money trail yet to speak of."

"Maybe it wasn't about money." Norbert is thinking out of his usual realm of thinking.

"That much money," Steve says, "it is always about money."

"Then where is it?"

"According to Heffelfinger, the accountant, Alvin was making bad trades, lousy investments, throwing money down a sink hole," Steve answers.

"Maybe it was a mercy-killing; do him in before he does himself in?" Norbert surmises.

"Or maybe they were trying to stop him before he lost it all?" I ask.

"Maybe he's not dead?" Tiffany perks up to say. "He faked his own death?"

"Remember, we found the body?"

"Oh, yeah," Tiffany remembers now. "I saw this movie on cable about a guy who did that."

Colin brings over plates of greasy food and refills of beers. We dig in with gusto. Tiffany abstains.

"What else do you know that we don't know, Sherlock?" Steve asks, being his usual self.

No matter what I say, it won't matter because Tiffany's reaction to the question is unmistakable.

"I've told you everything."

"How dumb do you think we are?" Norbert says.

I try to get out of my own lie. "The only thing I'm sure of, is that whoever wanted Alvin dead wasn't taking any chances. Shoot him, blow him to kingdom come or stone him, they were going to get him one way or another, either by doing it themselves or hiring out. You would believe it was all carefully planned out; but the act of destruction sure doesn't point in that direction. And what was he doing the night before? Why kill him at home, and why take

Joey, the junior trader, down with him? Too much of it doesn't make sense. And where the hell is the money?"

"Hopefully in your pocket, Sherlock." Norbert passes me the bill.

"You're holding back, Sherlock," Steve says.

"I don't have it all straight in my head, yet. When I do, I promise, you'll be the first to know." I hand the bill to Tiffany.

The three detectives stare at me while Tiffany asks, "What happened to chivalry?"

"You women want to be equal," Steve says, "this is where it starts."

27
Like Prada on a purse

The envelope comes in, addressed by name to the detective in charge. The person opening the mail sees it has no return address. The handwriting is odd, and the stationery is as common as can be. Ah-ha, the mail-opener realizes, an important clue in the big case!

All parties go into evidence mode: Handle the envelope only by its corner, don a pair of latex gloves. Then with painstaking skill, slit the piece open and peer inside to see the one folded page. Yes, it must be an IMPORTANT key to the case. Pull the letter from its envelope with a tweezers and unfold, without a foreign finger or substance contaminating the evidence. Lay it upon an inert blotter, free from any disruptive chemical or agent. Hold breath as you examine. Search for smudges, ink types, or paper fibers that can be traced back to the store where purchased or the pulp manufacturer. Use a magnifying glass to discover any typed letters where the strike key may be off center, chipped, or out of proper ink; so the typewriter can be found and linked for a positive identification. Use a camera of quality and take photos from every conceivable angle. Then the detective in charge orders the evidence techs to proceed in a full investigation.

Unfortunately, this never happens. Never.

Mail comes into a police station like it does to any business. Whoever sits at the spot where the mailman drops it off, rifles through the stack, separating the magazines, and tossing out the circulars, post cards, promises of a once-in-a-lifetime deal on carpet cleaning, and oversized ads for twenty percent off at Bed Bath and Beyond. The remaining mail, which is probably merely more cleverly designed junk, is put on a pile to be opened whenever time permits. Then, when the low person on the totem pole finally gets around to the stack, more pieces hit the circular file; and the remaining envelopes and whatever are sorted by addressee and slipped into the cubbyhole mail slots of the folks who work the precinct. Why should it be any different in a police station than at any other home or business in America?

In this case the letter, addressed to "Steve Burrell, Detective," isn't noticed as being odd, even though it is first class mail; and who gets first class mail anymore that isn't a bill? The handwritten envelope sits in Steve's in-box for two days. By the time Steve gets around to ripping it open, it has been manhandled by the desk sergeant, two secretaries, the cleaning people, and patrolman Timmy Badau, who constantly pulls the mail from the wrong slot.

Too bad. The letter is a confession to the crime.

Except for two spelling mistakes and one misplaced comma, the letter is very well written. It begins with: *I can no longer live with myself. I am the person responsible for the death of Alvin J. Augustus.* It continues, noting how Alvin swindled him out of his business, savings, house and car. It goes on about his wife leaving him, kids refusing to speak, parents being heartbroken, blah, blah, blah. It was very touching. If it was a woman writing, it could have been the basis for one of those Lifetime TV *I Hate Men* movies.

The best part of the correspondence, by far, was the explanation of how the deed was done. It described how Alvin was lured into a rock garden he personally help design; and met his death by being forced to watch a wall of stones fall upon him and crush him like the "vermin he had become."

Not only was it all bullshit, it was bad bullshit.

In almost any murder case, there is bound to be one, two, or twenty nuts out there who will confess to the crime. The bigger the case, the bigger the confession pile. It is my theory that the confessors are only trying to spice up their lives after days of working the grill at Burger King, or picking up trash alongside the expressway.

In a high-profile case like Alvin's, phone calls, letters, personal notes, untraceable emails and text messages always come in, confessing to the crime. Detectives hate them because each has to be checked out, a boring, pointless, time-consuming waste of manpower and energy.

The rule of thumb is: Whomever the mail is addressed to, it is that person's responsibility to check it out. Steve isn't happy about it. He stops by my apartment on his way downtown. "I hate these things."

I read it quickly. "I like this," was my initial reaction.

The reason this confession was of particular interest was that it was sent to Kenilworth, where there is only one station house, and postmarked 60601, which is the zip code of the Board of Trade. Confessors might be loons; but no self-respecting self-incriminator would ever send it from anywhere close to where he lived or worked. Or be dumb enough to mention something that wasn't in the papers or on the news.

"Whoever wrote this had something to do with the murder."

"The reference to body position?" Steve asks.

"And the timing of the delivery."

Confession letters usually arrive while the body is still warm; maybe there is a contest among confessors of who can be first. This one was postmarked a week after he was charbroiled.

"Sent to throw us off?" Steve asks.

"Pretty stupid way of going about it; wouldn't you say?"

"Stupid is what stupid does," Steve quotes Forrest Gump. "Want to tag along as I check this out?"

"Can't. Jonas called and he's got a match on Lizzy's prints."

"Come on, I'll give you a ride."

————

Steve must be mellowing, because on the way downtown he asks about my daughters, speaks of his family, and tells me of he and his wife's vacation plans, to visit his brother and family in Vermont. I can sense a bit of worry since, if the case isn't closed, he won't be able to go.

"That's the problem with buying non-refundable airline tickets."

"Tell me about it," he says.

Jonas is waiting for us and, *surprise-surprise,* Tiffany is with him.

"You were right, Mister Sherlock."

"Why should that amaze you, Tiffany?"

Jonas has a mug shot of an Amy Zebelski, aka Lizzy, taken a few years back. She has blond hair, black roots, a snarl on her lips, two piercings above her right eye, yellow teeth, and dirt on her cheek. Flattering, it's not.

Why is that people take such lousy mug shots? Of course a nobody such as Amy, aka Lizzy, doesn't count; but Mel Gibson, Gary Busey, Glen Campbell, Lindsey Lohan, and the hottie from Baywatch-people who make their living looking ravishing - all take terrible mug shots. Why don't they ask for a comb, and time in the washroom to freshen up? And why, oh why, don't they ever smile, or at the very least pose in a thoughtful and professional manner? They're actors, for Christ's sake. There is no law that says you have to frown for your mug shot. Somebody famous getting busted has to know that the next picture snapped of himself is going to hit the internet, and be seen worldwide in a matter of hours. So why don't they make the slightest effort to perk up and look good? Isn't that a part of their job?

In the interim between when Amy's mug shot was taken and when I met her as Christina's lover, her looks sure have improved. Could this mean that becoming a lesbian has agreed with her?

"She got busted in a Boston confidence game back in 02," Jonas tells us. "I got a call in to the arresting officer."

"Could you fax a copy of the picture of our mystery man? So he'll have it before you speak with him?" I ask, then explain, "I have a feeling we're going to find lovebirds."

"I'll get Norbert right on it," Steve says, dialing his cell.

"I knew she was no good," Tiffany adds.

"It's about time we started checking cell phone records, emails, and test the printers to see if we can match up." I still hate my job, but I'm more animated than I have been in weeks.

"No judge will allow that," Jonas says.

Steve asks, "Maybe we should bring Romo in to check out the phone records?"

"You want to work with him?" I ask.

"FBI's got better resources than we do in that area," Steve says.

"You must really want to take that vacation."

Steve nods.

I suggest, "Could we get Norbert to fax the picture of our guy to every motel on the Northside, so we know where to look when we need him?"

"Send a picture of Lizzy along with it. I'm sure these two

hooked up along the way." Steve adds to my idea.

"This is so exciting," Tiffany says. "What do I get to do?"

"Take this stuff back to Lizzy's office," I say.

"But how do I do that without blowing my cover?" Tiffany says she doesn't watch a lot of TV. Yeah right.

"Leave it all in a stall in the women's bathroom. Lizzy will find it sooner or later."

"Excellent idea, Mister Sherlock."

"And at five, when she's off work, I want you to follow her."

"I'll be on her like Prada on a purse."

Jonas says, "I'm seeing Joey Villano's parents this afternoon. I'll check out his bank account."

"What are you going to do, Mister Sherlock?"

"It's Tuesday, Tiffany, my kid day."

———

The instant Care gets in the car, she talks a mile-a-minute of the fact that there are only nine days before summer vacation begins. Kelly isn't so talkative. She is either in a snit, or some element of preteen life is troubling.

"What's the matter, Kel?"

"Nothing."

I cook burgers for dinner, but don't tell the girls I use half beef, half tofu, supposedly healthier than pure cow. By the time they slather it with ketchup, mustard, mayo, lettuce, onion and tomato, even a professional taste tester couldn't tell the difference.

Homework follows dinner. They do math and social studies. I rearrange the cards on the wall. They finish well before I do.

"Figure out who did it yet, Dad?"

"Nope."

For the next two hours we mix and match the cards according to suspect. Doris, Clayton, Brewster, Christina, Joan, Heffelfinger, escorts, Millie, Joey, Lizzy, "mystery man," and an "x" factor for a person yet to materialize. This is exhausting.

"Dad, we're not getting anywhere," Care says the obvious.

"Duh," I speak their language.

There is something I'm missing, an aspect that I have not

seen, a way of thinking I haven't yet tried. It is all right in front of me; I just have to arrange it so it all makes sense.

"Maybe you should figure out who couldn't do it," Care suggests.

"And work backwards," Kelly adds.

I sit at a loss for words.

"Just trying to help," Care says, noticing my funk.

"And I appreciate that."

I put the girls to bed without a story. I call Tiffany, wake her up. She is parked outside Christina's condo where Lizzy went right after work. "Go home," I tell her. She doesn't argue.

I call Steve next. Nothing new from him and he tells me nothing new from Norbert either. Jonas tells me that the Villano family is still in shock.

I can't sleep. I place the cards back over the *Original Carlo* the way they were when the three of us entered the apartment that night. Back to square one, except for one difference. I leave a hole right after Lizzy and before the "mystery man."

"Dad," Kelly says, coming out of the bedroom.

"What's the matter?"

"I can't sleep."

"I miss my old friends," she says.

"The girls you used to sit with at lunch?"

"Yeah." She sits on the couch next to me. "The new table doesn't have as much fun."

"I hate that."

"I don't know what to do. If I leave the table I'm at now, they'll never speak to me again; and I'm not sure my old table wants me back," she pauses to yawn. "It's a conundrum."

"A lot of those going around lately."

"What should I do?"

"Well, Kel, I'm not going to tell you what to do, because you got yourself into this and you're the only one who can get yourself out."

"But that's not fair."

"Get used to the 'not fair' part of life. It'll happen a lot from this point forward." I pull her closer to me. "All I can tell you is that, when you are young, these things seem to change at a much faster rate. What happened today can be quite different tomorrow.

So, you might want to merely wait it all out. Don't forget you only have a few days left to eat lunch in the cafeteria, anyway."

"I didn't think of that."

"Don't feel bad, the obvious is often the most difficult to see."

I give my oldest a kiss, put her back in bed, come back to the *Original Carlo* and take every card down, leaving them in a big pile. I sit in front of the pile for about five minutes, then begin placing the cards back up on the painting, this time by suspect. Who could do it and who couldn't.

Three hours later I fall asleep.

28
Well, I'll be doggoned

Augie Rinaldi is the mystery man. A small-time hood, Mafia wannabe, hailing from upstate New York, his first stretch was two years for assault when he was eighteen. From there he had a number of minor infractions and short incarcerations. At twenty-six, he was convicted of running a real estate Ponzi scheme in Wooster, Massachusetts, but doing only eighteen months after he turned state's evidence against his accomplice, Amy Zebelski. This fact alone would question his quality as boyfriend material; but Amy might have known something I didn't, or maybe love does have no bounds. Reading his resume tells a cop that Augie is not the tastiest morsel in a criminal pot of stew.

The detective in Boston, Mickey Flynn (and what better name could a Boston cop have?), was kind enough to send along a one-sheet of Augie's driver licenses, all with the same picture; but with the names Paul Lennon, John McCartney, Harrison Starr, and Buddy Ringo. Two things astound me: why stores and businesses consider a driver's license proper identification, since it is probably one of the easiest documents to get; and how totally unoriginal criminals can be in choosing phony names. If I ever become a criminal, one of the first items I would steal is a "What Should We Name the Baby?" book.

Norbert finds Augie registered under the name Keith Jagger, at the I Love Chicago Motor Inn on Peterson, where Ridge and Clark meet. If not the noisiest intersection in the city, it ranks close to the top of the list. Actually, the name of the place wasn't "I Love," but "I", followed by a picture of a heart and the city's name. Augie has a ground-floor room.

Norbert kept his distance from our man, as was the plan. Steve and I meet Norbert and check into Room 135, bringing the day manager with us for a friendly chat.

While Steve snaps photos of out-of-shape Augie sunning himself by the pool, we quiz the Heart's manager. "This guy been doing anything while he's been here?"

"Not much," he says.

"Does he do her?" Norbert asks, showing him Lizzy's photo.

"Yeah, I thought she was a professional girl." The manager would be one that would know.

"How long will he be here?" I ask.

"He paid for the month."

"In cash?"

"Yeah."

"Good, that means he'll stay at least six weeks," Steve says.

"You know which car he's driving?"

The man points and Norbert writes down the license number.

"If you think he's checking out early, you call us," Steve tells the man.

"What do I get out of all this?" the manager asks.

"Our undying gratitude."

The manager is not happy. He looks like he needs sleep.

"You don't think we should pull him in now?" Steve asks.

"Trust me on this boys, there's a lot more we have to find out about Augie, before he finds out about us."

The two detectives look at each other. They agree, but not happily.

"I have a request," I tell them as we watch Augie get up out of his deck chair.

"What?"

"Would you consider exhuming a body?"

"Alvin was cremated, Sherlock."

"Another body."

"Joey Villano's?"

"Not Joey."

"Who, then?" Steve asks.

"Lucy."

"Arnaz?"

"No."

Norbert is perplexed. "Sherlock what the hell are you up to?"

"I'm just trying to help Steve's vacation plans."

Steve turns to me. "Where do you want me to start digging?"

We watch Augie wade into the pool, but hold onto the side as he makes his way to the deep end. Augie can't swim.

"I only need a few more cards on my wall and I'll be ready to rock and roll."

"You sure, Sherlock?"

Every case I've ever worked on has a lightbulb. When it pops on, the light hits you in the face like a prison searchlight.

"There are only a few more aspects that have to be checked out."

"What do you need?" Steve asks.

"I need the help of the detective in Boston."

"Jonas can set that up."

"I need Alvin's financials from his account at Northern Trust."

"Why?"

"Mister P. Carrington Vogel is holding back and I got to find out why."

"Pace is picking up," Norbert says. "I like that."

"Music to my ears," Steve adds.

"Give a criminal enough rope and he will invariably figure out a way to hang himself," I tell the boys, "time to prepare the gallows."

————

Tiffany meets me at my apartment and we pull up EscortsRus.com on my computer.

"I bet I could make a lot of money if I were an escort, Mister Sherlock."

"Yeah, but you'd have to have sex with guys like Alvin."

"Oh, gross," she says.

"And Herman."

"Oh my God, I'd rather die."

I scroll down to Diane and Alexis' pictures. "I need you to pull these two photos off, print up the head shots and take them around to every bartender in town until one recognizes a love connection."

"Why?"

"Because you're so good at doing stuff like this."

"Thanks, Mister Sherlock. I love flattery."

"But first, I want you to visit Romo at the FBI, and go through the family's phone records. All you have to do is find the ones with the 617 area code and report those back to me."

"Maybe while I'm there I can get one of those baseball caps with "FBI" on the front."

"Why would you want one of those?" I ask. "If you run into a criminal and he sees the hat, you'd be the first on his list to shoot."

"I didn't think of that."

"You'd be better off wearing one that said CRIMINAL on the front."

"Then wouldn't the cops want to shoot me?"

"Cops don't shoot pretty girls, they harass them."

While we speak, Tiffany figures out she can't print the photos on my crummy printer. "I'll have to do this at home."

"That's okay; you're going to need a nap since you'll be working late tonight."

"I'm not sure I can sleep. I mean I can feel the energy of the case bubbling to the surface."

"Well, if you want to tag along, I'm going to see Herman."

Tiffany yawns. "Maybe you're right. A little nappy-poo would do wonders."

———

I call Herman before I show up to be sure his butt is in gear when I arrive.

"What have you found out?"

"Not only has he been skimming Alvin's account for years, he's had help."

"Little Miss Millie?"

"She'd be the logical Target Team Member."

"How'd they do it?"

"When all the trading chits are tallied each day, they merely take a few for themselves."

"Alvin didn't see?"

"He's too busy jumping up and down on the floor to remember every time he makes a bet."

It makes sense. Heffelfinger didn't go out of town to find Alvin's money; he went to visit his. And, maybe Millie isn't moving in with her sister in Florida; but traveling farther South to live out her days with Heffy in the splendor of some South American posh resort.

"There are a few more aspects of the case that I want you to figure out, Herman."

"More?"

"Don't worry, I'm almost done."

"You're leaving me with a lot of porn to catch up on, Sherlock."

I give him his own to-do list to do.

Next stop, I meet Jonas at Joey Villano's parents' house. Parked in the front with a FOR SALE sign is a new Pontiac Grand Am.

"I've seen enough."

"You drag me all the way out and we don't even go inside? What fun is that?" Jonas asks.

"Want some fun?" I ask him. "I'll take you someplace for some fun."

Jonas is too good of a detective, not to take my bait.

We head north to Kenilworth.

Mrs. Coulter is not too thrilled having her backyard dug up for a second time; but Steve was smart enough to arrange it during school hours.

"We're digging up a dog?" Jonas asks.

"Yep."

The bag containing Lucy's remains stinks to high heaven when the unlucky Peter Patrolman pulls it out of the ground.

"Whew!"

"Want it back?" I ask the Missus.

"Ah," she says, speaking through her handkerchief, pushed against her nose and mouth. "You keep her. We're good."

"It'll never get back to New Trier High School, I promise."

"Super."

The bag containing the remains is placed in another, more airtight bag, and loaded into the trunk of Norbert's car. "This all better pay off, Sherlock, or you're going to owe me a month of lunches," Norbert says after rethinking his dinner plans.

We leave patrolman Peter to fill in the hole.

———

My cell phone sings "Breakaway." I answer and take down the phone numbers Tiffany found with Romo.

"You did good," I tell her. "Now get out there this weekend and drink enough martinis to make us both proud."

"Will do, Mister Sherlock, will do."

I dial the reverse directory for area code 617, discover exactly what I expected. Jonas and I call Mickey, the Boston detective. We have a nice chat. He is more than helpful.

———

I catch Conway Waddy before he leaves for the day.

"Time to untie the purse strings," I tell him.

"About time," he says. "I need my fee."

"But there is one more person who should be in on the festivities." I give him a paper with the name, address, and phone number. I also hand over what is left of the four hundred dollars Tiffany withdrew for my escort foray. "All you'll have to say is that you're handling Alvin's estate and there is something here waiting for her."

"This is all news to me," Conway says, hiking up his pants.

———

Later, the entire team meets at Barleycorn's in Lincoln Park for beer and burgers. We take a table in the back, away from the Friday night dinner crowd.

It is time I held court for my comrades.

I get a mind-eye Polaroid of the *Original Carlo*, filled with index cards; and recite one by one every conceivable aspect of the case. I hold back Bennie, Clarence's real name, and the boys in the caddie at Leon's, but I leave no card unturned. I review my thoughts on the murder scene, Alvin's last night, the scam at the Board, accountants, Doris, Joan, Clayton, Brewster, Christina,

250

friends and foes, the whys, wherefores, what has gone down, and what I think will go down soon. They go through three pitchers of beer while I pour out my thoughts. They have questions, lots of questions. I can't answer all, but I answer enough. I can see it in their faces. It all makes sense. By the time the burgers arrive, all at the table have heard everything I know, and all I suspect.

Steve is feeling better about his vacation plans.

After dinner they take out their notepads. I rattle off one duty after another. By the time dessert arrives, each has a to-do list that will eat up most of their weekend. No one complains.

My final bit of information is that the Augustus Family Reunion is scheduled for Monday 11 am in Conway Waddy's conference room.

———

It is late Friday night, and I'm tired. I have a list of stuff to get done this weekend. My back is starting to hurt and I can't wait to get inside and go to bed.

"Excuse me." A man steps out of the shadows and approaches me.

Instinctively, I go for my gun, but I'm not wearing one.

"Are you Sherlock?"

My lousy life passes before my eyes, as his hand goes into his coat pocket.

"No, don't please," I beg. "I got kids."

"I know that," he says, and pulls out two sheets of paper. "Here." He pushes the papers into my hand. "You've been served."

"Oh, no, please, not now."

"Sorry, buddy, only doing my job." The man walks away slowly. "I've been trying to find you for three days."

I read the first paragraph, which is all I need to read.

My ex-wife is taking me back to court, under an emergency order, to get more money.

Timing in life is everything.

29
Order up a paddy wagon

The morning starts off with my back so stiff, you could use it as a cutting board. I crawl to the shower, hoping a combination of the ibuprofen and hot water will give me some relief.

Little, if any.

Hunched over like Quasimodo, I try to force-feed myself the most important meal of the day. I take two more pills before leaving the apartment. I've got five in me now. Getting into the Toyota is excruciating. The ride downtown fighting the traffic isn't much better.

I arrive at the Daley Center at a few minutes before nine and have to wait to get through the metal detectors. The sheriff's department has set up a display of the knives and homemade blades confiscated from people entering the building. I'm not sure what is more thought-provoking, the number, sizes, and types of weapons on display, or the absolute idiocy of the jerks who actually thought they could get through a metal detector carrying such hardware.

On the ninth floor, I find the assigned courtroom, and peer through the glass doors to see Judge June Shay, already on the bench, berating some couple. I take one step inside the room and I'm in shock.

"What are you doing here?" I shout.

The entire courtroom quiets and stares as I stand over my two daughters.

I continue, as loud, or maybe a bit louder than my last outburst. "You're not supposed to be here."

My ex, seated in the middle of the row, pretends she's never seen me before in her entire life.

"Mom wanted us here," Kelly says, embarrassed as all eyes in the courtroom focus on her.

"She said she needed moral support," Care fills in with no concern whatsoever of being on stage.

"Excuse me," Judge June says.

"Are you out of your mind?" I ask my ex-wife, ignoring the judge.

The bailiff comes out from behind the witness box and takes my arm. "Maybe you better wait outside, buddy."

"Me?" I say. "If anyone shouldn't be in this place, it's my kids. They don't need to hear any of this crap."

The bailiff grabs me a bit tighter.

"He's right," the judge speaks over all of us. "Take the children outside."

Kelly and Care exit past me. I give my ex the meanest glare I can muster, and find a seat on the other side of the room.

"If I may continue." Judge Shay gavels once, returning to the case at hand. "Mister Jones, if you don't pay support next month, you're going to jail."

"But, Judge..."

"Pay up or be shackled up." She gavels. "Next case."

"Sherlock versus Sherlock," the Court Clerk announces.

I hobble to the bench, my back somewhat better. I'm semi-Quasimodo.

"Nice to see both of you again. It seems like only yesterday." Judge Shay and I share a particular brand of caustic humor. "Let's see... what is it this time?"

"Guess, your honor," I say.

"Quiet."

My ex speaks, she knows the drill well. "I need more money to support my two girls. They're getting to be teenagers."

"Really?"

"You know how it is, your honor."

I stand, wondering if the two are going to start discussing the costs of acne medications.

"The pittance that he gives me now is barely enough to keep them in clothing. They deserve more." The ex finishes with her best hound-dog face. "They're growing up."

"How much more are you requesting?"

"Two hundred," my ex-says.

I attempt to break in. "Excuse me, judge."

"Not your turn yet, Mister Sherlock."

"They're getting to the age where they want to get out and do things. My Lord, movies are ten dollars, sports events, birthday parties, classes, camps - it all costs money."

"I know I have two of my own," Judge June says.

"And since the original judgment on the amount was made when the girls were much younger, it only seems fair that the situation should be revisited." My ex loads it on and finishes with: "And don't forget inflation. A dollar doesn't buy what it used to buy."

"Anything else?"

"No, your honor." The ex has rested her case.

The judge pages through the case file.

"My turn?" I ask.

"Not yet," the judge says. "How much was the increase the last time you were before me?" she asks my ex.

"I can't remember, but it wasn't much."

"And the time before that?"

"I don't remember."

"And the time before that?"

No answer.

Judge June turns my way. "Your turn."

I stay calm. "Ask her about the horse."

"Horse?"

"The horse she bought."

My ex butts in, "I didn't buy a horse."

"That was two guys inside a costume the girls were riding last weekend?"

"I didn't buy the horse. I'm share-boarding." My ex turns to plead before the court. "The girls needed a hobby to get their minds off the divorce. Horseback riding is very therapeutic."

"So is an afternoon walk, but a lot cheaper."

"You don't want them to have what the other kids have?"

"How many of their friends have horses?"

"All of them at the stables."

"You see the reasoning I have to deal with?"

"Enough," the judge says ending our quarrel. She pauses.

"The girls want a horse, fine. Mister Sherlock you are ordered to pay an additional two-hundred dollars."

"What?"

"For the next two months."

"I got to support a horse, too?"

Judge points her gavel at me and shuts me up. "I'm not done yet. Ms. Sherlock, if you feel a horse is that important, then you have one month to find a part-time job to pay for the animal." The gavel comes down. "And don't ever bother me with this brand of nonsense again. Next case."

Outside the courtroom, the girls rush to their mother. I hear, "Do we get to keep our horse?"

"No."

I immediately correct her answer. "You get to keep the horse if your mother wants to keep the horse."

"No, that's not it, girls," the ex says.

No matter what I say, I'm the evil guy from the glue factory coming to take their beloved pony.

This is certainly therapeutic.

I glance at the clock on the wall; I'm late. I walk to the elevator bank and call out to the girls who have turned their backs to me, "Hey."

Neither moves, but I know they're listening. "I figured out who did it."

Kelly snaps to attention, "Was it Brewster?"

"Who snuffed him, dad?" Care calls out.

Both girls run to my side. I give a double hug. "And I couldn't have figured it out without you."

"Please."

"Tell you Tuesday, I love you both."

———

I'm a half-hour late. The Augustus family reunion is in full swing.

Tiffany has done a marvelous job. The conference room is festooned with streamers, a personalized sheet cake in the middle of the table and Augustus Family tee-shirts have been passed out, although no one puts one on. Tiffany has assembled individual goodie bags, complete with soaps, matchbooks, napkins, pen and pencil sets, and multi-colored Augustus sun visors. She has the bags lined up on the back table ready to be taken home and treasured. I certainly hope she made enough so Lizzy, the three detectives, and the other special guests also have a remembrance of this happy day.

"Sorry I'm late, everybody," I announce to the crowd.

Romo and my other compatriots have brought along their weekend findings, which are stacked in the back of the room. Last night he set up a conference call so we could all talk from the comfort of our own homes.

"What the hell is this idiocy all about?" Doris is the first to shout at me.

"I figured it would be fun to get everyone together."

"I got better things to do than this," Clayton informs all.

"Clayton," I say, "this is going to be not only fun, but educational."

"I'm leaving," Brewster says, making his way to the door, which Peter Patrolman blocks and will continue to block until the party is over. Brewster returns to his mother's side.

"First of all I want to thank Conway Waddy for graciously offering up the use of his conference room. I was going to do this in Alvin's rock garden, but it wasn't cozy enough. Special thanks to Diane and Alexis for coming, they're not used to getting up this early. And, last but not least, a extra-special shout-out to my assistant Tiffany for giving the proceedings such a festive nature." I applaud.

Tiffany beams.

Horace Heffelfinger is seated at the table, Millie alongside. "You can't hold us here against our will."

"No, we can't," Steve Burrell says, "but we can arrest you for suspicion of murder. Which would you prefer?"

"And," Norbert asks, "did you have a nice time in the Caymans?"

"I wasn't in the Caymans."

"Yes, you were," Norbert says, pulling a sheet of paper from the pile he has brought.

"No, he wasn't," Millie defends her man.

"I have the flight logs, if you'd like to see them."

Millie glares at Heffelfinger.

"Plenty of time to go into all that," I say, and suggest, "Why don't you all have a seat around the table, have some punch, relax, get cozy, and I'll begin the entertainment portion of the program."

They sit where I figured they'd sit. Brewster next to Doris, Clayton next to Joan, Christina and Lizzy, Diane and Alexis, Millie and Heffelfinger. I hold court at the head of the table. The lawmen stand spread around the back of the room. Miraculously, my back no longer hurts. I clear my throat and begin.

"At first, I and my fellow detectives thought this case was about money, and in a lot of ways it is. Heck, the only reason you're all here is because Tiffany's daddy wants an end to this whole shebang."

"It is about time we get our money," Doris yells.

"Patience," Norbert says. "Patience."

"But the case is really about technology." I pause to see the expressions on Romo, Tiffany, and the detectives' faces. They each stare at me like I'm changing the script we agreed upon.

"You see, technology is creeping in on the Board of Trade. All the guys like Alvin who made fortunes jumping around waving hand signals can see their manner of business going the way of the Model T, Betamax, and Oldsmobile. Alvin knew he had to do something before the computer emptied the trading floor, so he set out on an ambitious plan.

"Some of you are of Alvin's blood, some related by marriage, so I apologize in advance for what I'm about to say; but old Alvin J. Augustus was a real jerk. I really can't blame anyone for wanting him dead. He cheated, lied, finagled, stole. The guy had more enemies than Bernie Madoff.

"Let me also preface by saying that you shouldn't feel too rotten about being a dysfunctional family. All families are dysfunctional in some way shape or form; you should see mine. But you, Alvin's immediate family, bring a whole new dimension to the term."

Norbert can't wait any longer. He reaches in and cuts the first piece of cake, a corner with the most frosting, scoops it onto a paper plate, grabs a plastic fork, and digs in.

"The first step in Alvin's plan is to move off the floor into his upstairs offices, staffed by Mister Heffelfinger and Millie, who immediately hate having Alvin around all day. Right?"

Millie nods her head.

"Alvin tries to trade via computer and he's awful. It's not the same as being on the floor, elbowing and out-shouting the little guys. He tries bringing in clerks to trade on the computer for him, but that's a disaster. What Alvin can't do from his upstairs offices, that he could do on the floor, was cheat. No more listening in, ripping up chits, lying, getting insider information. He hated it. He's losing millions, so he decides to change tactics a bit.

"Alvin has a huge pile of cash, which he rolls forward one year to the next to avoid paying taxes on it." I see Heffelfinger stare at the desk before him. "In Alvin's mind the worst thing that can happen is to have the government come in and take its share, so he decides to lose the money by investing. He'll write off his losses against his gains and come out way ahead by paying hardly any taxes. His first investment is Clayton's company, Incubate Inc., which was great for number-two son who takes most of daddy's money and invests it in himself. Clothes, cars, townhouse, women, drugs, booze, gambling. The rest you merely wasted, eh, Clayton?"

"That's not true," Clayton defends himself.

"Son number one, Brewster, gets his dad's investment dollars in the form of a seat on the Board, where he maintains an unprecedented losing streak. Brewster inherited certain qualities from his dad, but not his daddy's trading genes."

"I could have been great, if he would have left me alone," Brewster says unconvincingly.

Doris gives Brewster her second dirty look of the day.

"Millie and Mister Heffelfinger watch as money goes out the door like French fries at McDonald's. This is especially galling since Horace has been skimming money off Alvin and sinking it into a retirement fund for himself and Millie. At least that's what he tells Millie to assure her silence in the matter."

"You can't prove that," Heffelfinger snaps at me.

"I probably won't have to," I tell him, "and who really cares anyway at this point?"

"Alvin is smart. He pre-pays his next year's IRS taxes, based on last year's earnings. Smart move, for this will give him time to begin the second phase of his plan. And here's where Alvin gets really clever. He begins doing business with the NIVLA Corporation, located a few floors above him in the Board of Trade building. Alvin might be a genius when it comes to money, but he's lousy at creating company names, since NIVLA is Alvin spelled backwards."

"I should have seen that," Tiffany blurts out, as she slaps her forehead.

NIVLA becomes Alvin's personal, impenetrable piggy bank, created to be the recipient of Alvin's biggest losses. He needs this company not only to cheat the government, but to put a stop to his wife spending him blind, his sons milking him dry, and his accountants siphoning dollars off the top. NIVLA is going to put a stop to all of it, plus cheat the IRS. Brilliant."

Jonas, Steve, Romo, and Norbert watch the eyes of the seated shoot from one to another as if they were watching rats scurry around the room. To say the least, I have their complete and undivided attention.

"With the help of computer whiz, Joey Villano, Alvin begins losing and NIVLA begins winning. What he did was so simple, it's scary. Thank God, my friend Herman is as sneaky as Alvin, because it was so obvious, no one would have ever seen it. He fakes trades. He records one loss after another on his books, transfers the dollar amount of those losses, not through the Board, but straight into NIVLA. Millie and Horace are suddenly kept in total darkness as to what's going on, thanks to Joey.

"Panic sets in. There has got to be some way of stopping the money flying out the door. Besides Heffelfinger and Millie, I'm not sure who is in on the scam at this time; but one of you places an anonymous call to the FBI that a major trading swindle is taking place. The person who placed this call knows an investigation will stop all activity immediately." I ask Heffelfinger, "Did you call or was it Millie?"

"This is ridiculous." Heffelfinger harrumphs.

"If you have not had the pleasure of meeting FBI Agent Romo Simpson, who was assigned to the case, please make it a point to say 'hello.'"

Romo stands and waves at the assembled.

"Meanwhile, back at the ranch, wife Doris is happily spending her husband's money, until she gets a call from Heffelfinger, informing her that she has been taken off the payroll, credit card accounts, and joint checking. Pair this with Alvin hinting around that a divorce is in the offing; Doris is hardly a happy camper."

"I don't know what you are talking about," she says. "We were happily married. Why would he want a divorce?"

I answer, "Ask his other wives."

I continue, "Alvin has begun the third phase of his nifty little plan, which is to turn everything he has into cash, even his personal losses. He begins with Clayton, by withdrawing from Incubus' account, making it difficult for son number two to do business or to spend any more money himself. Clayton, I can't blame you for being mad at daddy scarfing up the cash; but, come on, you had been cooking your own books and daddy's turnabout was only fair play."

Clayton sits, tries to play it cool, but he's past the point of fooling anyone.

"Clayton confides in his mother, who has been the recipient of the cooked books for years; and Joan panics."

The second Mrs. Augustus sits perfectly still and doesn't say a word.

I move over and stand over Joan. "Joan here got royally screwed in her divorce from Alvin. Hey, Joan," I tell her, "I know the feeling." I speak to the assembled. "Joan, who grew up a nice Italian girl on the west side, is livid. She saw what Alvin did to her and can imagine what he'll do to his own son. She has to do something, but she's not sure what." I pause, leave Joan's side. "But back to you in a minute, Joan."

I wink at Tiffany and continue. "At this point, Alvin gets a visit from Agent Romo, who tells him to come clean or else. Alvin who is well along in his plan only needs time, so he stalls the FBI with a deal to turn state's evidence, and immediately picks up the slack everywhere else. He mortgages his house, sells off securities, liquidates stocks. Heffelfinger smells that Alvin s going to bolt. He tells Doris, who tells Brewster. Clayton gets wind and tells Joan. Little do you all know that the NIVLA Corporation is raking in the dough and funneling it into some offshore account, which, to be honest with you, we haven't yet found. If any of you would like to help..."

No volunteers come forward.

I pace over to Christina, tap her on the shoulder. "I'm sorry that I haven't mentioned your name in the story yet, Christina, but please be patient, your turn will come. You too, Lizzy."

I remind myself not to call Lizzy a lesbian.

"Doris visits Conway to go over the will, which hasn't changed, but Conway lets on that he thinks something is up. He's been talking to Alvin's banker at Northern Trust, P. Carrington Vogel, who reports Alvin has asked for a personal meeting. Clayton's business is now in arrears. Brewster is drinking his problems away with his new girlfriend. Heffelfinger and Millie hear their office lease has been cancelled and soon they'll be on the street. Boo.

"You all share the fact that your golden goose is cooking, your pot at the end of the rainbow has sprung a leak, and something has to be done. A decision is made. When in doubt, take him out."

Steve Burrell is the only one who laughs at my comment.

"At first I thought it was you, Doris, who hired the hit man; but where would you ever find a hit man? They don't advertise in the Kenilworth *Pennysaver*. Then I suspected you, Heffelfinger, but you already had your pack of cash, so why would you risk it? Finally, I suspect..." I place my hands on Joan's shoulders. "Somebody goes back into her rolodex of old and finds the right man for the job."

"Get your hands off my mother," Clayton demands. "This is all crazy."

"I do have an eyewitness of her making contact with a man who does this kind of work." I get a mental picture in my head of that dumb kid, who hangs out at Clarence's house, testifying in front of a jury.

"But not so fast," I put up my hand to interrupt myself. "As promised, it is Christina's turn," I smile and give her a wave. "At the same time all of the chicanery is going on with Alvin, Christina wakes up to find all her money is poof - gone, disappeared. Some dastardly folks have invaded her bank account and cleaned her out of the only real money she ever got from her old man. By the way Lizzy, the Girl Bar where you told us you and Christina met has been closed for years."

Lizzy takes her hand off Christina's arm and faces me. I have a feeling she knows what I'm going to say next.

"Christina, I hate to be the bearer of bad tidings, especially in the ways of love, but not only does your partner not have true feelings for you, she's the one who ripped you off; and probably worst of all, she's not even a lesbian."

"I'm as gay as a three-dollar bill, and I love this woman."

"Oh, come on, you couldn't even get a rise out of Tiffany."

Tiffany says, "He's right, you didn't even blip on my gaydar screen."

"Don't listen to him," Lizzy pleads to Christina. "We've been together too long for you to doubt my love."

"You cleaned her out and cleaned her out good."

Lizzy comes to her feet, "You are out of your mind."

"Jonas, would you be so kind as to bring in the reunion's first special guest?"

Peter Patrolman allows the Chicago detective to leave the room. In his absence, the entire room watches Christina's face crinkle with confusion and anger.

Jonas returns with Augie Rinaldi.

"Christina, meet Augie, Lizzy's lover and partner in crime. The two go way back."

"I've never seen this man before in my life," Lizzy screams out as Jonas handcuffs Augie to an empty chair at the table.

"Mister Rinaldi probably won't speak today. He's too smart for that, seeing he's been in this spot before. But don't he and Lizzy make a nice couple?"

Steve passes out copies of the Boston mug shots of the two when they were busted a few years back.

"Lizzy, I think you've really done wonders with your hair since this picture was taken."

"How could you?" Christina cries.

"Never give your password to anyone, Christina," I offer my advice. "Some things in life you should keep to yourself."

"What did I tell you?" Doris says, throwing in her two cents worth.

Christina wipes away tears.

"I'm going to give you a little time, Christina. I'm sure it is a lot to deal with all of a sudden." I pause to clear my throat, "Let's get back to Alvin and his little chipmunks."

I take a sip of the punch Tiffany brought to the party, a little sugary for my tastes. "It's a Saturday afternoon at the Augustus mansion in Kenilworth. Alvin is in his den, probably counting his money. A shot rings out. The bullet crashes through a leaded-glass window, missing Alvin by a mile and lodging in a bookcase.

"The instant Alvin hits the deck, he has figured out that someone is onto him. Interestingly, he never calls the police. The last thing he needs is to have cops snooping around his recent activities. Alvin deduces it must be a family member. Who else could it be? And, being the cheap, cunning, and heartless bastard that he is, he hightails it down to Richmond Insurance to add a rider to his life insurance policy, makes Conway Waddy the witness, but refuses to divulge what's in the rider. Alvin is pissed; and no matter if he lives or dies, he's determined to take every cent he has with him and screw everyone else. And they say you can't take it with you."

Norbert burps after finishing his cake.

"I know you people are sitting here saying you've never heard so much conjecture, and I will admit I don't have all the pieces of the puzzle filled in. Like, why did the hit man miss?"

"Joan, would you like to fill the rest of the people in, here?"

"I never hired any such man. You're just making this all up as you go along."

"Joan makes a five-grand deal, standard fee around town, to bop Alvin, but on the day of the dance, she decides to cut the price in half." I lean over the woman. "What did you expect the guy to do, Joan, kill half of Alvin?"

Clayton pushes me aside. "I told you to leave my mother alone."

"I wish I could, Clayton; but it was you who couldn't come up with the whole five grand, not your mother. Because it was your cash that paid him, you only have yourself to blame. Come on, you should have known better than to welch on a hit man. He could come back and shoot you for not paying."

Clayton avoids the stares of the others at the table. "You're nuts, Sherlock."

"Or Joan needed some extra cash and pocketed half, figuring the hit man would work for whatever. It really doesn't matter now," I say.

Conway Waddy has sat through the show, merely scratching his belly and fiddling with his suspender straps. I face the fat man.

"Conway watches the rider being signed and knows something big is up. He asks Alvin, but Alvin won't tell. He pleads with him, but Alvin won't budge. Conway decides not to keep this all close-to-his-vest; but figures Alvin's life must be hanging by a thread to go through all this rigamarole. The last thing Conway wants is to miss out on a piece of the estate Alvin will be leaving. Make sense, mister counselor?"

Conway smiles, plays with the end of his tie. "Absurd," he says.

"Conway goes back to his office and prepares a bill for thousands of dollars of fees to be sent to Alvin, dated the day before his assumed demise. Lawyer Waddy, being the executor of the will, will administer the payouts, no doubt paying himself first. It's a foolproof plan, almost."

"You can't prove any of this ridiculousness," Conway says.

Steve Burrell waves an invoice for all to see. "Ah, over here. Your invoice."

"That's no proof," Conway is adamant. "You could have written that up yourself."

I take a short pause to give time for some of this to sink in. "If only the hit man would have whacked Alvin, it would have all been so much easier, because the entire situation changed when the bullets missed.

"Alvin lies low, doesn't go home anymore, either staying in his condo or taking a room at the Hilton. The only person he talks to business-wise is Joey Villano, the trader he employed. Daddy's disappeared from your view. And you people can't find him.

"Time is of the essence. Something has to be done and done quickly. Cell phone lines are burning up, as all of you chat each other up. In criminal endeavors this is seldom a good thing, but none of you would have known that except for Augie and Lizzy, who have much more experience in these matters.

"The problem is simple. If any of you are going to see a dime from husband or daddy, he better get dead before he leaves the country for good. Six heads become one to solve the dilemma."

I take another sip of punch. "I admit you people really had me going in this case. I didn't know if it was six o'clock or Wednesday half the time. I'd go from one of you to the next, trying to connect the dots, and fail each time. It wasn't until my daughter suggested I try figuring out who didn't do it, instead of who did, that I began to see it was a family project in the truest sense of the word."

Norbert and Steve smile at me, as if to say they knew I'd get it sooner or later.

I continue. "And while all of you are talking, discussing,

plotting and planning, Alvin's wasting no time. He's got Joey Villano working overtime, cash is being transferred out of NIVLA into foreign banks and, as Heffelfinger discovers, Alvin pulls four-hundred large, in cash, out of his secondary account at Northern Trust.

"The red flags are flying high. The clock is ticking." I look across the table to see every eye upon me, in fear, in amazement and in awe. I decide it is time for a break in the action. "Before I go on," I say, "I'd like to bring in the last family guest of the reunion."

Jonas exits the room and returns with a fifty-something woman who has a striking resemblance to one of the people at the table.

"Christina, I know this has been a difficult day thus far, but maybe seeing your mom for the first time in years will help brighten it a bit. Ladies and gentlemen, coming to us all the way from Boston, Mass., meet Alvin's first wife, Didi."

Christina's eyes almost drop out of her head, "Mother?"

The woman comes in, escorted by Jonas to the chair next to Augie. She seems confused to see him, but says, "Hello, Christina."

"Didi has come all the way from Boston to finally get what she believes is coming to her."

I motion to Didi, as if to say welcome to the family, then start up again. "If you think you got hosed in your divorce, Joan, Didi here, got absolutely screwed. She never got a dime. Alvin skated from alimony, claimed he was broke, and must have hid every asset, because all he had to pay was a lousy child support amount. I don't blame you for being angry, Didi, and I applaud you on your persistence in never giving up; but using your estranged daughter to steer your ship, that was a little much.

"Didi lives in South Boston and had a neighbor named Lizzy, each has survived over the years by their wits. Didi comes up with a plan for Lizzy to move to Chicago, meet her lesbian daughter, gain her confidence, and clean her out of her cash. Didi figures little Christina will merely go back to dad and get more money, so nobody is really hurt in the plan."

I see a change in Didi's mood.

Christina is stunned at the news; but Tiffany seems to be the most shocked in the room. She didn't see this one coming.

"I'm not sure of the technology used; but once Lizzy moves in, she pokes around and sees a much bigger reward than Christina's lousy couple-hundred-grand trust fund. She sets off to get a piece of the bigger, better, Alvin-pie. To do so, she brings in her old buddy, Augie Rinaldi, who you've already had the pleasure of meeting, to help in the criminal endeavor, and satisfy, shall we say, her basic human needs."

I stop at Christina's side. "I know this is all tough to take, but hang in there, okay?"

Lizzy speaks up. "I had nothing to do with this and want to go home now."

Norbert uses his considerable bulk to sit her back down in her chair. "Have a piece of cake," he suggests.

"Lizzy begins making family inroads. Doris hates her, which means Brewster hates her. She's kept out of the family loop. But Lizzy is smart, and when she sees the opening, she's ready to jump in with both feet. And so is another person, but I'll get to her, later."

"I told you Lizzy was the one who did it, didn't I?" Clayton reminds us of our non-lunch, lunch conversation.

"Kinda," I tell Clayton, "but not really."

"This is like the plot of a bad TV movie," Brewster says, visibly upset.

Tiffany walks across the room to a small refrigerator, pulls out a beer, and hands it to Brewster. "Here, this might make the reunion a little more fun." Then she pulls the beer away from him, "But everyone has to promise not to say anything to Brewster's AA people if they ask if he's cheating."

Brewster takes the beer out of her hand.

"Now, what do you people decide to do?" I wait for an answer from my peanut gallery, but no one speaks up. "You decide to throw a party."

"Whee," Tiffany says.

"But you can't locate the honored guest." I pace over and stand between the two escorts. "Brewster's girlfriend, Diane, comes to the rescue." I pause to say to Doris, "You could have done a better job of teaching him about picking girlfriends."

Doris' head rivets to her son. "What is he talking about?"

Brewster shrugs innocence.

"I'm not saying you shouldn't date professional women,

Brewster, just women in her profession."

"He doesn't know what he's talking about," Diane argues.

"Diane can easily find Alvin. She merely waits for him to get horny and call Alexis, who has been Alvin's number-one hump for months, and doing him without the knowledge of her boss at the escort service. Diane, who has put up with Brewster long enough, and is anxious to finally get her share of Alvin's pot of gold, becomes the party planner."

"The only thing I did was have sex with him," Alexis says. "Can't bust me for that."

"Well, we could, but with everything else going on, it might seem a bit silly." I say and turn back to the group. "I'm sure it was to Alvin's great surprise when everyone shows up at his condo, his secret home away from his wife.

"Diane knows how to throw a party. She's got booze, weed, cocaine, and Alexis-all designed to wear Alvin down to a state of unconsciousness. Alvin drinks, smokes, and snorts; but the old man has a constitution worthy of a modern-day Rasputin. He won't drop. Finally, in desperation, Diane dopes Alvin's drink with a shot of Rohypnol and Alexis screws him into hibernation. Nothing is ever easy in love, war, or crime, but finally, it is time to proceed with the plan."

The three detectives and Tiffany stand stock still at the back of the room. They seem to be enjoying my little show-and-tell.

"This is when one of you, probably Diane because the others are too scared, takes out a syringe, plunges it into his vein and loads him with a concoction of drugs. Heck, you shoot enough drugs in him to open a pharmacy. The deed is done. Alvin's not moving, a clump of rubberized humanity on the floor. The plan now is to get him home and make it look like a drug overdose." I pause. "Next time, if there is a next time, spread his cheeks and inject him in his butt crack, so someone at an autopsy can't see the needle prick on his arm."

No one is arguing. Each participant sits back in his or her chair, pretending this isn't happening. "I'm pretty sure it is Clayton's and Brewster's job to get daddy downstairs, into a car and back to home-sweet-home in Kenilworth, because it had to be someone who knew to take the back way in."

I clear my throat. I want to make sure I get this next part as clear as possible.

"You park on the sand. Good move, no tire tracks. You lift Alvin out of the car, get him to the edge of the trees and bushes and what does he do? He comes to. He's alive. You stand back as Alvin flounders around to the bushes at the edge of the sand and vomits."

Clayton's mouth drops open a bit. Brewster swigs his beer.

"He's not dead. You can't believe it. If you two would have done your homework, you would have known that most druggies do vomit before they die, but you didn't learn that. You figure daddy is making a miraculous recovery. You probably look at each other as Alvin vomits what's left in his stomach with *what do we do now?* on your faces. You argue. 'You kill him. No, you kill him.' I have no clue how long this goes on, but neither of you has the guts to finish the job. So, "momma's boy" Brewster gets on the phone and calls mom. Doris calls Joan. Joan calls Lizzy. This is what I meant about technology. Aren't cell phones wonderful?

"Lizzy, the only good criminal in the group, immediately cuts a deal to get adopted into the family for a full share. She knows the perfect man for the job and in no time whatsoever, Augie arrives in Kenilworth."

"I didn't go nowhere and I didn't do nothing and I don't know none of these people," Augie says. Spoken like a true criminal.

"Augie, my good man, we have pictures of you at your motel with Lizzy in your room." This is a lie, but how would he ever know?

"I want to see a lawyer," he says.

"Doris has one that will work for a hundred dollars," I tell him. "And I think you'll like his suit."

I take a moment, move to Christina and ask, "You and Lizzy didn't share a bed that Friday evening, did you?"

"We certainly did," Lizzy belts out.

"You said you weren't feeling well, got up in the middle of the night," Christina says.

I move behind Augie. "So Augie shows up before daylight, has some choice words for the idiots who can't finish the job, picks one rock out of the lined path and whacks Alvin right on the forehead. How difficult was that? But suddenly, there is a whole new problem: How do you make this look like an accident? The overdose idea won't work anymore, nobody would believe a Kenilworth mugging and you can't drown him in the lake.

"Necessity, being the mother of invention, one of you comes up with a brilliant idea. Alvin is dragged along the path to the base of the rock garden, where he starts to twitch, which leads everyone to believe he has once again cheated death. So Augie drops a boulder on his head. Finally, with Alvin's brains draining on the path, there is no doubt whatsoever." I take a deep breath. "Whew."

No comments or questions or arguments from the assembled.

I change my tone of voice. "This reminds me of a joke. One guy tells another that he had a fire in his factory and got a million dollars from his insurance company. The other guy says he had a flood in his factory and got two million. The first guy asks, 'How do you start a flood?'"

Only my fellow detectives and Tiffany laugh.

"As is the case with most on-the-spot criminal decisions, something again is amiss. The crushing idea wasn't as complete as first thought. It doesn't look natural that one boulder could have rolled off and landed so perfectly on Alvin's skull. More must be done, but what? I can imagine the three of you standing there, trying to come up with the next great idea.

"You give up. Augie calls Lizzy, the junior architect, and she comes up with the idea in no time. She gives you directions, and the wall of rocks came tumbling down, covering Alvin's body. The deed is done. It is time to go home, except for one thing. One of you remembers Alvin has a pack of cash in his pocket; and to leave that behind would be a crime. So, you uncover the rocks from the left side of his body, remove the wad, split it up, and now you're finished. Talk about a long night.

"I will admit, you did an excellent job cleaning up. All wore gloves because nary a fingerprint was left, and you even smoothed the path back to the car so no footprints were evident. Bravo, good work. The party's over."

Clayton says, "This is the most absurd idiocy I've ever heard."

"And now comes the real tragedy of the story. The next day, Lucy, the dog from next door takes a break from playing fetch to eat Alvin's drug-filled, puke and less than an hour later Lucy the Labrador drops dead. Killing Alvin is bad enough, but killing a dog. That's cold."

Norbert holds Lucy's autopsy report, "What was in Alvin ended up in the dog. Got to be careful where you eat," he says.

I pause. "Guess what happens next?"

"Oh, tell us Sherlock, tell us," Brewster says.

"Worry sets in, which is usual in a case involving amateurs. So much worry, one of you actually places a phone call to the house that evening to be sure all went well."

"That was me on the line, if you didn't know," Tiffany says. "At first I thought you were a telemarketer."

"Next day, you see on the news and in the paper the Kenilworth PD has labeled it an accident and the cha-ching floodgates will open. All that is left is for Alvin's money to be disbursed." I take a deep breath.

"What you didn't know, but Heffelfinger and Waddy did, is that before Alvin died, he not only changed his insurance policy, but also removed the bulk of his cash from his account at Northern Trust. Why?"

I pace around to Millie and Heffelfinger. "Because there is one string still hanging out there: Joey Villano. The money is Joey's reward for all his fine work."

It is Horace's turn again on the hot seat. "Heffelfinger sees three things. One: a personal four-hundred grand payday; two: the last link to the one guy who can blow the lid off the scam; and three: personal retribution for Joey being the one who discovered and told Alvin his accountants were stealing him blind."

"You are out of your mind," Heffelfinger says.

"You followed Joey to the condo when he went to pick up his money, killed him, and stuffed him in the chest. To make it look like a break-in you trashed the place, but not very convincingly."

"I did not," Heffelfinger screams.

Millie sits contrite. She looks up at me and says, "I didn't have anything to do with killing anyone. I want you to know that."

The weakest link in the chain breaks. It is the first confession of the day. I have a feeling there will be more.

"Thank you, Millie. I never thought you were the type."

"How can you say such a thing?" Heffelfinger continues to scream.

"He was a nice boy," she says, "a little overweight, but a nice boy."

"Surprise, surprise, there is no 400k; but you do find a portion of that amount. You figure Alvin screwed Joey too. It certainly would be in character, wouldn't it?"

"I want to see a lawyer," Heffelfinger says.

"You visit his house in Kenilworth, flip off the alarm and trash it, looking for the rest of the money missing from the chest."

Heffelfinger clams up tighter than, what else, a clam.

"At the funeral you all play it pretty cool, but people are getting antsy. You can't wait to get your money and split. At Conway Waddy's office, the day of the disbursement, it all falls apart."

The detectives in the room begin to position themselves for the inevitable.

I continue on a roll. "It must have been one painful moment when you all heard that Alvin had outsmarted the lot of you. Not only was there no money in the corporation, but the life insurance policy holds a rider that could tie up the money forever. Four-hundred grand has disappeared. Most of you are already broke. Instead of one for all and all for family, it becomes every man and woman for his or herself. Let the other guy take the rap, and you take the money.

"Doris, figuring Heffelfinger knows more than anyone else, casts her lot with him and phonies up some of the most obviously forged travel documents imaginable. Clayton tries to pin it on Lizzy. Diane is so pissed at Brewster, that she plants drugs on him and has him busted. Alexis wants her money out of the deal, so she and Diane finagle to tap into whatever is left of the estate. Lizzy and Augie are the maddest of all. They did the deed and have only Christina's money to show for it; and they have to split the amount with Didi. One of you even has the audacity to write a phony confession note to throw us off track. Talk about an amateur stunt. And to make matters even worse, there is a sting at the Board of Trade. Then you read in the newspaper that an eyewitness has popped out of the woodwork. What a set of revolting developments this has become."

I stand at the head of the table where I began, and look at the players. What a sorry bunch of losers.

"The scramble is on. Millie decides to sell her house, and move to Florida with a sister she doesn't have. Doris, or Conway

Waddy, rehires Joan's hit man to miss Brewster this time, to throw off suspicion on themselves. Heffelfinger leaves town for the Cayman Islands, where he transfers the money from the account he shares with Millie to an account of his own. Lizzy and Augie have to hang around and hold out hope for a disbursement of the Insurance money or at the least wait for Christina to get hers, so they can clean her out again. Clayton's company is broke and in danger of an IRS investigation of his accounting practices. Brewster starts drinking again, which for Brewster is par for his course. Didi remains in Boston, happily spending Christina's money.

"The fact is, there is no way that Richmond Insurance will ever pay out. The police have changed the case from accidental to murder, and the IRS and FBI are involved. Oh, what to do, what to do? And that's pretty much brings us to the next party, which is today. Go ahead, have some cake."

I allow my stew to simmer for a minute or two before I add a pinch of salt. "And by the way, Agent Romo had your cell phone companies list all your calls over the last few weeks. Cell phone technology is great; but also is the technology of recording which calls you made. We needed something to tie it all together and your record of calls certainly helped. I would like to thank the four of you for being on the family plan, which made it especially easy to link this all together."

There is but one innocent face in the crowd around the table, and she speaks up. "How could you people do this?"

"He deserved it," Doris says, as good as a confession in my book.

"If you would have had the guts to kill him," Brewster says to Clayton, "we would have been home free."

"What about you, studly?" Clayton snaps back to his half-brother.

"I never collected a dime," Conway says.

"Neither did I," Alexis says. "I did the screwing and I end up getting screwed."

"It was all Doris' idea," Joan says.

"You bitch," is Doris' reaction.

It was only a matter of time before they all talked.

"Who was the eyewitness?" Clayton asks.

"Didn't have one," Norbert tells all.

"We lied," Steve confesses.

"That isn't fair," Brewster says.

Augie says, "I didn't do anything. I'm just visitin'."

"Spoken like a true professional criminal," I commend Augie. "Never, never admit any fault or guilt."

Augie smiles.

"Augie, if I may offer some advice, I have gone over your rap sheet; and if you ever do get out of prison, please try another life besides crime. All in all you are a pretty lousy criminal. Not as bad as these rank amateurs, but not very good nonetheless."

Lizzy says, "You have no physical evidence."

"We're getting there," Jonas says. "And worse-comes-to-worse, we can always nail you two on grand theft."

"It is all hearsay." Lizzy must be studying legal terms in her spare time. "You have to prove it beyond a shadow of a doubt."

"No, I don't," I tell her. "I could care less which of you idiots did what. My job is merely to stop the twelve million from being distributed."

"And a job well done it is," Tiffany calls out.

"How about me?" Christina asks. "I didn't do anything wrong."

"Unfortunately, by the time they all get attorneys, this case will drag along for years." I tell her.

Christina sinks into her chair. It has been a bad day, to say the least. I wonder if she is considering going straight?

"That's about all for me," I say. "I apologize if I bored any of you. By the way if you'd like a copy of the DVD of today's show, you can ask Agent Romo, who was kind enough to tape the audio portion of the program. And don't forget your goodie bags on your way out."

Romo pulls out two small microphones hidden in the cake, while Norbert, Steve, Jonas, and Peter Patrolman pull out pairs of handcuffs and begin to secure the players' hands.

Brewster finishes his beer. It is the last one he'll be enjoying for a while. Talk about going cold turkey.

"Don't say a word until we have a lawyer," Doris tells her son.

"And how are we going to afford one of those?" he asks.

"Hey, stop that." Alexis fights off Peter's handcuffs.

"You admitted having sex for money," Peter says.

"I didn't get any money. Didn't you listen?"

Peter carts her off with the rest, all of whom will fill a paddy wagon waiting downstairs.

The room is empty, the case closed-at least in my book.

Tiffany comes to my side. "That was really super, Mister Sherlock, my dad is going to be thrilled."

"Will I get a bonus?"

"I'll put in a good word for you."

Well, something good happened today.

"Come on, Mister Sherlock," she says with that youthful exuberance, "wasn't it fun standing up there figuring it all out?"

"I would have rather been bowling."

30
Bon appétit

Tiffany bought me lunch a week later. I showed her the postcard
I received from Steve in Vermont.

"Do you think they will find where Alvin stashed his
millions?"

"Someday," I say, "and when they do they'll confiscate the
money as ill-gotten gains and put it into the state coffers, so that
elected politicians can steal it legally."

"How about the four-hundred grand?"

"Good question, Tiffany."

"Yeah, where is it?"

"I'm waiting for you to find it."

———

The next day, I take a trip to Bucktown and empty out my storage
locker. I divide the money up carefully. Since it isn't mine, I can be
generous.

Five grand goes to Bennie, so he can finally afford to get away
for a vacation. Ten goes to Clarence, aka Preston, who remains out
of town and, I'm sure, out of work. I take five and hire an attorney
for Alexis, who I believe is more stupid than guilty. I take a grand
to Leon's Ribs with specific instruction that two guys in a
Mercedes eat "on me" until the money runs out. I pay in advance
for one year of boarding at the stables. I pay my rent, alimony and
child support for three months in advance. I ask for a receipt from
my ex.

The rest of the money I take in grocery bags to a condo in
Uptown.

"What do you want?" Christina says, seeing me at her door
loaded down with shopping bags.

"May I come in?"

I enter. Christina looks like she has spent the last week crying non-stop, kinda the way I felt going through the first week of my divorce.

"Did Herman ever find any of your money?" I ask.

"Not a dime."

To change her mood, I dump the stacks of bills on the floor. The pile reminds me of the rocks covering her dad. "Maybe this will help get you back on your feet."

She's in shock, holding her fist against her open mouth. "Where did you get this?"

"Don't ask, don't tell."

I fold the grocery bags up, place them under my arm and leave the condo.

———

Friday afternoon, I pick up my girls from their last day at school.

"Learn anything new today?" I ask.

"Nope," Care says.

"Kelly?"

"I took my lunch, sat at an empty table, started eating, and two of my old friends and one new came over and sat with *me*."

"Bon appétit."

The Toyota found its way back to my apartment where I cooked a turkey-surprise dinner, set it in front of my girls, who turned up their noses and said in unison, "This is gross."

Ah, family.

Thank you for reading The Case of the Not-So-Fair Trader. I certainly hope you enjoyed my novel, and if you did, please let others know of your good reading fortune. A review on Amazon.com, Amazon Kindle, Goodreads.com, and/or LibraryThing.com would be greatly appreciated. Also, if you could let your friends know via Facebook, Linkedin, and Twitter, I will be forever grateful.

Also by Jim Stevens

The Case of Moomah's Moolah
        A Richard Sherlock Whodunit

WHUPPED

And Coming Soon:

The Case of Tiffany's Epiphany,
        A Richard Sherlock, the Reluctant Dick, Whodunit

And Coming Whenever:

WHUPPED TOO

Jim Stevens was born in the East, grew up in the West, schooled in the Northwest and spent twenty-three winters in the Midwest. He has been an advertising copywriter, playwright, filmmaker, stand-up comedian and TV producer. To read about the next case of the reluctant dick, Richard Sherlock, contact Jim at:

JimStevensWriter@gmail.com

7|18

Made in the USA
San Bernardino, CA
25 June 2015